BOLD
BEN BRIERTON

BY HAL STRANGEWAY.

SPLENDIDLY ILLUSTRATED.

BOLD BEN BRIERTON.

CHAPTER I.

SHOWS THE KIND OF METAL OUR HERO IS MADE OF.

PEOPLE often wondered as they looked at the slim, handsome lad ; but the good people of the hum-drum, dreamy cathedral city of Cloisterville were always wondering. They wondered how the rest of the world lived, and not a few of them had reason to wonder how they contrived to exist, for Cloisterville, a once important centre of shawl weaving had gone to the wall, and left the majority of the inhabitants, as Iago says "poor indeed." Ben Brierton, the object of so much mental attention was in his seventeenth year, a lad of muscle, and brave and generous to a fault.

Poor fellow ! he had little to be generous with, as it was his misfortune to have been brought up from early childhood by an old man rejoicing in the name of Ebeneezer Chipps, but better known to sportive youth as Daddy Miser.

Ben Brierton called this mysterious individual " uncle," although the boy had an inborn notion that the humpbacked, wrinkled-faced, evil-minded, grasping old man was in nowise related to him.

To arrive at Ebeneezer's abode without accident great precaution had to be taken. There was a narrow, dark court-yard, terminating in a flight of greasy stone steps, and then, lo ! a change came o'er the scene.

The astonished stranger came suddenly upon a plain of flint-faced houses ; houses guarded by strangely carved porticoes, and surmounted by immense stacks of chimneys.

One of these ghostly old dwelling houses had been purchased by Ebeneezer Chipps on the very day that he, leading Ben Brierton, then a toddler of two years old, made his first appearance in Cloisterville.

Mr. Chipps was willing to buy and sell anything, indeed there was a half-believed-in rumour that he had sold himself for a chest of gold, any portion of which would turn uncommonly hot if touched by any fingers than his own.

And as Ebeneezer Chipps had never a good word to say, or a kindly smile to give to man, woman or child, was uncleanly in his habits, and always in rags, he gained the nickname of Daddy Miser.

Mr. Chipps when abroad did not lead a pleasant life.

He never shuffled out of his house without being armed with a stout oak sapling, a weapon capable of doing tremendous execution at close quarters; but the rising generation of the male gender having quick eyes and nimble feet, laughed derisively at the instrument of torture carried for their express edification, and drove the old man nearly mad.

He was often asked in a pointed manner whether there was any truth in the report that he made soup of empty match-boxes and bread of sawdust; and he was occasionally accused of having stolen a slice of bread and butter from a starving child.

And as these remarks were sometimes accompanied by cabbage-stalks, and other stray missiles of an antique pattern, freely abounding in the narrow courts and streets, Ebeneezer Chipps often went home in a state of mind bordering on ferocity, and very much the worse for wear.

One bitterly cold afternoon, when the leaden-hued sky was trying to make up its mind to snow, and a few particles were dancing aloft Mr. Ebeneezer Chipps staggered into the entrance of the court, and reached his house, clawing the air and foaming at the lips.

"If I could only get hold of one them," he almost shrieked, "I think there would be work for the coroner. The idle, dissolute, good for nothing ragamuffins! Why are they not imprisoned, or whipped at the cart's tail. Ah! that would be better. Their howls would be music—

sweet music—to my ears."

At that moment Ben Brierton opened the door, and appeared in the company of a freshed-faced, comical-looking lad, named Timothy Toppem.

Timothy looked up to Ben as in the days of old a henchman looked up to a baron. He hung upon every word our hero said, and so thoroughly believed in his mental and physical capabilities that had he been told that Ben had dispersed an unruly mob single-handed, and then calmly proceeded to give a lecture on astronomy, Tim would have expressed no astonishment.

Ebeneezer Chipps favoured the lads with a snarl which would have done credit to a surly cur, but neither seemed to be affected by this salute.

"Loafing and idling about as usual," said Chipps, addressing himself to Ben. "Didn't you hear the shouting? No! You are deaf to such sounds, and secretly rejoice at knowing that I am hunted and reviled as if I were a leper."

"It is no fault of mine," Ben replied. "If you had not taken any notice of the boys they would have long since ceased to annoy you."

"Bah!" said Chipps, with a malignant glare in his eyes. "What should I expect from you but protection in return for boarding, lodging, and clothing you? Yet I get nothing but ingratitude."

Ben Brierton sighed as he glanced down at his poor attire.

"I cannot always be fighting," he returned. "I don't want to grow up with every man's hand against me. You accuse me of loafing. Why don't you apprentice me to an honest trade in some other town?"

"Because I choose to have my own way so long as the law gives me power over you," Ebeneezer Chipps said. "Have you sorted the heap of rags that came in this morning?"

"No," Ben replied, "and, what is more, they will remain where they were pitched for ever for all the attention they will get from me."

Ebeneezer Chipps clutched his oak sapling tighter and took a step backwards.

"You had better not try that sort of argument," Ben said, squaring his shoulders. "You used to beat me when I was small and helpless, but that luxury is a thing of the past. I am strong, and have a way as well as a will. Don't tempt me to lift my hand against the man who is always taunting me with owing him so much."

"Hear, hear!" murmured Timothy Toppem, who had squeezed himself against the wall and in the dim twilight resembled an old-fashioned clock.

"Hold your tongue!" Ebeneezer Chipps cried, finding himself defeated in one quarter and attacking in another. "Get out of my house and never darken it again. I am master here, as you will find if I catch you hanging about."

"You had better go, Tim," Ben replied. "He is in one of his worst moods, but he will calm down presently. Have no fear for me; I know how to manage him."

"You know how to manage everything and everybody," Tim replied, with an admiring grin. "Lor! how cool you do talk to him. Well, good-night, Ben; and good-night to you, too, Mr. Chipps, though you don't like me. Didn't I hear something rattle down the steps just as you came down them?"

"Yes," Chipps replied. "A young miscreant hurled an old saucepan at me. Go and pick it up, Ben. We are running rather short of kitchen utensils, and it may come in useful."

"I'll chuck it down as I go out," Tim said, as he turned away.

Ebeneezer Chipps, still muttering and murmuring, hobbled into the gloomy house, leaving Ben standing just within the porch.

The snow was falling faster now, and the flakes whitened the cobble stones Ben was gazing pensively at.

But the lad's thoughts were far away. He was thinking of the miserable life he led, and of his many failures to obtain permanent work at Cloisterville.

Whenever he applied for a situation, the name of Ebeneezer Chipps always acted as a wet blanket, and people, though half-pitying Ben, shrugged their shoulders and declared they were suited.

As may be imagined, Ben's education was not of the best; but he had picked up scraps of information from some old books possessed by Ebeneezer Chipps, and when alone he would sit for hours practising and improving his handwriting. Thus, Ben Brierton, naturally quick, was no dunce, and could hold his own with many a boy who trudged to school every morning and afternoon.

"I can't stand this much longer," Ben said, half aloud. "There must be an end to it soon. I am growing fast into manhood, and when others are fighting the battle of life, I shall be as near to success as I am now. Heaven knows that the bread of charity is coarse, and, hard as it is, chokes me, but—"

"Shut the door!" roared Ebeneezer Chipps, down the staircase. "The wind is melting the rushlight as if it cost nothing."

Ben awoke from his reverie, and, obeying his gentle relative, walked upstairs into a room which seemed to be the very home of fantastic shadows.

The smallest of fires flickered in the rusty grate, and over it cowered Ebeneezer Chipps.

"Don't snuff the candle," he said, turning his head sharply. "It is the only one in the house, and must last two nights. I—I suppose you have had your tea?"

"I have had a crust, and a drink of water," Ben replied. "The tea-caddy is empty."

"What!" Chipps screeched. "Tea-caddy empty. Two ounces gone—wasted in four days. This is ruination. Fetch me the cold potatoes out of the cupboard, and keep your own fingers off them."

Ben said nothing; he merely complied, and then sitting down at a rickety table that complained bitterly when he leaned his elbow upon it, took up a book.

"What trash is that?" Chipps asked, for the want of something better to snarl about.

"A book of travels and adventure."

"Put it down, and go to bed if you are cold," the old man said. "I'll have you read no such rubbish. I didn't know there was such a book in the house; but I suppose it is one of a job lot I bought."

"No," Ben replied. "Tim Toppem lent it to me."

"Then pitch it into the fire," said Chipps; "it will make a good blaze, I dare say."

Ben Brierton paid no attention to this command, but went on reading quietly for a few minutes.

Suddenly he turned down a leaf, closed the book, and walked straight up to the old man.

"Mr. Chipps," said Ben, "I want to ask you a few questions."

Ebeneezer was so overcome with astonishment that he picked up the poker, and, applying it to the fire, extinguished it.

"Questions! What questions?" he gasped.

"I want to know where I can find the certificates of my parents' death?" said Ben. "And, moreover, I want to know how it was that I was left to your charge?"

"Haven't I told you over and over again that I am your mother's brother, and that you were left to me as—as a kind of natural debt," the miser replied, without raising his eyes.

"Yes; but I want you to tell me the truth now."

Ebeneezer Chipps was seized with a violent fit of coughing, interspersed with remarks which were not at all complimentary to Ben and his inquisitiveness.

"See here!" he cried, starting up. "You are what I have often described you to be—a beggar and a pauper. You have nothing in the world, only what I give you. But don't think of running away. I've prepared your path in life, and one day, when I think proper, I will tell you what it is to be."

These last words set Ben thinking.

Looking at the old man, he saw that he was concealing his emotion under a fit of passion, and the lad, after pondering whether it would be wise to say any more, took the candle from the table and went upstairs.

"Hi!" Chipps bellowed. "What do you mean by running away with the light and leaving me in the pitch dark?"

The echo of his own voice alone answered him, and Ebeneezer Chipps, groping his way back to the fireplace, crouched and huddled over the smouldering ashes.

"So," he muttered, "the boy is beginning to show his teeth. I might have expected it from one of his accursed race. But I will keep my word to— Ahem! they say walls have ears, and I must be careful. I will keep my word, and he shall be an outcast and a vagabond."

CHAPTER II.

THE ARRIVAL OF A MYSTERIOUS LETTER—BEN MAKES UP HIS MIND TO START ON HIS OWN ACCOUNT— THE LION KING, AND WHAT HAPPENED AT THE TRAVELLING MENAGERIE.

WHEN Ben Brierton come down the next morning he found Ebeneezer Chipps in a softened mood.

"Look here, Ben," he said; "we will forget what happened last night, and try to be on better terms. You are very late, but never mind that. I have a forgiving nature and to prove it I went out an hour ago and bought two rashers of bacon—expensive form of food, but we must be merry sometimes."

"I have no appetite," Ben replied, shortly.

"I'm glad—sorry to hear that," Chipps remarked. "Then we'll put the rashers away for Sunday's dinner. Hullo! Who is making that confounded din at the door?"

"It sounded like the postman's knock," Ben said; "now he is kicking at the panels."

Chipps jumped up, and almost flew down the stairs.

"Registered letter," Ben heard the postman say. "Make haste and sign the receipt. The wind cuts into a man like the edge of a razor in these draughty places. Here's a pencil."

When Ebeneezer Chipps returned to the room his eyes glaring, and his hands trembling with excitement.

"Ben," he said, stammering out the words, "I have had news from an old friend—a man who may do some thing good for me, and for you, too, if I hide your faults from him. I am going out for the day, and may not be home until late."

Our hero did not seem to be at all interested in the announcement, but stood at the window apparently watching some sparrows throwing up the snow with their feet and wings, and pecking vigorously away at nothing.

"Sulky!" Chipps muttered. "Whenever he is sulky he stays at home and reads hard. I shall find him here when I return. I—oh! dear me—suppose I had better leave him a few coppers to buy a loaf and a scrap of butter with."

Then a terrible thought flashed into the old man's mind, and he became violently agitated.

"Ben!" he said, in a pleading tone of voice. "Promise me that you will not touch the rashers. I know you will keep your word if you give it."

"You will find the rashers where you put them," Ben replied, contemptuously.

"That's right. You are improving, Ben," said Chipps. "Now then for my hat and stick; I must be off. Just run to the top of the court and see whether there are any of those young demons about. No! Stay where you are, and here's—oh! bless me, how money flies—here's fourpence. Keep some of it back, if you can."

Not a word did Ben say; but no sooner had the old man shuffled out of the house than he threw his head back and burst out laughing.

"It is my opportunity," he said, "and a better one could have been offered me. I will turn my back on this old house for ever, and face the world. I'll just run round to Tim Toppem, say good-bye to him, and then be off."

Hidden away in the garret, where he had slept from childhood, were a few shillings Ben had earned from time to time, and tying the coin in a knot in his handkerchief, he left the home of misery, and locked the door.

"What am I to do with the key?" he thought. "I'll thrust it under the door. My so-called uncle always had a mortal terror of burglars; but for once his house will be broken open by himself or the blacksmith."

Ben lingered a moment, gazing at the old dwelling with its windows of diamond-shaped panes, and as he stood there tears welled into his eyes; but not tears of weakness or occasioned by any pang of regret in leaving.

They overflowed from the flood-gates of his heart because of the dreary life he had endured, and that he, while other boys seemed so happy in cosy homes with loving faces round them, was so friendless and alone.

Ben's grief was natural enough, for he had only one tie to hold Cloisterville dear to him, and after he had shaken hands with Timothy Toppem and breathed the words farewell that tie would be broken.

Passing into the street he wended his way through several thoroughfares until he came to one in which a row of small houses, with green shutters, elegantly picked out with the brightest of vermilions, shrank bashfully at the ends of narrow strips of gardens.

It was here that Tim Toppem resided with his father, who was a widower, and, being rather too fond of the interior of the Briton's Arms, was more often out of work than in.

In a way Toppem senior was fond of Toppem junior, yet there were times when he remembered Tim's achievements at meal times as a destructive and non-productive source.

Tim had once served under a grocer; but having a "sweet tooth" the service was of short duration. Master Toppem then hired himself out to an aged lady, afflicted with an everlasting cough and a mangle; but the life proved too monotonous to the high spirited youth, who then exercised his talents in the adventurous pursuit of driving bullocks on market days, which ended in him being thrown over two sets of iron rails and providentially landing on a fat man, who kept an oyster stall.

So when we find Tim he was, like the proverbial naughty boy, "doing nothing at all," save waiting hand and foot on Ben Brierton, and going home regularly to dinner.

Ben knocked at the door, and Toppem the elder, with dishevelled hair, and a suspicious redness about the eyes, answered the summons.

"Tim in?" Ben queried.

"Did you ever know him to be out when there's anything to eat?" said Toppem, replying to one question by putting another. "You'll find him in the back kitchen."

Ben needed no further bidding, and the two friends were soon shaking hands.

"Tim," said our hero, after a few preliminary remarks, "I am going away—running away, in fact. I am sick and tired of the life I lead with my – my uncle, so I have given myself the order to march, and if it should ever be the case of right about turn, I shall be well off and independent when I come back."

Timothy Toppem sat down, and, leaning his elbow on the table, and his head on his hand, began to weep copiously.

Ben Brierton expected this, and waited until Tim began to cool down.

"Where are you going ?" Tim asked.

"That I cannot tell. Anywhere to earn an honest crust, and to lie down at night, thankful that I am free from the taunt of having eaten bread I have not worked for."

"Then." said Tim, brightening up, "you are in no hurry for a few hours. Your uncle won't be home till late, so we may as well have all the time we can together."

"I am afraid that every moment is precious to me," Ben replied. "I intend to start on the London-road like many others have done before me. Some have failed, some have succeeded, and I intend to take my chance."

"Don't go yet," cried Tim, clinging to him ; "don't— don't ! There's a menagerie just come into the town. It's full of monkeys, lions, tigers, wolves, and all sorts of nice things. And there's a Lion King, too—a man who goes into the cages, and—"

"But you see, Tim," said Ben, interrupting him, "these sights cost money."

"So they do," Tim acknowledged. "But we can walk round, look at the painted canvas, and listen to the band. Besides, I have so much to say to you."

Ben shook his head, but Tim would not be denied.

"The first performance is at twelve o'clock, and we

"The 'irons'!" cried the King, "or I am a dead man."

shall hear the Lion King fire off his pistols," he urged as a further inducement. " I'll let you go at one o'clock, Ben, so don't say no to me, unless you wish to break my heart.'

"Very well," said Ben, "I give way; but mind, old fellow, the moment the clock strikes one we must say good-bye, for I intend to put twenty miles between Cloisterville and myself before I sleep."

We shall see presently how all Ben Brierton's calculations were upset. When the boys arrived at the open space of ground devoted to fairs and such travelling shows as came to Cloisterville at odd times, " Wobstock's World-famed and Universally Renowned Menagerie," had not yet opened.

But the musicians, a singularly seedy and worn out number of individuals, were showing signs of activity, and sun-tanned men, most of whom wore earrings and tight unwhisperables, were hauling up marvels of artistic work on canvas, as if they were the sails of a ship.

The pay-box was fixed at the entrance, a flight of steps lowered, and then a showily-dressed man, in a white hat and wearing a watch chain capable of securing a desperate criminal, came to the front of the platform, and held forth on the marvels to be seen within.

If half what he said was true there was nothing so wonderful above the earth or under the sea as Wobstock possessed.

His elephants were the perfection of training, his bears as tame as kittens, and his lions and tigers as wild as when they were first trapped in their native jungles.

While Ben and Tim were looking on and listening, there was a sudden stir in the crowd.

A swarthy man, mounted on a horse, came dashing through, pulling double and shouting to the people to get out of the way.

Ben saw what was the matter in a moment.

The horse had taken fright at something, and springing forward he seized the reins and brought the rearing and plunging horse to a standstill.

"Well done, my lad!" said the man leaping from the saddle. "What is your name ?"

"Ben Brierton."

"And yours," with a glance at Tim.

"Oh! I am nobody," Master Toppem replied.

"Would you like to see the show?" the man asked, as he took the reins from Ben's hands—"of course you would. Here, Joe, pass these youngsters in, and give the tallest one five shillings for me. He prevented a nasty accident, and perhaps saved me from coming an awful cropper."

"Ladies and gentlemen," roared he of the prodigious watch chain, "you observe that we do everything on a liberal scale. I will also add five more shillings to the reward. Walk up, youngsters, and stay as long as you like."

"You are in luck," whispered Tim, delightedly.

"You must take half the money," Ben said, as they ran up the steps.

"I! What for?" demanded Tim. "Why I didn't know whether I was on my head or my heels. I thought the horse was clean over me."

The loud-voiced individual, facetiously termed "a barker" by his colleagues, made a great show about paying the money. It consisted principally of sixpences and threepenny pieces, with a dash of copper, and this exhibition of benevolence induced several people to ascend the platform and plank down their coins like independent Britons.

The menagerie was nearly empty when the boys entered its well sawdusted arena, and they had plenty of opportunities of looking about.

The show was arranged, as is usually the case, in an oblong form ; the elephants at one end, the camels, goats, and tame antelopes revelling almost untrammelled at the other, and the sides flanked with cages containing the birds and animals.

The caravan in which Wobstock and family resided when on the road was next door to the monkey cage—it always is in all travelling menageries, and in a Darwinian sense may have something to do with the missing link.

Half way down the space between the cages glowed a mass of burning coke in a hooped brazier or fire-basket, and between the bars were thrust a few stout pieces of iron, about four feet long and half as thick as an ordinary man's wrist.

"Ben," said Tim, "I don't know whether you sniff anything. This place smells like the b⸱ of white mice I used to keep. Ah! the poor things were ʼune and such beauties; but father came home one Saturday night and chucked them into the next garden."

Ben returned a sympathetic reply with regard to the white mice, and informed Tim that the strange and not altogether pleasant aroma was natural to animals when kept in confinement, no matter how careful their keepers might be.

A few more people strolled in, and then the lecturer of the establishment went from cage to cage, followed closely by the audience and explained the names and habits of the various specimens of natural history.

He made his last stand at a cage of lions, and after an exaggerated and thrilling account of how they were captured at the cost of running up the bill of mortality, informed the attentive listeners that the Lion King would now appear, and " put the hanimals through their facings."

The lions, hitherto quiet, crouching, and blinking sleepily, seemed to know what was coming. Rising to their feet they lashed their tails, and, pacing up and down, filled the menagerie and the surrounding neighbourhood with tremendous roars of expostulation.

"Oh! lor'," Tim gasped. "I begin to wish I was out of this. Suppose they should take it into their heads to dash up against the bars all of a sudden. Where should we be then?"

"Outside as quick as possible, I suppose," Ben replied, laughing.

Just then the Lion King made his appearance from the living caravan.

He was dressed in flesh-coloured tights, save that a leopard's skin was wrapped round his loins, with a strong leather belt, containing a brace of pistols, just above it. In his hand he carried a loaded whip, which he swung in a manner indicating that he was not in the habit of standing any nonsense from the animals he had forced to subjection.

The Lion King was a splendid specimen of humanity—tall, muscular, and firmness of will flashing from his great dark eyes.

"Why, bless me!" Tim cried, "it's the same man we saw on horseback."

"That is true enough," Ben replied, "but he looks quite a different creature now."

"There's as much difference in him," Tim observed, "as there is in a policeman a walkin' out with his missus, and when he's in all his gorgeous beauty of overcoat, helmet, and buttons."

The Lion King gave the lads an encouraging nod just before entering the cage, and then his powerful voice rang out—

"Lie down, Wallace! Come here, Bruce! Jump over me, Hector!"

Muttering like distant thunder, and snarling, the powerful brutes obeyed his every word and action.

The slightest sign of disobedience was visited by a taste of the cutting whip, and the lions flew hither and thither until some of the audience turned pale and looked towards the entrance as if they had seen more than enough and wished to go.

It being an afternoon performance the perilous entertainment was not of long duration, and the Lion King, with his face to the animals, began to back out.

Placing his hand at his back he disengaged the fastening of the cage, when the lion named Hector, and the one that had received most attention from the whip, sprang forward with an angry growl.

Quick as thought the Lion King leaped back into the cage, and seized Hector by his bristling mane; but in so doing he kicked the door wide open.

Then ensued a terrible fight between man and beast.

The people screaming, shrieking, and shouting, fled in all directions.

Timothy Toppem went down upon his back as if he had been shot, and exposed the soles of his boots to the canvas roof of the menagerie.

"The irons!" cried the Lion King, hoarsely; "the irons!

or I am a dead man."

Ben Brierton knew what he meant, and, rushing to the fire-basket, drew forth one of the heated bars, and dashing back again thrust it into Hector's gaping jaws.

Another keeper ran to follow his example, but the Lion King was already free, and Hector was roaring with pain in a corner of the cage.

CHAPTER III.—A STRANGE JOURNEY.

Now that the excitement was over, Ben stood as if he were dazed, and scarcely conscious that the Lion King was wringing his hands and pouring words of gratitude and admiration into his ears. But Wobstock awoke the lad by rushing at him and fairly hugging him round the neck.

"Bless my 'eart !" the proprietor of the menagerie cried. "And bless you my—my brave boy ! When I heard the people hollerin' 'A lion's loose !' I fell bang into the big drum, and it wasn't easy to get out or I should have been here before. Ted Barrett," he added, calling the Lion King by his proper name, "stand that other boy on his feet, and bring him along to the van. We must have a little chat about this affair."

He made another rush at our hero, who avoided him, laughingly.

"Please don't !" he said ; "you are rather heavy, and I don't feel over strong just now."

Wobstock linked his arm in Ben's and marched him off to the living caravan, leaving Ted Barrett to bring Tim round.

That youth still lay upon his back as if he never intended to get up again, and it was all the lion tamer could do to persuade him that the danger was over.

"It's all like a dreadful dream," Tim gasped, running his fingers through his hair. "I say, what do you think of Ben now ?"

"That he is the boldest and bravest lad I have ever met."

"You've hit it, for that is Ben's exact character," Tim said. "It makes my heart ache to think that he is going away, and," squeezing up his knuckles into his eyes, "per-perhaps I shall never see him again."

"Where is he going to?" the Lion King demanded, gruffly.

"I do—don't think he—he knows himself," Tim sobbed, "but—but perhaps I ought not to have said anything about it."

"I think I shall have a word or two to say," the lion tamer muttered. "If the lad and I part just yet it will be no fault of mine."

Meanwhile Ben had been giving Wobstock a brief outline of his history, and when Tim and Ted Barrett appeared, the proprietor of the menagerie was in a very thoughtful mood.

"Look here," he said, striking the table with his great fist. "I am a man of very few words, but what I say I mean. Ben Brierton, you may travel with us as far and as long as you like, and I'll pay you keeper's wages, and board you well. When you wish to leave us you will only have to say so, and you'll not start empty handed. Wild tigers and spotted monkeys!" he roared. "If Ebeneezer Chipps should ever come within reach of my arm, I'll make a hole clean through him."

Ben jumped at the offer.

Tim was almost as delighted as Ben, and proposed that they should have one more walk round Cloisterville.

"There will be no harm in doing that," Wobstock said, "and perhaps it will be just as well for you to be seen about the city until the last moment. We close at ten, and shall be on the road shortly after midnight. Our next pitch is at Macleton, two days' journey from here, and by that time I hope that Mister Chipps will have done mourning for his nephew."

"Tim," said Ben, as they left the menagerie, but not before they had dined well, "I have a notion that I should like a last turn round the old cathedral. I have spent many happy hours there. It has been to me like some good book full of peace and calm. Many a time when I have been very miserable a visit to the cathedral has eased my heart, checked my rising temper, and filled my mind with better thoughts."

"I wish I could think and talk like you!" Tim said; "I think I know what you mean. You have gone there to pray that you might resist temptation."

"Yes," Ben replied; "often when Chipps has cruelly beaten me, and so starved me that I dare not look at the good things displayed in the shop windows, I've gone there as a refuge from my thoughts."

Passing under a crumbling archway they entered the close.

The sky was now clear but the wind was keen and kept most people indoors.

The great doors of the cathedral stood open, for afternoon service was proceeding and the voices of the choristers filled the grand aisle and nave with melody that did not seem to belong to the earth.

"I think I will stay outside," Tim said, halting suddenly.

"Why?" Ben demanded.

"Because I fancy you would like to be alone for a little time."

Ben did not deny it, and he pressed Tim's hand.

"I shall go to the north tower after the service is over," he said, "and take a last bird's-eye view of the city. You will find me there."

Tim nodded his head, and watched Ben until his figure became enveloped in the dim mysterious gloom of the nave.

In about a quarter of an hour the service came to an end, and Ben pushing open a little door ascended a spiral staircase.

He had often gone to the north tower on account of the splendid view it afforded

Higher and higher he mounted past the belfry, where the wind was filling the deep-throated bells with a moaning sound.

Still higher up Ben went until the stairs ceased, and uninviting ladders took their place.

Here Ben stopped, and going to a window looked down upon the city lying beneath his eyes like some vast and elaborate model with the river winding its way to the ocean.

Suddenly Ben Brierton started.

He heard his own name called, but faintly and like the

echo of a despairing voice.

Our hero was not prone to superstition, but he felt an uncomfortable thrill pass through his frame, and he stood motionless trying to convince himself that he was labouring under some delusion.

But if it were a delusion it was a very remarkable one, for again he heard—

"Ben! where are you Ben?"

And then—

"Oh! Ben come to my help or I shall fall. I am growing giddy and cannot hold on much longer."

Our hero knew the voice now; it was Tim Toppem's, and rushing to the top of the staircase he cried—

"Here I am, Tim. Come along, the stairs are safe enough. Don't look down."

And yet again came the voice, now in accents of agony—

"Ben! Ben! I shall fall and be dashed to pieces."

Almost beside himself with doubt and terror, Ben ran to the window looking south, and thrusting out his head saw a sight that chilled his blood and often haunted him in his dreams.

Perched astride a gargoyle, fully two hundred feet from the earth, was Tim Toppem.

Terror was depicted on every feature of his face.

His eyes were glaring, his mouth wide open, and as he clung frantically, but with loosening fingers, to a narrow coping, his whole attitude was that of one who had given up all hope.

It was no time to ask questions, as every moment was precious.

Ben threw one leg over the window-sill, and holding on to the stone casement with his left arm, thrust down his right as low as he could reach.

"Courage, Tim!" Ben cried. "Keep up your pecker, old man! and give me one of your hands."

"I can't—indeed, I can't!"

The words came from Tim's quivering lips, as if they were uttered by an old man in his dotage.

"Nonsense," said Ben. "Do as I tell you, or you are lost. See, I can almost touch you. Make one effort, Tim?"

Tim's face grew deadly pale, and his eyes closed as he raised his almost strengthless hand, which Ben grasped in a moment, and held on with the strength of a young giant.

"You are safe enough now," he exclaimed, exultantly, "and may take time to breathe. How in the name of wonder did you get into such a position?"

"I—I thought I would give you a surprise," Tim stammered.

"And you have done it with a vengeance," Ben said, "but we will have no more talking until you are safe inside the tower. Hug the gargoyle with your knees, and draw up your feet carefully. That's right; keep your eyes on me, and trust to my strength."

In less than half a minute Tim was inside the tower; but no sooner did he touch the flooring than he fainted away in Ben's arms.

"This a nice day of adventures," Ben said, as he rubbed Tim's hands. "Open your eyes, old fellow. You are as safe as the very tower now."

"Shut the cage door! Look sharp, or we shall be all torn to pieces," Tim murmured.

He was thinking of the lion, and when at last he opened his eyes he looked round with a shudder, but smiled when he saw Ben Brierton leaning over him.

"Ben," he said, "I am coming to, and when I am a little more like myself would you mind kicking me a few times round the tower?"

"Upon my word I think you deserve it," Ben replied, "but at present as I am not quite sure who feels the worst, I will postpone the punishment. Now tell me how you managed to crawl to the gargoyle. You must have flown there, and flying is certainly a novel accomplishment in a mortal."

"If I had flown up I could have flown down," Tim replied. "I walked up to the stairs as far as the second gallery, and looking out on the leads, I saw a ladder, so I thought I would make the rest of the journey in the open air."

"Poor thoughtless Tim!" said Ben. "But what became of the ladder."

"Why, I had no sooner reached the gargoyle and seated myself upon it than two men appeared and took the ladder away. I shouted to them, but I suppose the wind carried the sound of my voice away. At all events, they paid no attention to me, and—well, you know the rest Ben, and—and this is second life you have saved to-day."

"We will leave that out of the question," our hero responded. "You ran an awful and useless risk, Tim; and I hope it will be a warning to you as long as you live."

"I am sure it will," said Tim Toppem, who was still too frightened even to shed tears. "Ben, do oblige me with a few kicks. I think they would warm me."

"No doubt, about that," our hero replied, "and so will a walk downstairs. I think we will try that instead."

When they reached the aisle of the cathedral, they found an old blue-gowned verger, preparing to lock up, for it was growing dark and the oil-lamps were being lighted.

As they passed out of the close, Tim suddenly wheeled round, and, grasping Ben's hands, looked him full in the face.

"Do you know why I did not join you at the service?" he asked.

"I had my own opinion about it. I thought you felt that I should like to be left alone for a few minutes."

"It was not that, Ben."

"What was it, then?"

"It was because I am going to do something very wrong."

Before Ben could question this remarkable statement, Tim Toppem took to his heels, and vanished up a narrow passage.

"The shock to his nerves has proved too much for his head," Ben cried, aghast. "Tim—Tim! If you wish to say Good-bye to me, do so in a proper manner."

But Tim was gone, and there was nothing left for Ben Brierton but to wander about until the time appointed for him to return to the menagerie.

Our hero was rather piqued at his friend's extraordinary conduct; but he could not feel angry, as for the life of him he could not understand what it all meant.

As the darkness deepened the sky became overcast, and snow fell heavily, whitening the house-tops and almost silent streets.

At last it was time for Ben to renew his acquaintance with Wobstock and the Lion King.

He found them waiting anxiously for him, but at the same time giving orders to a number of men.

The breaks had been removed from the caravan wheels, yellow shutters obscured the animals from view, the stage with its background of startling pictures was down, and between thirty and forty well-fed and sturdy horses were ready harnessed for the journey.

Mumbo, the elephant, was harnessed too, as it was part of his duty to drag the immense caravan in which he resided during the various "pitches," on the road.

Now that there were no more stale buns, biscuits as hard as pantiles, and such like delicacies to be had, the descendant of the mammoth stood sulkily swinging his trunk, half asleep, and probably dreaming of the jungle from which he had been lured by that ruthless creature, man.

"Come this way, my lad," said Wobstock, to Ben. "The snug quarters for you are quite ready. Ted, bring along the blankets; but I think that Ben— Bold Ben Brierton, I calls him—will be almost warm enough without 'em."

Our hero thought so, too, as a little door was opened at the back of a van containing a choice selection of tropical birds, and he crept into a den just long enough for him to lie down at ease, and sufficiently high for him to sit up.

"As I remarked afore," said Wobstock, as he shook hands with Ben and bade him good-night, "you're as safe as if you was twenty miles under the earth with a forest growin' a top o' you. If anybody finds you I'll— well I'll eat this 'ere white hat and never wear another of them."

In another instant the door closed; it went with a spring, and Ben not relishing his position for the moment experienced such a sensation as a captive of old may have felt when thrust into a dungeon from which nothing but the hand of death could relieve him.

However, Ben was not in the mood to trouble his mind about the mode of travelling so that he got away from Cloisterville and resting his head upon his arm closed his eyes and settled his limbs for repose.

But there was little sleep for him. The cracking of whips, the hoarse cries of the men encouraging the horses, the jolting of wheels, and the occasional roar of some wild animal vainly expostulating kept him in a state of wakefulness; but at last exhausted nature claimed her rights, and with the sounds dull upon his ears, he slumbered soundly.

When he awoke it was broad daylight.

The door was open, and Wobstock, with a mug of steaming coffee in his hand, was shouting that it was past eight.

"Steady, my lad," said Wobstock, as Ben started up, "or you will strike your head ag'in the boards. Take this as a refresher, and then come to my van. Breakfast is waiting."

CHAPTER IV.

HOW EBENEEZER CHIPPS MOURNED FOR BEN, AND THE PASSAGE OF ARMS HE HAD WITH TIMOTHY TOPPEM SENIOR.

ALMOST at the same time that Ben Brierton entered the menagerie Ebeneezer Chipps hobbled homewards through the fast-falling snow.

For once in a way the old man seemed to be in a thorough good humour.

Wherever he had been something had happened to please him, for he twisted his fingers until his knuckle bones cracked, and croned the words of a song he had learned in the long ago days of his youth.

His tormentors—the boys—were all in bed, and he passed unmolested until he reached the door of his domicile.

"Ah!" he muttered, glancing up at the windows,

"Ben has taken a lesson out of my book. He is not even burning a light. I wonder what he will say when his future master calls for him in the morning?"

Chipps stamped his feet on the threshold and knocked loudly with his clenched fist, but as these sounds brought forth no response he walked backwards a few paces and gazed up wistfully at the darkened house.

"This is strange," he said. "I don't think that he would dare to be out at such an hour, nor would he go to bed. Perhaps he has gone to sleep in the—ha! ha!—dining-room."

Thrusting his skinny fingers through the snow he grabbed a handful of earth and pebbles and hurled them at the window.

In so doing he broke two or three of the small panes, and then a sudden fit of rage seized him.

"Idle, sleepy-headed dog!" he yelled; "you are the cause of more waste as usual. It will cost sixpence to put in the windows; but you shall pay dearer for them. I'll get Jem Barker to keep you on bread and water for a whole week; I'll tell him to beat you with a rope, and—"

"Hallo!" demanded a gruff voice. "What's all this row about?"

The speaker was an individual skilled in making boots, and well known for his war-like proclivities when fairly roused to action.

"I cannot make my nephew hear," Ebeneezer Chipps snarled, "and in trying to rouse him I have run myself to a fearful expense."

"I don't think you are likely to rouse him in this part of the world," replied the follower of Saint Crispin. "He went out early this morning, and I could almost swear that I saw him lock the door and push the key under it."

"What!" Ebeneezer Chipps shrieked. "Ran away and locked me out of my own house? I won't believe it."

"Then don't," said the bootmaker, banging the window out of which he was leaning; "but if you kick up any more row I'll put a pail of water over you."

Ebeneezer could scarcely credit what had been told him, but there were two facts he realised.

He was getting bitterly cold, and to open the door he must summon assistance, as his own strength would not admit of the task.

Suddenly a thought flashed into his brain.

"That leather-spoiling villain told me a lie to frighten me," he said. "Ben has been spending the day with Tim Toppem, and doubtless I shall find him in that young reprobate's company. I'll fetch him home, and he shall dance every inch of the way. Ben, my lad, you are laying in a good store of miseries."

Off he went, anger lending him the power to walk at double his usual speed.

Toppem senior was at home, and he immediately answered the thundering knock which Chipps favoured the door with.

"You are the very man I want to see," said Toppem, with an angry glare in his eyes; "but I didn't think you'd have the cheek to come round just yet."

"What do you mean?" demanded Ebeneezer Chipps. "I came to fetch my nephew."

"Oh! you did, did you?" responded Mr. Toppem. "Then just walk in here."

Ebeneezer did as he was told, but with all sorts of doubts and conflicting emotions worrying his mind.

"Now, just listen to this," said Mr. Toppem, holding up a sheet of paper. "Instead of finding a good fire, and the kettle bilin' when I came home, I found this. It's what I call a staggerer."

Gnawing at his fingers, Ebeneezer stood like an ugly statue while Mr. Toppem read the following, with as much emphasis as he could throw into his voice—

"DEAR FATHER,—*I hope you will not think it unkind of me, but something has happened to make me leave Cloisterville. I know it is a very wrong thing to do, and I can picture how angry you will be; but don't take on too much, nor go straight off to the Britons' Arms, as you used to do when anything upset you. I don't exactly know where I am going, or how long I shall be away ; but if ever I should make money you shall have some of it.—Your loving but undutiful son,*

"TIM."

"Now," said Mr. Toppem, turning ferociously upon Ebeneezer Chipps, "perhaps you will tell me what you think of that?"

"Why, I think it has nothing to do with me," Chipps retorted. "I came here about my nephew, and not about your son."

"Don't you see that this is all Ben's doings?" Toppem roared. "Who put such things as reading and writing into his head?—Ben! Who taught him?—Ben! I was forced to learn to read and write when I was a youngster at a place where—where there was a beadle, or I'd have had none of it."

"I don't want particulars of your early days—I want my nephew," Chipps murmured.

"Then," bellowed Mr. Toppem, "when you find Ben you'll find him. They've sloped together, and if you weren't an old fool you'd have thought so before."

"But where could Ben go to without money?" gasped Chipps.

Toppem put the same question with regard to his son, and then pointed sternly to the door.

"Old man," he said, "get out, or I'll set upon you in a way you will remember to your dying day. If I ever get hold of your precious nephew—"

"If I ever get hold of him," cried Ebeneezer Chipps, interrupting the irate and sorrowing parent, "I'll have him loaded with chains and treated like a criminal of the vilest order."

Toppem took a step forward and Chipps several backwards, but before he could reach the open air in the orthodox fashion he was assisted by a singularly heavy hob-nailed boot, and a fist that collided unpleasantly with the nape of his neck.

Vowing vengeance, and smarting with mental and physical injuries, Ebeneezer Chipps hurried off to the blacksmith, and after much haggling and groaning on his part made a bargain with him to open the door.

No sooner was this done, and the miser was alone, he went from room to room, with some vague hope that Ben might be playing him a boyish trick, and still be hiding in some part of the old building.

"Gone!" Chipps cried, when he had discovered the futile nature of his search. "Gone, and thwarted me!"

"Thwarted me!" replied the echo of his own voice.

"But I'll find him," he continued, "I'll find him, if it costs me my life."

"Costs me my life!" answered the echo.

Ebeneezer Chipps had dived down into the cellar as a last forlorn hope, and now, throwing aside a heap of rubbish from a corner, he went down on his knees and began to claw the earth like a wild beast.

Presently his hands came in contact with a hard substance, and a grim smile stole over his face.

"No, no!" he said, "the boy has not pryed into my secrets or touched anything. I did not think he would, but—but never mind, it is still there, and that is one comfort."

Ascending the rickety staircase, he threw himself upon his bed of straw and rags, and, overcome with fatigue and the strength of his violent temper, fell asleep, and lay dreaming and kicking until the dawn of a cold wintry morning stole through the windows, and told him that he had one day less to live.

"It is time that Jem Bosker was here," he said, as he turned out of bed; "but I dread to think of what he will say when he finds that the bird is flown."

The toilet arrangements of Ebeneezer Chipps were of a light description, as he generally slept in his clothes, and had no great love for soap and water.

Thrusting open the window he looked up the courtyard and saw the object of his remark approaching—and a most villainous-looking object it was.

CHAPTER V.

A SURPRISE FOR BEN BRIERTON—TIM TOPPEM'S VOW—
COMING EVENTS CAST THEIR SHADOWS BEFORE.

BEN and his appetite were quite ready for the breakfast.

consisting of steaks, and eggs to fill up with, in the living caravan.

The party consisted of four in number—our hero, William Wobstock, and Mrs. Wobstock, a strong-minded and business-like woman, whom we have not had occasion to mention before, and Ted Barrett, the lion tamer.

Sundry little Wobstocks partook of their morning meal with the keepers and helpers in the open air, and Ben Brierton wondered, with natural curiosity, where the Wobstock olive branches were stowed away at night time.

He thought it quite possible that they might be slung in oblong baskets under the caravans.

At all events, it was the first time that he had seen anything of them, and a shock-headed, rosy-cheeked, healthy lot of youngsters they were, varying in age from fourteen to four.

Mrs. Wobstock performed the ceremonies of the table in a matronly style, but she went a little out of her way in calling coffee "corfee," and an urn "a hurn," but such trifles were excusable under the circumstances; as in her skipping rope and hop-scotch days there were no such blessings as Board Schools.

"Will—i—am," she said, "please remember our guest !"

"He's never been out of my mind since I first saw him," Mr. Wobstock replied.

"Then, my dear," said the partner of his joys and sorrows, "will you pardon me if I say it is not perlite to eat in a hurry before strangers."

William Wobstock, who had demolished a steak weighing fully a pound and was well on the way with a second, put down his knife and fork.

The rebuke took him so much aback that in tilting his chair he nearly lost his balance.

"Hangelina," he said, "I have no wish to have any words, but when I took you for better or for worse, it was an arrangement that I should never be interfered with, and, dash it ! I won't be told how I am to get rid of my wittles."

Ben Brierton was desirous of pouring oil on the troubled waters which promised to rise under the domestic storm but he did not see his way clear how to do it.

Ted Barrett happily came to the rescue.

"Look here," he said, "you two shake hands. It's better that Bill should swallow his steak whole, and even choke himself than there should be any words about it."

"Ted always puts us right," Mrs. Wobstock observed. "Will—i—am, take your wedded wife's 'and in your own."

"There's mine, old gal," Wobstock replied, "and I mean it 'arty. Hullo! who's this."

A man had opened the door of the caravan just wide enough to admit of his head and shoulders.

"Somebody wants to see you," he said, looking at Ben Brierton.

"He can't and sha'n't see anybody," Wobstock said, leaping from his chair. "Higgins, you must be a born fool to say that he was here."

"Then why wasn't I given my orders," Higgins retorted, "I didn't know that there was a secret about his being here. It's only a young chap as wants to see him."

"Then," said Ben, his eyes rounded with astonishment, "it must be Tim Toppem."

"Go out and see," remarked Wobstock. "If it's your friend, bring him here, but if it ain't give him one straight from the left, and foller up with your right afore he knows what's the matter."

It was scarcely likely that Ben Brierton would follow this advice unless he was in danger of being violently assaulted, himself, and he left the caravan with few misgivings.

Near a tree, and eyed curiously and not a little suspiciously by the young Wobstocks, stood Tim Toppem.

"Good gracious!" Ben cried. "What brought you here?"

"My feet," Tim replied.

"I suppose so," Ben said. "But what is your object? You have some news to tell me? Don't be afraid to speak out."

"That is what I am going to do," Tim returned. "I told you when we parted that I meant to do something wrong, and I've done it."

"Tell me what it is?" Ben demanded, half guessing the truth.

"It won't take me long. I ran away from home, and I followed the caravans at a distance all through the night. Ben, you've been the only real friend I ever had, and you don't think that I am going to leave you now?"

"But, my dear boy," Ben Brierton said, "think of the awkward position you place me and yourself in. I am living with these people, who have befriended me out of the goodness of their hearts—"

"And gratitude," Tim put in. "I don't wish them to take me, because I know I am not much use to anybody. I only want to be near you, and near you I will be. I daresay I can pick up my living somehow, but if not I will starve cheerfully. Don't turn me away, Ben; don't say the words that will send me back with a broken heart; only let me be within sight and hearing of you and I shall be satisfied."

CHAP. VI.—TIM IS TAKEN INTO CONGENIAL QUARTERS.

TEARS welled into Ben Brierton's eyes, for Tim's noble nature now shone out in all its truth and glory.

"You shall share my last crust with me," he said; "but it is nevertheless a serious step you have taken. What will your father say?"

"I fear that he will come it strong for a little while," Tim responded; "but he will cool down and perhaps think that he has got rid of a bad bargain. Besides," he added, smiling, "I promised to send him a little money if I made it, and it will give him something to do to look out for the postman."

"You wrote him a etter?"

"Yes, and leaving it on the table made tracks for fear that father might come home early."

Just then Wobstock, with the lion tamer's ponderous whip tucked under his arm, appeared on the scene.

He was not displeased to see Tim personally, but it had dawned into his mind that the youth might have fallen a prey to the allurements of Ebeneezer Chipps, and consented to act as a spy.

"Now, then, my lad," he said, "you see this little article? I want to know what you are doing here, and, being a man of few words, I want few from you, and the exact truth."

"Let me explain how matters stand," Ben said.

He did so, and William Wobstock listened, rubbing his chin with his hand.

"I suppose there is no blarney about this?" he demanded, fixing his eyes on the runaway. "I suppose you didn't say to anybody 'I know where Bold Ben Brierton is, and if you want to catch him all you have to do is to follow me?'"

This implied accusation nearly lifted Tim Toppem off his feet.

"What do you mean by talking to me like that?" he retorted, clenching his hands and striding forward. "Do you think I'd be so mean, and low, and lost to everything that is straightforward and manly as to sell Ben after he has been so good to me? Your words have made my blood hot. You'd better be careful, or I shall ask you to put down that whip and come on."

Poor Tim did not look as if he could stand a pugilistic encounter of long duration.

He was footsore, half frozen, hungry, but plucky withal, and Wobstock marked his demeanour and attitude with pride and admiration.

"My lad," he said, "when I saw you on your back, I didn't think that there was much sound metal in you, but I was mistaken. I'm sorry I doubted you for a moment, and here's my hand upon it—a hand that was never lifted against any man without good cause."

Tim Toppem's wrath vanished in an instant.

He shook hands with the proprietor of the menagerie, who suddenly eyed the youth's waistcoat with a wistful and critical eye.

"I was just wondering," he said, "whether you were in a fit condition to spoil the look of a steak."

Tim felt inclined to reply after the fashion of the proverbial boy who, when asked whether he could eat a tart, forthwith answered that he was ready to annihilate forty; but he merely expressed his thanks, and said he would do his best to settle the question satisfactorily.

"Then come along," said Wobstock. "Bold Ben Brierton next to you, your faithful friend, Tim Toppem, is welcome. Hyenas and halligators!" he exclaimed, smiting the crown of his hat; "the world seems to be full of young heroes just now."

Tim was introduced to Mrs. Wobstock and Ted Barrett, and the ceremony having been performed as quickly as possible a fresh steak was soon hissing pleasantly on the grill.

It made Wobstock almost hungry again to see Tim eat, and he watched him with as much satisfaction as a doctor regards a patient of whose life he has despaired returning to health and strength.

"Hangelina!" Wobstock said, in a stage whisper. "More bread and butter, and cut it thick."

"Will-i-am," his mate replied, "being the mother of boys 1 think I know what they are capable of when hungry.

Mr. Wobstock silently confessed that such was the case, and, putting on his hat, he went forth to attend to some business connected with the menagerie, the lion-tamer following him.

"Ted," said Wobstock, "it's almost a pity that a menagerie don't admit of a clown. That boy Tim is a ready-made one. What is the best thing to do with him? Come! you are never lost for an idea."

Ted Barrett rolled his massive head on one side, and reflected.

"Suppose we taught him to look after the monkeys?" he replied. "He might get up a comic lecture about their tricks to make the people laugh. I think it would draw."

Wobstock smote his thigh, producing a sound as loud as a pistol shot.

"Draw?" he echoed. "There's money in it. And look here, ha—ha! I've got an idea, too."

"You'll forget all about it if you laugh like that," Ted Barrett said; "and too much laughing isn't good for a man of your weight."

Wobstock was fairly roaring now.

His head was well back, his mouth wide open, and his cheeks growing dangerously purple.

"What's come to you?" the lion tamer demanded, in an alarmed tone of voice. "Here! hold up. Your feet are slipping away from you. Look here! I shall have to call the missus."

This brought Wobstock to a state of semi-gravity.

On a previous occasion, when seized with a sudden fit of mirth, Angelina had put a summary end to it by throwing a jug of cold water over him, and completing the cure with an effective application of a mop over his back and shoulders.

"Ted," he observed, "if you hadn't mentioned the missus I think I should ha' gone. I feel double my size, and dreamy like. Why shouldn't we get a fur dress for Tim, and advertise him as the only tame gorilla in the world?"

"What!" exclaimed the lion-tamer. "Put the boy in the cage?"

"Why not?" said Wobstock. "He would only have to appear twice a day for a few minutes. We could keep a curtain drawn over the cage, and when he was wanted he could slip in at the back."

Ted Barrett did not like to discourage Wobstock, but he was rather dubious as to the result of the venture.

"Here he comes, and you can speak to him about it if you like," he replied.

Tim, now thoroughly refreshed and looking like his old self, came up with Ben Brierton, and Wobstock was so full of the gorilla idea that he broached it immediately.

The notion made Tim laugh almost as much as it had done Wobstock.

"If you think I am capable of it," he said, "I shall be only too willing to try. I suppose I should have nothing to do but to climb about and make horrible noises?"

"He knows his part already!" Wobstock cried, enthusiastically. "We'll have the cage fitted up with a bit of a tree, and you shall have a club as big as the one that killed Captain Cook. We'll keep the people back as far as possible, but if they should be too inquisitive, why—"

"I'll rush at the bars and yell at them," Tim interposed. "You leave it to me, sir; I'll give 'em fits!"

Wobstock was delighted beyond expression.

He took a careful measure of Tim there and then, and was not contented until he had written to London for the dress and posted the letter.

"Now I feel happy," he said, "and there's nothing more to be done but to get up a fetching bill, with a gorilla takin' a walk with a huge tiger under his arm, or something of that sort."

The boys, finding that their services were not required, resolved to take a walk, and no two happier lads ever set out together.

"We've dropped on our eet," said Tim, stopping, and leaning his back against a mile-stone, "but it's all through you. And I say, Ben, tell me again that you are not angry that I ran away from Cloisterville to find you?"

"I am only too pleased to have you near me," Ben replied; "but I am still haunted with visions of your father arriving unexpectedly."

"Well, I must risk that," Tim said; "but I think you have more to fear from—"

At that moment a dog-cart, drawn by a spirited horse, driven by a middle-aged man of aristocratic appearance, rattled round a turning in the road.

"Is this the nearest road to Cloisterville?" he asked, pulling up.

"So the sign-post says," Tim replied.

"Thank you, I did not notice it," the gentleman returned. "What is that noise? It sounds like distant thunder, a rather unusual thing for this time of the year."

"That's a lion, sir."

"A lion?"

"Yes," said Ben. "There is a menagerie just under the hill."

"Then I must avoid it unless I want a spill," the gentleman remarked. "My horse would bolt if I took him within a hundred yards of wild beasts. I suppose you lads belong to the show?"

He looked hard at Ben Brierton as he put the question, and at the same time a puzzled expression came over his face.

Ben was at a loss to know what sort of reply to make, but Tim came promptly to the rescue.

"If my father knew that I was within a mile of the show," he replied, and with perfect truth, "there would be a jolly row."

"I must find another road," the gentleman said, laughing, as he turned the horse.

But still he seemed reluctant to drive away, and again directed his eyes wistfully at Ben.

"If my memory does not mislead me," he said, "I think I have seen you at Cloisterville.'

"I have been there," Ben replied.

The gentleman drove off but slowly, as if he had given up the conversation reluctantly.

The two boys looked after the dog-cart until it vanished out of sight, and then Ben spoke.

"That man seems to know me," he said; "and he has left an uneasy impression behind him. I feel as if his shadow still lingers near me, and that his life is in some way bound up with mine."

It was the old story of coming events casting their shadows before.

Ben Brierton was destined to meet the occupant of the dog-cart again, and under strange and eventful circumstances.

CHAPTER VII.

RETURNS BRIEFLY TO EBENEEZER CHIPPS, AND TELLS OF THE GREAT DISAPPOINTMENT OF HIS FRIEND, SAMUEL RUSHMORE—AN ELEPHANT WITH A SWEET TOOTH.

THE disagreeable object that met the gaze of Ebeneezer Chipps was a human one.

A lanky, villainous-looking fellow, clad in a jacket of thick pilot cloth, corduroy continuations, a fur cap, and heavy boots that made the hard-frozen ground ring again.

This individual, named Samuel Rushmore, *alias* Jem Bosker, gave out to the appreciative public that he was a dealer, a rather vague term that might imply anything.

Judging by Rushmore's appearance his dealings were

not of a kind such as would always meet with the appro-
bation of a judge and jury of his fellow countrymen, and
as he came swinging over the stones with his head down
and his hands deep in his pockets, he might have been
taken for a garotter returning from a successful ex-
pedition.

Chipps ran downstairs, and greeted him at the door
with—

"It's all up, Sam; the boy's bolted."

Rushmore said never a word until the door was closed
behind him, and he was well into the house.

Then he took Ebeneezer Chipps by the ears, and gave
his head a sounding bump against the wall.

"Don't!" Chipps gasped, as his eyes filled with water,
"I am too old to be treated in that way."

"I'll treat you to somethin'," Rushmore growled.
"Tell me again that the boy isn't here, and I'll knock
your head off your shoulders."

"It's a painful fact—a mournful fact," Ebenezer Chipps
groaned. "I left him here while I came to see you, and
he bolted during my—oh! don't, please don't, Sam—
absence. The little villain locked the house up, and—"

"Hold your tongue," Rushmore interrupted. "I must
have time to get over this. I'll sit down while you fetch
some brandy—a bottleful."

"Brandy, my dear friend, is an expensive article,"
Chipps observed, faintly. "Once, when I was very
ill—"

"You'll have a sudden illness, which will end fatally,
if you don't do as I tell you," Rushmore bellowed, starting up and shaking his brawny fist in the miser's face.
"I want something to string my nerves together.
Bolted! And just when everything had been so neatly
arranged. Brandy, you mumbling, mouthing old sinner!'

"But surely not a whole—"

The only article available as a missile within Rushmore's
reach was a three-legged stool, and this gentle persuader
followed Chipps into the hall, just missing his head, and
accelerating his movements to a superlative degree of
activity.

During the miser's absence Sam Rushmore crouched

over the grate, clutching his knees and contorting his face.

"It ain't likely," he muttered, "that I'm goin' to let two hundred pounds slip through my fingers. It's all the more aggravatin' because I'd got the boy a nice crib which the police have got their eyes on, and intend to make a raid soon."

Rushmore was so virtuously indignant at our hero's ungrateful conduct that he seized the poker and dashed it into the cinders, scattering them right and left, to ease his feelings.

It was not long before he heard the return of the miser's footsteps; but something else came to his ears—a heavy fall, accompanied by a gasping cry and the smashing of glass.

"The old fool has tumbled down and broken the brandy-bottle," Rushmore said, starting up.

This proved to be the correct state of the case, and Chipps, white as a sheet, staggered into the room.

"I'm a ruined man!" he howled; "five shillings gone in one moment. Sam, my dear friend, you won't let me bear all the expense; you haven't the heart to do it?"

"I have the heart to knock what little sense remains in your addled pate out of it," Rushmore replied, laughing in spite of himself. "Well, I suppose I must do without the brandy. Sit down, and let us talk the matter over. What are you going to say to Mr. Reginald when he comes to settle up? He will expect to find that I have gone away with the boy."

"You mustn't meet him here, on any account," Chipps moaned. "I'll do my best to wheedle him over. Leave it to me to break the news gently."

"But the boy must be found,

"Of course he must. We must start after him as—as soon as Mr. Reginald comes down with the money for travelling expenses."

"I suppose we must leave the affair where it stands," Rushmore growled, pitching his fur cap on to his head. "I'll hang about the city for a few hours. At what time do you expect Mr. Reginald?"

"At one o'clock."

" Then," said Rushmore, striding towards the door, " if I look in in an hour or two the force of his fury will have spent itself. All I know is that I've come by appointment ready to do the work I took in hand, and I mean to be paid for it."

Just two hours after this conversation had taken place, and Sam Rushmore had departed to follow his favourite pursuit of "hanging about," Wobstock's menagerie was on the move towards Macleton.

The town was not many miles distant, the journey was soon completed, and if all went well everything would be in order in the cattle market by noontide.

Accidents occur in the best regulated establishments, and it so happened that Mumbo the elephant upset all the peaceful arrangements.

The huge brute was relieved of his trappings and was allowed to stand untrammelled to be admired by a gaping crowd, while the caravans were got into position.

Never before had Mumbo misconducted himself in any way—indeed, he had been looked upon as a pattern of docility.

But lo ! a change came o'er the spirit of the beast.

Jack Wyatt, Mumbo's keeper, happened to be called away for a moment, and the elephant forthwith displayed an amount of skittishness which commenced in his swinging his trunk at a furious rate, and finally trotting playfully through the crowd.

Speechless with fright, the people fled in all directions, leaving the ground bestrewn with hats, caps, umbrellas, shawls, and, here and there, an article of feminine head-gear.

Three stout old ladies dashed down the steps of a greengrocer's shop, destroying the symmetry of a pyramid of potatoes and a handsome pile of cabbages.

The curate of the parish—a mild little man, with scarcely the strength to lift a fiddle—skipped over eight flights of sheep-pens, and went up a lamp-post with the agility of an organ-grinder's monkey.

A schoolmaster who had brought his boys to view whatever could be seen for nothing, and who had been delivering a lecture on the subject of elephants in general, was seized with a sudden desire to flee, and, deserting his flock, bolted headlong into a public-house, and before he could be stopped to give a word of explanation, became a livid spectator of the scene from the topmost room.

All this, and more, happened in much less time than it has taken to record it.

The keeper, snatching up a pitchfork, and followed by Ben Brierton and Tim Toppem, gave chase.

Mumbo, however, had made up his mind to enjoy a holiday, and, increasing his speed, thundered up the High-street.

He had it all to himself; for such people as were about performed the vanishing trick quicker and neater than it has ever been presented on any stage.

In vain Jack Wyatt shouted to Mumbo, varying endearing cries with threats which had more than their ordinary share of violence.

It so happened that half-way up the thoroughfare was a confectioner's shop, kept by a Mr. Crumbles.

He was a stout, bald-headed man, rather deaf, and always obtuse, save when his customers came to pay their accounts.

Mr. Crumbles was pleasantly engaged in placing the stale pastry over the new, when he saw several people scamper past.

"A fire, I suppose," he murmured. "Well, it's nothing to me. If I were fool enough to leave my shop some villain would rush in and prig the till. I'm well-insured, thank goodness, so, if the whole street is burnt down, why—"

The rest of the words he intended to utter trembled on his lips.

Something like the sudden overcasting of a thunder cloud darkened his shop.

The next instant the plate glass front gave way with a terrific crash, and Mumbo, stalking calmly in, began to help himself to the dainties displayed on the counter.

Even if the elephant had been gifted with the power of speech he would have had no chance to ask the confectioner any question with respect to the price and quality of the various articles.

Mr. Crumbles expected instant death, the all-devouring monster.

In the first place, Mr. Crumbles took a violent leap into the air, accompanying the involuntary action with something that sounded like—

"Good gracious! what the deuce is it?"

And then took a header under his counter in a manner a professional diver might have envied.

Even in that moment of supreme agony he knew that he had bumped himself severely.

His bald head, knees, elbows, shins, and pet corns seemed to have come simultaneously in contact with pain-producing agencies, but it was not the time to think of such trifles.

Mr. Crumbles expected instant death, and closed his eyes so that he might not gaze upon the all-devouring monster.

Just then up came Jack Wyatt, with our hero and Tim, in hot haste.

"Come out of it, you ten tons of destruction!" the keeper roared, striking Mumbo over the head with the pitchfork. "You shall wear chains for the rest of your life."

Mumbo took the blow as lightly as if a feather had fallen on him, but the sound of Jack Wyatt's voice recalled him to a sense of duty.

Having finished the last bun he prepared to back, and whisking his ears and blinking in a manner denoting that he had thoroughly enjoyed himself.

"Here's a pretty smash!" cried Tim, who was bare-headed, and his hair sticking up like birch twigs. "This will cost something."

"Never mind the cost," Wyatt gasped. "Only let me get this brute back, and I'll teach him manners."

"It's an unfortunate affair," Ben Brierton observed.

"Unfortunate?" the keeper groaned. "If you don't find Wobstock in a fit it will be a wonder to me."

At this moment Mr. Crumbles crawled out from under the counter.

He looked as if he could have sung "Is this a dream" with demi-semi-quaver variations.

His mind was in such a confused state that he had not as yet fully realised what had happened.

"Buns are seven for sixpence to-day," he said, with quivering lips. "If you do not object to stale ones, and they toast well, I will say eight."

It dawned on him that there was too much ventilation in his shop; and then, as his vision cleared and his senses returned, he gave a cry of horror and rushed into the street.

"Hi! there," he shouted, "come back and settle for this damage."

"What, come back with this thing?" Jack Wyatt retorted, pointing to Mumbo. "Not if I know it. You'd better see the guv'nor later on, if he's in a fit state to be spoken to."

Mr. Crumbles went back for his hat and coat while Wyatt and Ben Brierton were escorting the elephant back to the menagerie.

Mumbo was already on good terms with our hero, and kept touching him with his trunk, as much as to say —"A fellow must have his fling sometimes, let the cost be what it may."

A sad sight met the gaze of the returning party.

Wobstock, who had heard what had happened, sat upon his white hat, with nothing but the whites of his eyes visible, and Angelina was was fanning his face with a tea-tray.

"Will-i-am," she cried, in accents of anguish, "don't look like that! Think of me and the children."

"I'm thinking of the county court," he gurgled. "Action for breakages and shock to the nerves. Fifty pounds damages. Fifty pounds at five shillings a month, if they get it, will hang round my neck like a millstone for more than sixteen years. Oh! Ben, is that you? It's a pity that we were not near at hand at the moment. Wyatt, get out of my sight. I'm dangerous just now."

"Whatever there is to pay you can stop out of my wages by instalments," the keeper grumbled. "If you hadn't called me away this bother wouldn't have happened."

"There's some truth in that," Wobstock replied. "I'll let you down easy, Jack. Your wants are few, and being a single man, money is of little use to you.

Where's my hat?"

"You are sitting upon it," Tim said.

"Why so I am," Wobstock returned, dismally, "and, worse luck, it takes me years to get used to a hat. Jack, this must go down in the bill."

Wyatt said nothing, but walked away, vowing vengeance against the cause of the mischief.

"I think," said Ben, "if you were to have a few bills struck off about Mumbo's performance, nearly all the town would come to see him."

Wobstock wrung our hero's hand.

"So they would, my boy," he cried. "We'll turn the accident to good account yet. We must have the bills out at once. I'll run out and find a printer."

In less than an hour the town was fluttering with bills containing the following headlines: "Laughable incident at Macleton! An elephant in the tuck-shop! Mr. Crumbles under the counter! Come and see Mumbo! who walked through a shop-front. Great excitement! The police going to bed in a hurry! Flight of the populace! Don't forget Wobstock's menagerie! Mr. Crumbles, having recovered from his shock, has promised to ride three times round the menagerie on Mumbo's back. To-night! To-night! Mumbo and Crumbles, and all the other wild animals. Prices as usual."

When Crumbles, who had formally lodged his complaint at the menagerie and the police-station, read the bill, he almost exploded with indignation.

Ruthlessly crushing a jar of raspberry jam with his heel, he swore by his kneading-trough that he would run up such a bill as would make Wobstock as bald as himself.

CHAPTER VIII.

THE MINION OF THE LAW AND WHAT BECAME OF HIM—
A LITTLE DISTURBANCE AT THE MENAGERIE AND
WHAT IT LED TO.

THE aforesaid bills had the desired effect, in spite of all Crumbles could do or say.

The people poured into the menagerie in such numbers that they were almost suffocated. and a portion of the canvas roof had to be removed to give them air.

The Lion King's daring brought forth thunders of applause, the tricks of the monkeys shrieks of laughter, and Mumbo was the darling of the hour.

The elephant was so fed that, even with his enormous capacity for stowing away edibles, he was compelled to cry, "Hold! enough;" and Jack Wyatt had his work cut out to keep his charge from going to sleep.

"Where's Crumbles?" was the shout again and again indulged in. "Why isn't he here to keep his promise?"

Wobstock paced up and down, rubbing his hands and his face beaming like an amiable harvest moon.

"I'd like a shop front to be busted in every day if it would draw like this," he said, pinching Ben's arm affectionately. "We'll try it on something a little smaller than Mumbo. We might do it with a runaway camel."

As he was speaking a stout police-sergeant stalked up.

"Now for it," Wobstock thought. "There's a look in his eyes that means summonses."

"Where is the proprietor of this show?" demanded the officer.

"He is here," Wobstock replied, putting his damaged hat straight for the fortieth time. "What can I do for you, sir?"

"You can clear out of the town as soon as you like, and look sharp about it."

As the sergeant spoke a weedy youth, hitherto unseen, darted from behind him and tapped Wobstock familiarly on the shoulder.

"Writ, sir," said the youth. "Crumbles v. Wobstock. Would you like to see the original?"

"Blow the original," Wobstock gasped. "Who let you in?"

"Paid my shilling, like a man."

"Well then, you've a right to be here," the proprietor of the menagerie returned. "Now, sir," he said, turning to the police-sergeant, "perhaps you will explain what you mean by my clearing out. I've taken this ground and paid the money down for three days, and here I mean to stick."

"Oh! you do, do you?" cried the officer, swelling out

his chest. " Here is the magistrate's order, and—"

" If you or the magistrates think you can move me, try it on," Wobstock interposed, indicating the whole of the ponderous caravans with a sweep of his arm. " There's a lock brake on every wheel, so the job would take some little time."

" The magistrates have come to the conclusion that there is danger to life and limb to the general public in such an exhibition as this," said the sergeant, growing very red in the face, " so they have given you six hours to leave the town."

" I see how it is," Wobstock responded ; " they are afraid of Mumbo. Now, if a horse ran away with a man and pitched him through a window, would the magistrates have the power to prevent that man from ever driving another horse?"

" I'm here to do my duty, not too argue," said the officer.

" Then you can do it by marching out of this place at once," Wobstock replied. " This is my land while I pay for it, and my house, too, because I live in it. You have no more right to come marching in here without leave than you have to break open a door without a warrant.'

" But that is a warrant," persisted the sergeant.

" Pooh !" said Wobstock, crumpling up the slip of paper and pitching it into the fire-basket. " That's what I think of it. When my time's up I'll go to the minute, and as to the writ, I'll stand the racket of it. Now you've got my answer. Be off."

CHAPTER IX.—THE POLICE SERGEANT DISCOMFITED.
NEVER before had the bold sergeant been spoken to in such a manner.

" Be off " to him ! Why, if it went forth to the people of Mucleton that he put up with such an indignity tamely he might as well tear the stripes from his arm and retire from the force. .f the stars had fallen, or a collection of thunderbolts had paid him an unexpected visit, the ser* ant could not have looked more astonished

Wobstock was not a nice looking man to openly offend, therefore, the sergeant, who felt that he must find an excuse for attacking somebody, looked round for a weaker victim.

His wrathful eyes fell upon Ben Brierton.

"Go away," he said, pushing the lad roughly by the shoulders; "who told you told you stand there listening?"

Ben lost his balance and fell, but was on his feet in an instant, and in another the bold sergeant's legs were waving in the air, and the sound like the crushing of a band-box proclaimed that his helmet was well over his eyes.

"Bravo, Ben!" cried Wobstock. "He had no right to assault you. Don't think of his uniform—it's only cloth and buttons—the law is on your side. Put him out."

Amid a tremendous uproar, Ben, with Tim Toppen forcing a passage through the crowd, carried the dazed officer out, and dropped him carefully down the flight of steps.

The proceedings, summary and violent as they were, did not seems to interest the sergeant much.

For some seconds he sat on the bottom step without even attempting to remove his helmet.

But suddenly it dawned upon him that he was in the same plight as Moses when the candle went out, and that the use of his eyes were necessary.

"If there's a man about with an ounce of good feeling in him," he gasped, "he will help me out of this thing and send for a cab. I'm all in pieces."

Somebody came to his rescue, and the sergeant, after staring wildly round him, and shaking his fist at Angelina Wobstock, who was counting up the money, walked away at a wonderful rate for a broken man.

"Ben," said Wobstock, "you had better go to bed. There's a red light loomin' not far off, and that sergeant will be here again with every man at his disposal."

"So much the better," Ben Brierton said. "Why should I be afraid of him or all he can bring? Surely you wouldn't have me sneak off to bed, as if I had been guilty of a mean thing?"

Wobstock shook his head gravely.

"No," he said. "But, on the other hand, you see, trouble might come of it in another way. If the sergeant can get one warrant he can get another, and he might march here with the whole force at his back and demand your arrest. I think we had better take Ted Barrett's advice."

The Lion King, when consulted, seemed to share Wobstock's opinion, and drawing him aside whispered something in his ear.

"The very thing!" Wobstock said. "If nobody has taken the old mill, and it was half in ruins last year, it will be a safe hiding-place."

"They say the mill is haunted, and that is why nobody will take it," Barrett observed.

"Haunted by rats and mice you mean," said Wobstock, contemptuously. "Ben, my lad, come here."

Our hero, fully aware that he had been the subject of the whispered conversation, advanced a little anxiously.

"I suppose," said the proprietor of the circus, "you wouldn't mind sleeping in a place said to be haunted by a few ghosts, witches, hobgoblins, and such like?"

"Not a bit," replied Ben, wondering what he was driving at.

"Let us put it in this way," Wobstock continued. "Suppose Ted Barrett and me have come to the conclusion that you had better be stowed away in some place until we were on the road again; and suppose that we knew of a certain old mill which had not been tenanted for many a day where you could stay?"

"I should say that it would be a most undesirable place of residence," Ben Brierton replied; "but I see what you mean, and I will do just as you wish."

"There's sense for you!" Wobstock cried. "There's intellect! We will look after you, Ben; your friend shall bring you plenty to eat and drink, and, take my word for it, we will make you as comfortable as possible."

"The only thing that makes me vexed," said Ben, "is that I must hide at all."

"Which shows your pluck, of course," Wobstock observed; "but, you see, if you got before the magistrate, and I was called forrard to answer questions, somebody might turn up to claim you, and off you'd go back to Cloisterville as sure as gooseberries are sour before they are ripe."

"Never !" Ben said ; "I would sooner die first."

"But as you don't want to die, and I don't intend you should afore your time, you'll put up with the old mill for a day or two. Ted, put up some blankets and other things you think may come in useful, and drive Ben off at once."

"What, to-night ?" our hero cried, in astonishment.

"As soon as the horse is ready," Woodstock replied, in a tone of voice that admitted of no argument. "I'm on thorns for fear that the sergeant and his men may be back before you make yourself scarce."

Ben Brierton did not relish the arrangements made for him, but not liking to throw any obstacle in the way, such as might displease those who had his welfare at heart, he said nothing.

Tim Toppem's mind hovered between fear and admiration when he heard the use the old mill was to be put to.

"Ben is a match for any number of ghosts, I know," he said, as he helped Barrett to put the horse into the trap, "and I'm sure he'd just as soon sleep in a church as anywhere for the matter of him being afraid. But a musty old mill, with boards rotting, wheels groaning and rusty chains cranking—oh ! lor', the very thought makes one shiver."

"Better that than find himself on the police books, and be marked for life," the lion-tamer replied. "When you take Ben his breakfast in the morning I don't think you will find him much the worse for his night's lodging."

"Then I am to go with you ?"

"Yes, or how do you think you'll find your way to the mill ?"

CHAPTER X.

THE HAUNTED WATER-MILL—HOW TIM TOPPEM WAS FOLLOWED, AND WHAT HAPPENED WHILE BEN BRIERTON WAS TAKING A NAP.

THE old water-mill spanned a stream about two miles from Macleton cattle-market, where the menagerie was pitched, and no sooner was Ben on the road, than the somewhat damaged and altogether wrathful sergeant, with sixteen men in blue, with buttons gleaming like shining armour, made their appearance.

Wobstock was equal to the ordeal.

The musicians had played the National Anthem, and the people were gone, when the representatives of the law, advancing in single file, appeared before the platform.

The steps were up, and Wobstock had no intention to let them down again.

"Well, my lads," he said, cheerfully; "I suppose you are out for the night."

"Somebody will be run in for the night," retorted the sergeant, savagely. "Where's that boy of yours?"

"Young Henery, aged nine, is in bed, with a sudden rash pecooliar to Macleton," Wobstock replied; "and as for the hinfant Jacob, just gone seven months, he is, to the best o' my knowledge, bein' lured off to sleep with a hempty feedin'-bottle."

"Blow Henery and Jacob!" gasped the sergeant; "I mean that strong feller, who—er—took a mean advantage of me."

"Oh! him," said Wobstock. "Ah! now I know. Poor boy, he was so frightened, that he went straight off. I had some notion that he went to the station to give himself up for high treason. At all events, I have nothing to do with the row, so Good-night."

"That man," roared the sergeant, as Wobstock disappeared, "has defied the whole bench of magistrates, and jeers at us. I order you to arrest him!"

Several of the constables leaped upon the platform, but retired precipitately, for something long, black, and pliable whisked round the corner.

Wobstock had brought Mumbo to the entrance, and that sagacious animal, guessing what was required of him, did his best to catch a constable.

The guardians of the public peace appeared to think that they were a little out of place, and retreated, the invisible Wobstock roaring after them—

"Afore I'd be taken for doin' nothin', I'd open every blessed cage and turn the town into a jungle."

In the meantime Ben Brierton and his friends had reached the old water mill.

It was certainly not a very encouraging looking place.

A portion of the roof had fallen in, and the wheel once so busy was choked with weeds, and silent, save that the water gurgled and splashed drearily through the open floats.

Leaving Tim Toppem to mount guard over the horse and trap, Ted Barrett, shouldering a bundle of blankets, led the way to a railed-in gallery that ran round the ruinous building.

"Mind how you plant your feet, Ben," the lion-tamer said. "Some of the boards are loose, and others are as rotten as tinder."

The warning came just in time, and Ben pulled up sharply on the brink of a hole which would have dropped him into the very midst of the rusty machinery.

Barrett pushed a door open, and entered the lower room of the mill.

"Now, Ben." he said, encouragingly, "you must make the best of your lodgings. Tim shall bring you a good hot breakfast in the morning, and a newspaper. Here's a lantern, but don't show a light unless you are compelled to do so. And now, Good-night."

Ben shook hands heartily with the lion-tamer, and Tim came to take his leave of our hero.

"Ben," he said, "you must have plenty of pluck to consent to stay in such a place as this. My goodness i the very thought is enough to give me fits; but, then, I am such a dreadful coward."

"You are nothing of the kind," Ben returned; "I know better. Don't worry yourself about me—I shall be all right."

"Now, then, Tim," the lion-tamer sang out, "it i time that we were on the road back. Jump up, and we will be off."

Tim Toppem did not appear to relish the notion of leaving Ben ; but he tore himself away at last.

Our hero stood listening to the sound of the wheels until it became muffled and indistinct.

He then closed the door, and took a survey of his quarters.

"Well," he said, "if any place in the world is haunted, this should be. What's that?"

His self-control almost failed him as something clanked and jangled above his head.

It was nothing more than a piece of chain hanging from the ceiling, which had been set in motion by a sudden gust of air, but it made Ben's heart beat high.

"How foolish I am!" he said. "Well, so much for ghost number one. I'll go to sleep at once or I shall be scaring myself with all sorts of visionary alarms."

Ben made a pillow of one blanket, and, rolling himself up in the others, closed his eyes, and was soon in the land of dreams.

While he slumbered, three men stole along the banks of the stream, and reached the mill.

They were Ebeneezer Chipps, Sam Rushmore, and the man of aristocratic appearance who had spoken to Ben and Tim in the morning.

"I own, Mr. Reginald," said Chipps, humbly, "that I ought to have been more careful; but who would have thought the boy would have bolted? Dear me! the world is full of ingratitude."

"Well, we've got him safe enough now," Rushmore whispered; "but what on earth they have put him in the mill for puzzles me."

"Hold your tongue!" Mr. Reginald said. "All we have to think of now is to catch him napping. I suppose he would show fight, if he had the chance?"

"Yes, sir, he would," Chipps replied. "I think he would even turn upon me."

"That," observed Rushmore, grinning, "I should think wery likely."

The ruffian, leaving the others, advanced on tiptoe, and tried the door.

It was not locked, for the very simple reason that the enterprising rustics had long since appropriated every lock and bolt in the mill, and Ben had been able to do no more than to secure the door with a wedged-shaped piece of wood.

This Sam Rushmore pushed back with the point of a huge clasp knife, and crept into the room on his hands and knees.

Ben lay sleeping soundly and dreaming happily.

Rushmore took a handkerchief from his pocket and scattered a few drops of fluid from a glass-stoppered bottle upon it.

In another instant the handkerchief was pressed over Ben's mouth and nostrils.

The lad tried to rise, but Rushmore, planting his knee on his chest, kept him down.

Ben struck out with might and main, but soon his hands moved feebly and aimlessly.

"No doctor could have performed the trick better," Rushmore said, rising to his feet. "I hope I haven't overdosed him with the chloroform, but if so, it can't be helped. You can come in," he cried aloud; "the boy is off sound enough, and likely to be so for some hours to come."

Ebeneezer Chipps came rushing in, his companion following in a more dignified style.

"It does my heart good to see him again," Chipps said, grinning hideously; "and if I didn't think that Mr. Reginald would object I'd ease my mind with a few kicks. Ho—ho! Ben, you have fallen into a nice trap."

"No thanks to you," drawled the swell. "I claim the credit of his capture, for it was I who brought the news of where to find him to you."

"That's right enough," Chipps returned. "How lucky you came upon him and that imp Tim. Don't you think I ought to action those wild beast people for luring my nephew away? How nice it would read in the papers, 'Chipps v. Wobstock—heavy damages.'"

"I know the sort o' damages you'd get," Sam Rushmore growled. "Let well alone, I tell you. We must be satisfied that the boy has fallen into our hands so easily. Keep your eye upon him while I bring the trap up."

Ben, unconscious of all that was passing, lay stretched upon the floor, pale to ghastliness, and breathing so faintly that Reginald placed his hand on the lad's heart to assure himself that he lived.

Then he drew Chipps aside, and held a whispered conversation, which lasted until Rushmore came back.

"Well," said Chipps, "why have you not brought the horse and trap with you?"

"Because the horse is dead lame," Rushmore replied. "I tethered him to a tree in the wood, but the brute broke the rope, and must have picked up something in one of his hoofs. It's all up for to-night, unless we hire one."

"That would be as good as sending for the town crier, and telling him to give out what we have done," Reginald said.

"But what is to be done?" Chipps demanded. "We must get away somehow."

"I will go and see what is the matter with the horse," Reginald replied, "and in the meantime we will guard against surprise. There is a smaller chamber under this, and we had better lower the boy into it."

As he spoke he pointed to a trap-door, which Ebeneezer Chipps opened, and held the lantern over it.

"A nice cosy place, full of cobwebs and dust," he said. "It's much too good for a runaway, but I suppose we must temper justice with mercy."

Rushmore had meantime secured the door, and now, stooping down, raised Ben in his brawny arms.

"Lend a hand, guv'ner," he said. "This 'ere job is a little more than I can manage."

Reginald complied, and Ben was carried slowly towards the open trap.

"Quick!" Chipps shrieked, suddenly. "I hear footsteps and a voice. Down with him!"

But before it could be done there was a crash at the door; one of the lower panels gave way, and Tim Toppem crawled through with a stick in his hand.

"Come along!" he shouted, as if he had a crowd at his back; "I've caught the rascals."

Ebeneezer Chipps dropped the lantern through the

crap, and made for the door.

But ere he reached it he received a tremendous crack on his head, protected only by a velvet skull-cap, that made him stagger again.

"Rushmore! Sir—sir," he cried, "surely you are not going to leave me to be killed! Oh! murder."

His voice brought no assistance.

The other cowards had fled, and Chipps ollowed their example, leaving Tim to sob and laugh in turns over Bold Ben Brierton.

CHAPTER XI.

ONCE MORE ON THE ROAD—THE ONLY TAME GORILLA IN THE WORLD.

"Oh! Ben—Ben," cried Tim, "open your eyes and speak to me? Say you aren't dead. Please do?"

But our hero did not move, and Tim went nearly frantic.

"They can't have killed him," he said, as he wrung his hands. "No—no; they wouldn't dare to go so far as that."

Tim had no fear that Ben's enemies would return.

He had scared them by pretending that he had brought assistance, whereas he was entirely alone.

After listening at the door he ran down to the banks of the stream, and, filling his cap with water, dashed it over Ben's face; but our hero showed no signs of returning consciousness, and it was not until the rosy light of dawn stole through the mill window that he opened his eyes.

Tim had never left Ben's side a moment during the night, and he felt that he was fully repaid for his faithfulness.

"Let me help you, Ben," he said. "There—there, that's better. How do you feel?"

"Giddy and confused," Ben Brierton, replied. "Where am I? What has happened? How early it is! Surely you have not brought my breakfast yet?"

"No," Tim replied. "I came to supper instead, and found you entertaining a nice little party."

"I don't understand you," Ben replied. "I remember nothing but a hideous dream, and now I feel as if I had been ill for weeks."

Tim Toppem then explained what had happened.

On going back to the menagerie he felt so uneasy that sleep was out of the question, and he made up his mind to return to the mill, even at the risk of incurring Wobstock's wrath.

Arming himself with a stout stick, he stole away, and ran along the road at the top of his speed.

"I thought I could hear you calling me all the while," he said; "and precious glad I am that I did come."

The rest was told, and Ben could do no more than listen in amazement.

"So," he said, "Chipps is in league against me with ruffians. What can I have done that he should take so much trouble about me? Who is this man of aristocratic appearance? Tim, I hope you have not been dreaming like myself."

Tim smiled as he pointed to the window where the casement was torn away.

"One went out there, and two out of the door," he said. "Chipps was lost, and I gave him something to remember me by. Ben, I wish it was a dream for your sake. One thing is very certain."

"What is that?"

"That Chipps is no more your uncle than he is mine," Tim replied. "There's a mystery somewhere."

"A very great one," Ben said, "and it must be solved. I shall know how to treat Chipps now. I don't think we shall hear anything more about the uncle and nephew business."

Ben grew stronger every moment, and was soon able to leave the mill and return to the menagerie.

The lion-tamer was engaged in the invigorating operation of cooling his head in a bucket of water, and Wobstock was instructing his men with regard to the business of the day.

"What's this?" he cried, as he caught sight of Ben. "Come, now, this is too bad."

"I don't think you will say so when you have heard all," Ben said.

On hearing our hero's voice, Ted Barrett took his head out of the bucket in a violent hurry, and listened with gaping mouth and staring eyes as the story of what had happened at the old mill was retold.

As for Wobstock, he became limp with rage and astonishment, and leaned heavily against a post.

"'Stonishing! 'Strordinary!" he gasped, at intervals. "We're betwixt two fires, the police and a pack of scoundrels. Ted, this has floored me! What is to be done?"

"I think somebody had better see the sergeant and square the matter with him," Barrett responded. "I'm not a good hand at the soft-soap dodge, but I think I can soften his heart."

"Give him what you like,' Wobstock said. "I suppose it wouldn't do to mention Chipps and his gang?"

"No," Barrett replied; "I think we will take that matter in hand ourselves."

The lion-tamer was as good as his word. He not only turned the wrath of the sergeant aside with a few coins of the realm, but managed to get the magistrates' order rescinded.

Wonderful was the business done, but at last the time for departure came, and the caravans were on the road once more.

Wobstock had ordered the suit intended for Tim to play the *rôle* of gorilla to be sent to an inn at Wundall, the next pitch, and there sure enough it was, neatly packed, and, when unfolded, hideous enough to satisfy the most morbid-minded sightseer.

"There's a fortune in that skin," Wobstock said to Tim, "and you shall share it. We'll have the bills out to-day, and the first performance shall take place to-night. I'll do the lecture."

"I hope I sha'n't make a failure," Tim said, rather nervously.

"You can't; it isn't possible unless you speak," said Wobstock. "If the people chuck you nuts, or stir you with walkin'-sticks, fly at the bars an' shake 'em."

It was an anxious time for Tim, and Ben shared in the anxiety.

The boys now walked about boldly, having no fear of harm in the day-time, and at night-time Wobstock put on another watchman, with special instructions to sound an alarm at the sight of any strangers hanging around the menagerie after it was closed.

"Ben," said Tim, as they were strolling up and down just before the doors were opened to the public, "I did not say so to Wobstock, but I feel that I am going to pass through a fearful ordeal. Do you happen to know the customs and habits of the gorilla?"

"Very little, indeed, and those that I picked up in a book I don't think can be relied on," Ben replied.

"Stand near to encourage me," Tim pleaded. "The beastly mask which is to cover my face haunts me, and I can't get it out of my mind. Suppose the imposture should be found out?"

"I am afraid that the people would make some little noise."

"And I might stand a good chance of being lynched," Tom remarked, rather dismally. "Well, it's almost time for me to dress and take my place in the cage."

At that moment Wobstock came up with news that the man with the bills was out, and that already people were clamouring to be admitted.

"Here goes, then," said Tim. "Ben, I want you to make me a promise."

"I will, and keep it, too, if it is in my power."

"Whatever happens don't laugh at me, or I shall break down."

"Not for worlds," Ben replied. "You had better be off now, Tim; Wobstock has commenced pattering about the gorilla."

"And the awful whoppers he's telling makes my flesh crawl," Tim gasped.

In less than a quarter of an hour the "gorilla" was sitting mournfully in his den, holding a club in one hand, and grasping a limb of a tree—fitted up for the purpose—with the other.

His heart beat fast as he heard the people pattering

down the steps of the menagerie.

At present a stout curtain, fastened down, concealed him from the public gaze, and a placard warned one and all to keep a respectful distance from the cage.

An overture by the band did not raise Tim's spirits.

To his ears the music sounded as dismal as a funeral march, for he felt that something of an appalling nature was going to happen.

In the semi-darkness of the cage he sat, until Wobstock whip in hand, approached.

"Ladies and gentlemen," said the proprietor, "I have much pleasure in introducing to your notice the only—keep back there, please—gorilla from the wilds of Ameriky."

"There ain't no gorillas in Ameriky," observed a man in the crowd.

"I should have said Africa," Wobstock said, correcting himself, "and, ladies and gentlemen, I challenges the whole world to produce a similar specimen."

"That's true enough," Tim muttered, under his breath. "There's nothing like me above the earth or under the sea."

"It took seventy men to capture the gorilla," Wobstock went on, "and even they had their hands full. They threw nets, made of twisted wire, over the animal, but he chewed them off like waste paper. For three nights and days the fight went on, and at last the huge creature gave way."

"This is horrible," Tim groaned, "and I can't stand much more of it."

"Now please to keep back," Wobstock said, striking the curtain with his whip to prepare Tim; "the gorilla though tame and docile to them as he knows don't always take kindly to strangers."

Wobstock loosened the curtain and drew it aside.

A prolonged "Oh—h—h!" burst from the throats of the victims, and Tim, flourishing his club, and crawling up the tree, produced sundry sounds that might have emanated from a red Indian on the war trail.

"Dear me," said a venerable old gentleman, gazing through a pair of blue spectacles, "this is a remarkable sight, and worth more than the money charged."

"Thankee, sir," said Wobstock; "and you're right. All the learned men in the country say the same. Why, I've got testimonials about the creature enough to fill a volume of a thousand pages."

This was too much for Tim.

He came a cropper from the tree, and bawled unmelodiously.

"That's only his fun," Wobstock said; "in fact, it's the way he laughs. We will now pass on to the next cage, but the gorilla will be on view for a few more minutes. Them as wish to remain may, but I warns em' to keep well back, as I will not be answerable for the consequences should anybody foolishly get within the gorilla's reach."

Tim thought he would settle that matter himself.

Uttering a tremendous roar, he banged the club about, and the people forthwith fell back upon each other's toes, and followed Wobstock round the menagerie.

"It went off better than I expected," Tim thought; "but I had a hard job to keep from saying something once or twice."

At that a moment a man who had come in late advanced towards the cage.

Tim gazed at him with emotions that may be better imagined than described; for in the new-comer he recognised his doting, and probably sorrowing father.

Toppem senior had been sent to do a little work at Wundall, and, as was the case with hundreds of others, the "gorilla" had drawn a sixpence from his pocket.

As he approached the cage, Tim retreated to the further end of it.

"I'm blowed if the critter ain't afeared of me," said Mr. Toppem. "I'll stir him up a bit. I thought as how the gorilla was afeared of nothin' and nobody?"

On his way to the menagerie, Tim's parent had fallen a victim to a slight temptation, and had refreshed himself in a manner causing him to be hilarious.

Mr. Toppem looked about for something long enough to worry the gorilla without running any danger himself.

CHAPTER XII.

AN AWKWARD MEETING.

THERE happened to be a pole leaning against an adjoining caravan, and satisfying himself that none of the keepers' eyes were upon him, Mr. Toppem annexed the weapon and favoured his son and heir with a tremendous dig in the ribs.

"Now then," bellowed Tim, flinging the club at the bars. "You drop it. You're old enough to know better. Why don't you go back to Cloisterville?"

Mr. Toppem did drop it. He dropped the pole as if it had turned red hot in his hands, and he walked backwards at such a pace as might have warranted the supposition that he was performing the feat for a wager.

A cage full of birds checked his career.

A particularly lively old pelican took a piece out of the nape of his neck, causing the sufferer to plunge wildly forward and expostulate in a manner that brought Wobstock to the spot.

"What's the game?" he demanded. "This isn't the place for a cellar-flap dance. Don't stand there kicking up the sawdust as if it was your own property."

"Who are you?" demanded Toppem, fiercely.

Wobstock enlightened him just as emphatically, and also informed him that his boots were in an excellent condition for kicking.

"There's no need for more wiolence," Mr. Toppem remarked. "I say, do you know that your gorilia talks like a Christian? He told me to go back to Cloisterville, where I came from, but—"

Wobstock took Mr. Toppem gently by the arm and led him away.

"How much did you pay to come in?" the showman demanded.

"Sixpence."

"Then," said Wobstock, "I don't mind paying you a shilling to go out. This place ain't a lunatic asylum. You've got 'em on, but I'll be obliged if you'll take 'em somewhere else."

"Do you mean to insinuate that I'm intoxicated?" said Toppem, wrathfully.

"I mean to say that you aren't accountable for your actions," Wobstock replied, moving him towards the place of exit. The man who hears a monkey speak must be in a bad state. Now, will you go?"

"I'm a goin'!" Toppem said; "but there's no need to shove me about as if I was a sack o' taters instead of a man. I don't believe it's a gorilla at all, but somebody dressed up like one. I'll take my apple-davit of it, for I'm as sure as I'm speakin' the truth — as my name is Toppem."

It was Wobstock's turn to be amazed now.

He started in such a manner that his hat fell off, and his face went red and then ashy grey.

"Come outside with me," he said, hoarsely. "I can't allow a man with such notions to be abroad. You'd better see a doctor at once."

"Blow the doctor and you too!" Toppem roared, as he reached the open air. "I'll expose this swindle, I'll—

"Will somebody tell me which is the nearest establishment where a straight-jacket can be purchased?" Wobstock interposed, appealing to some loiterers. "Look out, some of you. This fellow is dangerous, and I shouldn't wonder if he took it into his head to bite somebody."

Mr. Toppem turned almost black in the face with rage, and made a good show of pulling off his coat.

In a moment Wobstock was off the platform, and facing the irate individual.

"Just listen to me a moment," said the showman. "If you were anybody else, I'd teach you not to come here kicking up a row. But there are reasons why I have the strongest objection to punching your head. Take five shillings and go away."

"What!" Toppem roared. "Do you think that five shillings is enough to heal the mental wounds you have inflicted on me? I'll—I'll take the money on account, and call again to-morrow."

"If you're a wise man you'll keep away," Wobstock returned. "If I see so much as your shadder hangin' about here, I'll let the gorilla out after you, and I think that will about settle your hash. Go home and get into bed, and if you have any more of these 'ere delusions, take a short cut to the nearest lunatic asylum."

The five shillings had a softening effect on Toppem senior. He tested the goodness of each of the coins with his teeth, and then slouched away.

Wobstock rushed back to the interior of the menagerie and found the blue-spectacled old gentleman offering Tim an orange on the end of the pole his parent had prodded him with.

But "the gorilla" was in no mood to receive gifts of any kind.

He was perspiring through his artificial skin, and Wobstock at once hid him from view with the curtain.

"The hentertainment is over," said the showman. "Ladies and gentlemen will please to pass out quietly and as quickly as possible. We've got a tiger with the toothache, and we're just going to bring him from his cage to pull it out."

"I don't believe it!" cried the shrill voice of a boy. "This is only an excuse to get rid of us."

"Very well," Wobstock replied, calmly, "you can stay if you like. I dare say that there is a large family of you at home, and may be your parents won't miss you much. Mr. Barrett, will you kindly see about bringing the tiger out. If these people like to be so obstinate, why—"

This was enough.

In less than a moment the menagerie was clear of all save who had business there, and Wobstock, peeping behind the curtain, discovered that Tim had taken his departure.

As Wobstock walked towards the caravan which served Tim as a dressing room, he looked very grave, and rolled his head from side to side, as if it had offended him, and he desired to cast it from his shoulders.

Ben Brierton, who had wisely refrained from keeping with Tim while the exhibition was going on, opened the door for the showman.

"Where is he?" Wobstock demanded.

"In bed," Ben replied, "with his feet on the pillow and his head through the rail."

"I don't wonder at it," Wobstock replied, feelingly; "only fancy his father turning up. I can forgive Tim for speaking to him, but it nearly spoilt the whole business. I'll comfort him."

The caravan was divided by a movable screen, and at the further end of it lay Tim, wriggling about as if he had accidentally made the acquaintance of an ant-hill.

"My boy," said Wobstock, seeing that Tim was still in his gorilla attire, "you must take that thing off. This ain't the Arctic regions, you ain't a polar bear, and I don't want to have it on my mind that you suffocated yourself for my sake."

"I daren't take it off," Tim moaned. "I am doomed to wear it all my life. It's part of myself, and I must wear it for ever."

"What on earth does the boy mean?" Wobstock gasped. "Surely he hasn't taken leave of his senses?"

"He means that he's afraid of meeting his father," Ben observed.

"Oh! if that's all the matter," cried Wobstock, bursting out laughing, "I think he's the kind of party to be easily dealt with. Cheer up, Tim, and be yourself again. If the old 'un catches sight of you leave me to deal with him."

These drops of comfort did not soothe Tim much.

"You see," he said, "if dad knew that I was playing this game he might take it into his head to travel the country with me. Ah! Mr. Wobstock, you don't know my father as I do. If he could see a way to make profit out of me, I should lead a life of misery. He'd keep me at it day and night until I went silly and believed myself to be a monkey."

"I'll find out where he is," Wobstock mused, "and settle the difficulty one way or the other. I can't afford to part with the boy now. Tim," he added aloud, "trust me to see you out of this difficulty, and I'll do it before another day is over I'll leave you now. Ben, help him out of that rig, and both of you join the men at supper."

As Wobstock was passing out of the menagerie he tapped Barrett, the lion-tamer, on the shoulder.

"Ted," he whispered, "I want you to join me in a little excursion. Let us slip away before Hangelina catches sight of me. She's the best woman in the world, but she has a temper of her own and knows how to use it."

"She does," Barrett assented.

"Somethin' has upset her to-day," Wobstock continued. "I ain't quite sure what it is, but she's in one of her broomstick moods, and as I ain't inclined for war, why—"

"Will—i—am," said a hollow voice, from the living caravan, "there's a look about you as if you meant to go out to-night. Come in !"

But Wobstock had already beat a somewhat ignominous retreat, and Barrett took a harlequin-like dive after him.

"Whatever I get for supper," Wobstock said, as they halted in a narrow street, "will be curried. Ted, can you tell me why women are so unreasonable ?"

"Not being a married man I'd rather be excused answering that question," Barrett replied ; "but I'll tell you one thing. I'd rather find my lions out of sorts when I entered the cage than face an angry woman."

"I think you are right, Ted," Wobstock said ; "but there, let it all go. We'll find Tim's father, if we can, and see what can be done in that direction."

It so happened that they had not far to seek for Toppem senior.

Presently they heard somebody singing "I will stand by my friend," and ran against the very individual they were looking for.

To all appearance the five shillings received for compensation had not done him much good.

His voice was husky, his legs shaky, his hat was on the other side of his head, and his eyes had an expression which might have been taken for extreme melancholy.

"This is a lucky meeting," Wobstock said. "How do you find yourself, Mr. Toppem ?"

"I'm the most miserable man on the face of the earth," Toppem replied. "I've lost my only boy, and I shall oversleep myself in the morning, and lose the job I'm on."

"Better sit up all night and make sure," Ted Barrett suggested.

"I don't require no adwice from a stranger," Toppem retorted, "unless he wants to act like a man and be convivial. I never was in such a thirsty place as this."

Finding that Toppem displayed a strong tendency to sit down suddenly, Wobstock took him by the arm.

"I want to have a few words with you about your son," he said. "We'll go somewhere, and have something light and refreshin'—lemonade for instance."

"Lemmingnade!" cried Toppem, contemptuously. "I wouldn't touch the stuff for a pension. I had a bottle once, but I got the cork fust—right in the heye—and the neighbours swore I'd been fightin'."

"Well—well," said Wobstock, "do as you like. You heard what I said about your son?"

"I heerd," Toppem replied; "but what can you know about him? Tim ran away from his poor old father. Ah! many's the time I stood a tripe supper to him on Saturday nights. And now he's left me—stung me like the hadder you read about in Allsopp's fables."

Meanwhile they were on their way to a hostelry, Toppem going to it as readily as a needle is attracted to a magnet.

"Now," said Wobstock, when they had seated themselves, "suppose I were to tell you that I knew where your son was—what would you say?"

"Say?" echoed Toppem. "Why, I'd say that you was a-trying to delood a broken-'earted man. Don't pile it on; let me keep my sufferin's to myself."

"But I do know where he is," Wobstock persisted, "and he's as comfortable as can be."

"Tim comfor'ble, a-thirsting like a castaway on a hocean!"

Mr. Toppem covered his eyes with his hands and sobbed bitterly.

"Why did you tell me this?" he moaned. "Why did you stab me in a wital part? Tim promised to send me some money, but I looked for the postman in wain. Once I told him that I was sure he must have a letter for me, and his reply wasn't perlite."

"But see here," said the showman, "Tim has not had much money as yet for himself. I think we can settle this matter if you are a sensible man. The lad is in respectable employment, and the man who's got him is willing to take him as a 'prentice. How much do you want?"

Mr. Toppem drank up his beer hurriedly and gazed at Wobstock out of one eye.

"What?" he cried. "You want me to sell my own son?"

"Don't talk like a fool!" said Ted Barrett. "It strikes me that you are putting this on to serve your own purpose."

Mr. Toppem did not deny it.

He reflected deeply for a few moments, and then made a startling proposition.

"If I parted with Tim for a number of years," he replied, "I'd want fifty pounds down and thirty shillings a week."

"Suppose we say five pounds and nothing a week," Wobstock said, laughing.

"It's orf—it's orf," Toppem returned; "and yet five pounds air five pounds. Have you got the money about you?"

"Yes, but I mean to keep it until the morning. Meet me here at eleven o'clock, and I'll have the papers ready for signing."

"My friend," the fond parent replied, "there's no time like the present. If it ain't conwenient to pay the lot down, I'll take a little on account."

"Give him a few shillings, and let us get away," Ted Barrett whispered. "He so disgusts me that I can scarcely keep my fingers off him."

Wobstock complied, and he and the lion-tamer were not out of the house five minutes before Toppem, after singing "Be kind to your father," went sound asleep.

While in this condition the door of an upper room opened, and Ebenezer Chipps, looking furtively about him, came gliding downstairs.

To say that he started at the sight of Toppem would but ill convey the change that came over him.

He darted upstairs, and then stole down again, to make sure that his eyes had not deceived him.

"What's to be done?" he muttered. "If he should chance to wake up and find me here there would be a pretty kettle of fish. Confound him! I suppose he is looking for that vagabond son of his. Here am I, skulking and hiding like a fox, waiting for another chance to get hold of Ben, and this fellow appears like a Jack-in-the-box. Hang him! I wish Rushmore would give him an overdose of chloroform

At this moment the landlord, a burly, thick-set man, came round the counter and ejected Mr. Toppem with such force as the law allows on such occasions. It consisted of a punch in the nape of the neck, followed by a well-aimed kick that not only awoke the slumberer, but shot him to the other side of the street.

"Good—good!" chuckled Chipps. "That's the way to serve him."

"Do you know him?" demanded the landlord.

"I—I know him?" the miser stammered. "Certainly not. My dear sir, do you think I would keep such company?"

"The company you keep is bad enough, and I'll be obliged if you take it away with you. I don't like the look of you, nor the other fellows who have come to see you to-day. Clear out!"

CHAPTER XIII.

A GRAND HOLIDAY FOR THE MONKEYS.

EARLY in the morning, when Toppem senior went forth from his humble lodging, with a notion that his head had developed into a barrel of stale ale with the fumes of tobacco hanging about it, and almost convinced that his legs did not belong to him, chance took him to the fields.

It was an aimless walk.

His mind was in such a confused state that he could not collect his thoughts.

Not even his son Tim and the forthcoming five pounds interested him.

The only thing that occupied his brain to any extent was a strong presentiment that he would never be well.

Like many another fool, he cursed the vile stuff which with his own hands he had put into his mouth to sting away his faculties, and made him an object of contempt to the lowest animal breathing.

Slouching along, with his head down and his hands in his pockets, he came to a deserted shepherd's hut, and curiosity caused him to peer through the little window.

Toppem received a severe shock to his nerves and staggered back, for on the other side of the glass was the face of Ebeneezer Chipps.

" Bless me !" cried Toppem ; " this must be a wision."

The " wision " stalked out of the hut and stared at Toppem in a manner that made him gasp again.

" What are you doing here ?" Chipps demanded, clawing the air with his hooked fingers.

" That's a nice question to put to a man after scarin' him out of his wits," Toppem retorted.

" You are employed to spy upon my movements, I suppose," the miser snarled.

" I, a free-born Briton, turn spy !" Toppem returned, indignantly. " I came here by accident, just as I heard of Tim by accident. A wild beast-man's got him, and I'm goin' to meet the man at the Golden Stag at noon to settle Tim's 'prenticeship."

" Humph !" Chipps muttered. " Ben is in the same hands. Toppem, I believe that you are an honest man, and I want you to do me a favour."

" I'm open to do anything if I'm paid for it," Toppem replied, " but I don't think you're the sort o' party to come out lavish. What's in the wind, Daddy—Mister Chipps ?"

" I want you to go back to Cloisterville, and take charge of my house until I return," the miser replied. " You will live rent free, and I will allow you five shillings a week into the bargain."

" Done," said Toppem ; " I'm your man, but what am I to say to people when they ask about you ?"

" Tell them to mind their own business," Chipps re-

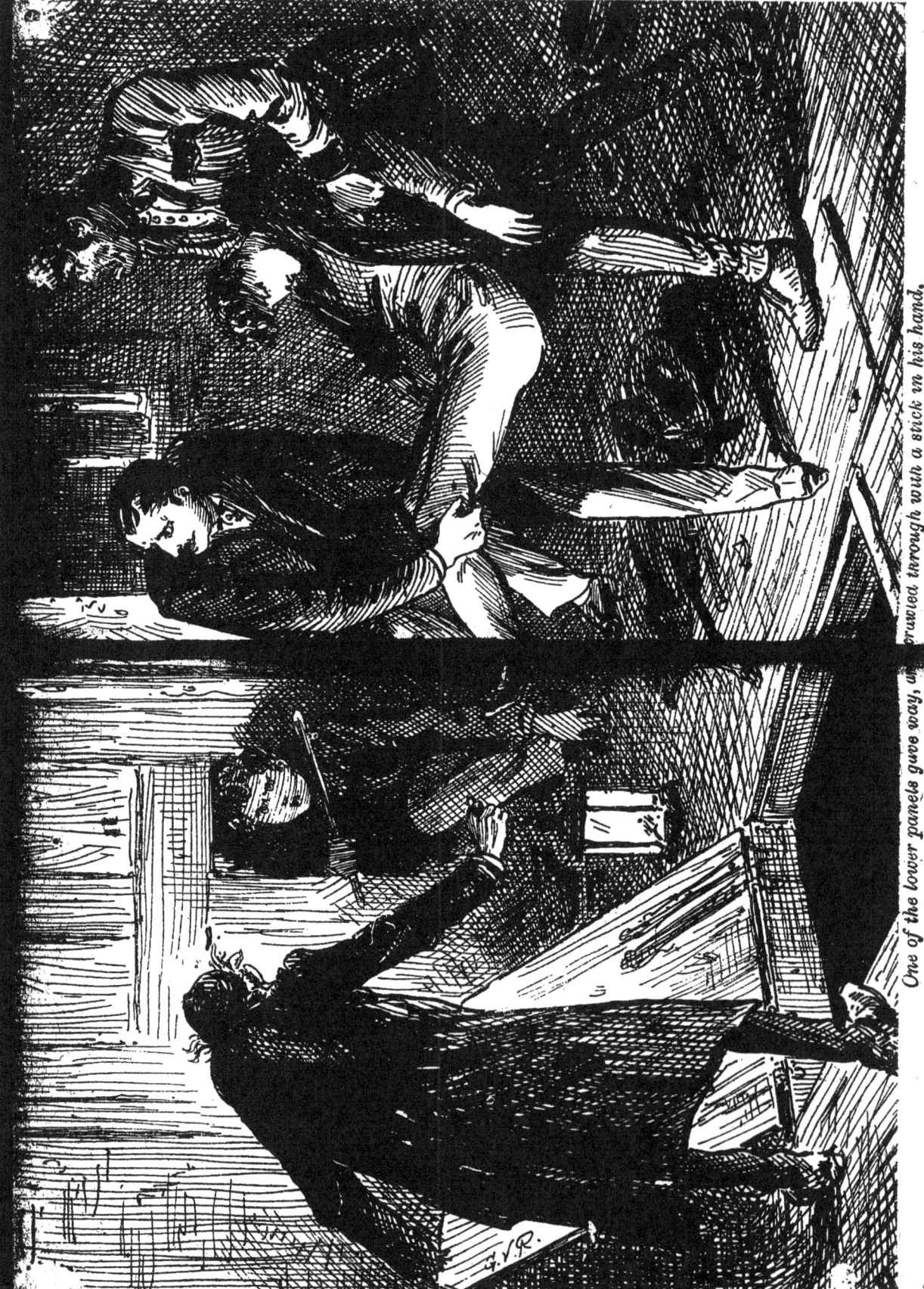

One of the lower panels gave way, and crawled through with a stick in his hand.

sponded. "Don't admit anybody inside the house under any pretence whatever."

All this was very mysterious to Toppem, but the offer was too tempting a one to refuse.

"Here is the key," Chipps said, "and I will send you a written authority by post to act as caretaker. Now go, and remember this—I do not wish it known that you have seen me."

"I'll be as dumb as a drum with a hole in it," Toppem declared. "I—I suppose you won't object to pay a little in advance?"

With many a groan Ebenezer Chipps produced two half-crowns, and with a few more words of caution bade Toppem take himself off.

The free-born Briton returned dreamily to the town.

"This all comes about through Ben," he thought. "I always said that Chipps was no relation of his. P'raps the boy is a son of a dook or a hearl! Who knows? I must keep my weather heye open, and see if I can't turn all this to good account."

Precisely at twelve Wobstock appeared with a printed and stamped indenture form, with the blanks filled in and signed by Tim.

"I suppose," said Wobstock, "you are not very anxious to see your son? If you are, say so."

"Well, no," Toppem replied. "I'm afeared that the parting would break us both down. I've a tender 'eart, and when I do start cryin' I'm a perfect woman."

Wobstock folded up the paper when Toppem had signed it, and paid over the money.

"Do you happen to know a man named Ebeneezer Chipps?" he asked.

"Oh! yes, I know him," Toppem replied, starting.

"If you should ever happen to see him let me know," Wobstock said. "We are just starting on the round of fairs, and if you want to find out where the menagerie is, all you need do is to consult any penny almanack."

Toppem sat still for some moments.

Speech failed him, for it appeared to him that he had fallen into the meshes of a net of the most bewildering pattern.

"Business is business, you know," he began, after a long pause. "I suppose—"

"You want to be paid for the information?" Wobstock interposed. "Make your mind easy on that score; I will pay you fairly And mind this, when once you see Chipps don't lose sight of him until I am on his track."

"I—I won't," Toppem gasped. "I'll stick to him like a leech. One thing I can tell you."

"What's that?"

"Chipps has bolted from Cloisterville."

"But he may return."

"If he does," Toppem said, "I will let you know."

"Look here," continued Wobstock, as he rose to go, "you are Tim's father. Tim is as good a lad as ever breathed; you may well take a lesson from him. Crush the glass under your heel, and have done with it for ever. And that is the advice of a man who have seen hundreds impoverished and come to untimely ends."

"Thank'ee," Toppem said. "I'll think over it."

"And," resumed the showman, "with respect to the matter in hand, there must be no double dealings between you and I. If I catch you selling me to Chipps I'll break every bone in your body and give your carcase to my lions."

Having delivered this tremendous threat in a style that made Toppem's blood run cold, Wobstock strode out of the house.

"Here's a game of battledore," Toppem groaned, "and the showman and Chipps are the shuttlecocks. I'll keep 'em movin' pretty lively. I'd better be off to Cloisterville before somebody turns up and ask me to look after the pair of 'em. I never knew that I was born to be a detective, but so it seems. Oh! Fate, what a wonderful thing thou art."

At the proper time the menagerie moved from the town, and Tim, being fairly settled and at peace, set to work in right down earnest.

In his new capacity of custodian to the monkeys he soon became friends with the frolicsome creatures and used to their habits.

He soon learnt their names by heart, and encouraged them to come to the bars of the cage when called.

A halt was made on a piece of common land to feed tne animals and clean out their dens.

Tim was very busy and the monkeys very lively.

They persisted in clinging in a heap and snatching the food from each other.

"You greedy beggars!" cried Tim. "I'll give you a taste of the whip. Just stand aside, Ben, while I fetch that Jacko a crack."

Jacko, a fine specimen of the ring-tailed species, retaliated by stretching out a long, hairy arm and annexing one of Tim's ears.

"Oh—h—h!" Tim yelled. "B—B—Ben, save me, or the brute will pull my head off."

Ben Brierton struck the brute sharply over the knuckles, and away went the monkey to the further end of the cage, chattering and gibbering furiously.

"Upon my word, this is too bad," Tim cried, snatching up a stick and throwing open the door. "Only let me get at him, and I'll make him sore for a month."

It was a fatal act.

No sooner did Tim insert his head and shoulders inside the cage than the monkeys swooped down in a body, and Tim, leaving several tufts of hair behind him, staggered back. Out rushed the monkeys, rolling over each other, shrieking for very joy.

Some climbed a tree, some disported themselves in the road, and one took liberties with Tim's hat, and enveloped its own hairy poll in its depths.

Ben Brierton could do nothing but lean against the caravan and roar with laughter; and as for Tim, he took his usual position when startled, and sitting down with sudden violence, stared aghast at the result of his indiscretion.

"I've ruined Wobstock," he cried. "Oh! Ben, did you ever see such a muddle as this?"

"Muddle!" bellowed Wobstock, as he ran up; "it's a howling chaos. How, in the name of wonder, do you think the monkeys are to be got back to the cage again? They'll be all over the country in less than an hour. Here, Ted! Dick! Harry! Come here, all of you. Ben, my boy, there's nothing to laugh at."

"I couldn't help it if the penalty were death," Ben replied. "Suppose we try what throwing some food into the cage will do?"

By this this time every keeper and helper in the menagerie had arrived, and armed with sticks, and anything that came handy, they formed a circle, and contrived to keep the monkeys within it.

Meanwhile, Ben laid a train of food intended for the jubilant throng, up to the caravan, and scattered the bulk inside.

The ever-greedy Jacko made a dart to secure more than his share, and his example was followed by the rest. Bang went the cage-door never to be opened again by Tim.

"Mr. Wobstock," he said, almost hysterically, "I deserve a sound thrashing for my foolishness, and if you give it to me I won't murmur."

But Wobstock was too limp and overcome to avail himself of the opportunity.

"It's a mercy all has ended well," he almost groaned. "Only fancy England being swarming with monkeys again. Pray be more careful, Tim. These shocks hit me like a sledge-hammer."

Tim was not only truly repentant but savage with himself, and especially with Jacko.

"I'll have revenge for this," he said, shaking his fist at the monkey. "I'll—I'll fill a nutshell full of pepper and give it to the brute to crack."

The laugh went against Tim that day, and the chaffing he got from the men was awful.

"But, after all," said Ted Barrett, "there is no wonder that the monkeys yearned for liberty, considering that our gorilla walks about as he pleases."

"That accounts for the sudden rush," added Ben. "They were jealous of the privileges accorded to Tim."

"Perhaps," said Wobstock, who was now inclined to laugh at the adventure, "Tim would not mind living with them altogether. A perfect knowledge of their language would come very handy to him."

Tim, knowing that he could not reply with effect, remained silent, and to soothe his ruffled feelings, started out for a short walk by himself.

" Let him go," said Wobstock ; "there's nothing like a spell of solitude for a shock to the system. I must confess that I did feel riled with him when I saw him sittin' on the ground doing nothin' but keeping his mouth working like a clockwork figger. But let it all go, and I think we've said enough to him."

Tim took his way towards a small copse, and as he approached it a pheasant flew out with a sudden whirr, its gorgeous plumage gleaming brightly in the sun.

For the moment Tim, whose experience of game was limited, thought the bird might be some novel kind of firework.

As Tim was gazing up in wonder and admiration at the pheasant it suddenly closed its wings, and fell lifeless almost at his feet.

Tim heard no sound and saw nothing to account for this sudden change from life to death, and he was in the act of stooping to pick up the bird when a strange-looking man came crashing through the under-growth.

A more savage-looking individual never met mortal gaze.

His clothes were such as may be often seen waving in the breeze as a warning to rooks. He was bareheaded and barefooted, and a tangled mass of black hair fell below his shoulders.

Almost as swarthy as a mulatto, and with features as evil and repulsive as to be absolutely demoniac. Tim recoiled upon his heels.

The man carried an air-gun in his hand, and came on, growling like a surly dog, and breathing threats.

He ignored Tim until when within a few paces of him, and then he reversed the gun, and swung it threateningly in the air.

" I suppose you mean to go down to the village, and tell what you have seen ?" he hissed. " If you've got such a thing in your mind you'd better close your eyes, and say your prayers."

" What do you mean ?" Tim gasped. " What have I done that you should threaten me in this way ?"

The fellow pointed to the pheasant, and then directed his eyes in a manner that seemed to pierce him through.

"You know that is my doing," he said, "and if you are not a fool you must be aware that if I am caught I shall be laid by the heels in gaol."

"Then I am a fool, for I know nothing of the kind," Tim rejoined.

"You are not a country lad—eh?"

"No; I was born in a town. I am travelling with Wobstock's menagerie."

CHAPTER XIV.

DANGER FOR BEN BRIERTON.

"I HAVE heard of Wobstock. 1 don't suppose he's particular what he picks up on the road?" the poacher said.

"Mr. Wobstock is an honest man," Tim replied, wrathfully.

"All men are honest until they are found out," the fellow said, grinning. "Well," he added, throwing open his ragged coat and thrusting the pheasant into an enormous pocket, "it seems that I have nothing to fear from you, so I'll be off," and with a wild, ringing whoop he plunged back into the wood again, and Tim drew a deep sigh of relief.

"That's a nice sort of man for a select tea-party," he said. "I wonder if there are any more like him about? There's a gorilla without a make-up! Ugh! I shall dream of him for a month."

Tim hastened back to the menagerie and told what had happened.

"The man you saw is Sable Wallack for a sackful of guineas," cried Wobstock. "He's the leader of a desperate gang of gipsies, the terror of every place they visit. There's a dark suspicion that he has blood on his hands."

"He looked capable of doing anything," Tim remarked.

"And he is," Wobstock assented. "Oh! I know the rascal—a poacher, mean thief, and footpad; in fact, anything that will bring him gain without honest work. As for the pheasant, that is no business of ours. Let the keepers of game look after it themselves."

Wobstock looked a little uneasy as he spoke, and

seemed to breathe more freely when the caravans had started again.

"Ben," he said to our hero, who sat on the driving-box beside him, "if we don't reach our pitch before nightfall we shall camp out. I have no wish to hamper your movements, but if you will take my advice you won't rove out of sight of the vans."

"I will do exactly as you wish," Ben replied; "but I ear nothing now. I only wish that I could meet the scoundrels who drugged me in the mill face to face. There would be a sharp and short reckoning, I can tell you."

"You've got the strength, pluck, and will to do it," Wobstock said; "but when there's danger in the air it is better to keep under shelter."

"Danger?" Ben echoed. "Surely you don't think Chipps and Co., as I must call them, will venture to follow us?"

"There is always danger in a country where there are wolves," Wobstock replied. "They skulk in the rear of their prey until the opportunity comes, and then swoop down upon it in a body."

The showman's words made Ben Brierton very thoughtful.

He was thinking of the miserly old rascal with whom he had lived so long, while, strangely enough, Wobstock was thinking of Sable Wallack, and the probability of Ben's enemies falling in with him and his gang. It was a presentiment which was fulfilled in a remarkable manner.

As the day advanced the sky became overcast.

Magnificent storm-laden piles of clouds rolled up from the west, bringing snow and wind with them.

Wobstock called a halt at a convenient place, for the horses could not struggle on with the fine, powdery snow driven into their eyes, nor could the men endure the bitter cold.

All hastened to shelter, as soon as possible after the horses were tethered in groups, in an improvised stable of tarpaulin sheets, secured with ropes to stakes driven firmly into the ground.

It was a memorable storm.

It's fury increased every moment ; vast wreaths of snow whirled in the air, blocking up the roads, and forming huge mounds where anything resisted its progress.

Strong and heavy as the caravans were, the tremendous gusts of wind made them rock.

"Heaven help the poor fellows at sea!" Wobstock said. "It's bad enough to sit here, with the prospect of waiting until we are dug out ; but think of the ocean on such a night as this."

The juvenile Wobstocks had been packed off to bed in a van appointed for that purpose, and the showman and his wife, with Ben, Tim, and the lion-tamer crouched over the fire, listening to the wind as it came roaring from the moorlands.

They were silent and depressed, for outside the horses were whinnying their complaints bitterly, and every now and then Mumbo sent forth a tremendous note of expostulation, and Wyatt had to struggle knee-deep through the snow to quiet the ponderous brute.

It may be very jolly while sitting over a cosy fire to read how travellers are snowed up, but to realise the fact is anything but pleasant, and so our friends found it.

"If this storm goes on all night," Ted Barrett said, "we are booked for a week, unless a rapid thaw sets in."

Wobstock nodded his head gloomily, and his wife went to one of the windows, and, thrusting it open, looked out.

In a moment her hair was as white as the head of a powdered footman.

"I can see nothing but snow," she said, dismally, as she returned to her chair, "and I do believe that the caravans are all smothered up."

"Never mind, old gal," Wobstock replied ; "we must make the best of it and cheer up. Ted Barrett, give us a song."

But the lion-tamer was in nowise inclined for melody.

"I think we had better go to our own quarters while we have a chance," he observed, glancing at Ben and Tim. "Mercy ! Did you ever hear the wind shriek and howl like it in your life?"

Our hero and Tim took the hint and followed Barrett.
Outside the scene was terrific.

Huge trees were bending like saplings, tossing their
bare limbs to the pitch black sky, and snapping, creaking,
and groaning as the tremendous gusts of wind swept past.

"Ben," said Tim, "I used to think a snow-storm jolly
good fun, but this is forty rolled into one. Which is our
van?"

"I was just asking myself the same question," Ben
rejoined. "The whole menagerie is one vast ridge of
snow. Steady, Tim; keep your feet. If you go down
you may not get up again in a hurry."

After some difficulty they found their van, and Ben,
letting down the steps, they set to work to clear the door,
which was completely blocked up.

Ted Barrett shouted a cheery Good-night to the
youngsters, and went to his own quarters.

The gloom and drifting snow swallowed him up in an
instant.

Once inside the caravan Ben lit the lamp and brushed
the snow from his clothes.

"We'll jump into bed as soon as possible and try to
forget this scene," he said. "I think the wind is
dropping, and to-morrow the sun may come to our
rescue."

"The sun will have to be in a good humour to melt
these mountains of snow," Tim returned. "How those
poor horses must suffer. Even the animals are too
frightened now to cry out. Here comes another gust
like a peal of thunder."

It was the last of its kind. The wind dropped as if
by magic, but the snow still fell thickly and steadily.

The lads were soon asleep, but their rest was not of
long duration.

Ben was awakened by strange sounds, like the working
of a pump-handle, mingled with the strains of a barrel-
organ very much out of tune.

Tim was the offender, and Ben shook him up rather
unceremoniously.

"What do you call that noise?" he demanded.

'Snoring, I suppose," Tim replied, rubbing his eyes.

"I knew I was doing it, but couldn't wake up. Oh! Ben, I have had such an awful dream. I thought that fellow whom Wobstock calls Sable Wallack was cramming a pheasant as big as a turkey down my throat."

"Nightmare," Ben replied, wearily. "Let us go to sleep again, and I hope your dreams will be of a gentler nature. I'm awfully tired."

Tim apologised, and was soon off again, and did not wake again until Ben woke him and told him that day had come.

Leaving the menagerie for the present, we will return to Sable Wallack.

With his prize in his pocket, he ran, or rather leaped, through the wood until he came to a tiny dell, so surrounded by bushes and brambles that a stranger might have taken a downward flight before he was aware of the trap which Nature had set for the unwary.

Within the shelter of a cave, near by a tree which had fallen and torn up the earth in its descent, sat two men, huddling over the warmth of a fire.

Two guns lay near to their hands, and a shaggy brute of a dog was curled up at the mouth of the cave, sleeping, as dogs are said to do, with one eye open, and twitching his ears to catch the slightest sound.

Suddenly, the dog started up and gave vent to a short, sharp bark, followed by a deep growl and a display of white, gleaming teeth.

"Lie down, Fury!" the poacher said; "you ought to know my footstep by this time."

As he spoke, he plunged through the briers as an ordinary being would through hay, and confronted his companions.

"We must put up with this," he said, pitching the pheasant down. "The covers must have been shot lately, as there is scarcely a bird to be seen."

"A pheasant ain't much for three," observed one of the other two, taking a black pipe from a pair of leathery lips.

"It's better than nothing," Wallack returned, sweeping his hair back. "Fury will come off worse than all, as he will only get the bones to pick. Any news of Rushmore, Faro?"

The man addressed looked up and shook his head.

"I can't make out what he wants with us," Sable Wallack continued. "If he's coming at all, it's time that he was here."

Fury was up barking and growling again; but in a moment Wallack's hand was over the dog's mouth.

"Go and see what it is," Wallack said.

Faro, with gipsy-like instinct, crept like a cat to the top of the dell, and, crouching down, placed his ear close to the ground.

He heard the sound of several voices, and recognised one to be Rushmore's.

This he reported when he returned to the cave, and then hung moodily over the fire.

"Put the pheasant away," Wallack said. "I'll be bound that Sam will not come empty-handed. Strangers with him, eh? Then there must be work for us, lads."

Some minutes passed away, and then the cracked and wheezy voice of Ebeneezer Chipps whined out.

"Where are we going?" he cried, in accents of despair. "Where are you taking me? I'll go no further, I tell you. I'm scratched and torn to bits. There goes another piece of cloth! Oh! dear—oh! dear! this is very dreadful. I've put all my toes out of joint by kicking them against the roots of trees."

"Why don't you hold your tongue?" hissed Rushmore, who led the way. "If the keeper should come down on us I shall know who to blame and what to do."

"You are a very violent man—a dreadfully violent man," Ebeneezer Chipps groaned. "Oh! there goes another thorn into my leg."

"If there were fifty you'd move a little quicker," Rushmore retorted. "Hold your tongue! We are near the place where I promised to meet Wallack, and I am going to give him the signal."

Rushmore put his hands to his mouth, and imitated the twittering of a blackbird startled from its nest.

This he repeated thrice, and was rewarded by the appearance of Sable Wallack.

"All's snug and quiet," said the weird-looking creature. "Come into our parlour and make yourselves at home.

So this is the old gentleman," he added, quizzing the miser's features. "Well, I can't say that he looks very happy.

"Happy!" Chipps repeated. "How can you expect a man of my age to be happy after being dragged through such a dreadful country as this. I don't think I shall have the courage to get out of it again."

Rushmore and Sable Wallack laughed in chorus, and the former, unslinging a bag from his shoulders, gave it to the gipsy.

"I thought you might be short of provisions," he said, "so I brought some with me."

"We shall want it," Sable Wallack replied, glancing up at the sky; "there will be a big storm ere long. I noticed this morning that the plovers were huddling together in the furrows, and that is a sure sign of bad weather. Come along. It's rather steep just here; mind you don't slip, old gentleman."

"I've done nothing else for the last hour," Chipps declared. "I'm one mass of bumps and bruises. I'm like a red-hot jelly, and so shaken up."

Sam Rushmore lost his temper, and gave the miser so violent a push that he shot neck and crop into the dell, where, happily for him, Faro caught him and bore him off to the cave.

The bag contained a good supply of cold beef and bread, and refreshment of a liquid nature had not been forgotten.

The select party fell to work on the viands, and even Ebeneezer Chipps forgot his woes as he polished off his share in a somewhat wolfish fashion.

He reflected that the meal cost him nothing, and the thought filled the apology for a heart he carried under his waistcoat with joy.

When the fragments of the feast were returned to the bag for future use, the precious crew laid their heads together and began to whisper.

"There's a mighty risk attending the job," Wallack said aloud; "but it shall be done, if, as you say, the swell will come down handsomely."

"He will come down to any extent," Rushmore replied.

"He is too generous—much too generous," Ebeneezer Chipps cackled. "When I went to see him in London, some years ago, I saw him give a cabman sixpence over his fare, and it made my heart bleed."

"So will your nose, if you ain't quiet," Rushmore cried, flourishing a brawny fist under the threatened nasal organ. "Keep quiet, and hear what Wallack has to say."

"I say this," Sable Wallack returned. "If I am treated well, the boy you call Ben Brierton will be out of the country in less than a week, and in such hands as will hold him tight."

"Good! good!" Ebeneezer Chipps murmured; "this is very soothing and satisfactory. My dear sir, you have taken a great weight off my mind."

"We had better follow the track of the menagerie," Sable Wallack said. "I know of a better shelter; for if we stop here we may be snowed in, and have to wait for spring to thaw us out."

Lightly as these words were spoken, they nearly frightened Ebeneezer Chipps out of his wits.

"Dear me!" he said, "you don't say so? Let us go at once. I, for one, am quite able and willing. I have the greatest horror of snow; it creeps into a man's boots and completely spoils them. I bought mine at a sale for eighteenpence, so I must be careful."

CHAPTER XV.

A DASTARDLY DEED—IN THE HANDS OF HIS ENEMIES —THE LONE HUT IN THE FOREST.

NATURE smiled after frowning so darkly, and the sun shone out bravely after the terrific storm; and the atmosphere became so warm and genial that the great bulk of snow vanished almost as breath upon the polished surface of the mirror.

Where it had drifted it still lingered in heaps; but in the roads channels of water ran, rivers overflowed their banks, submerging the meadow-lands, and tiny brooks, that in summer-time made laughing music in the air, were converted into roaring torrents, and thundered down the slopes.

Great and satisfactory as was the change, Wobstock determined not to move the menagerie that day, as some unexpected block on the road might be met with and cause no end of trouble.

As he put it, if the weather held fine there would not be quite so much damp about.

He and Ted Barrett drove back to Wendal, and returned with a cart-load of rough meat and bones for the carniverous animals.

There were plenty of provisions for the other species, so all fared as well as usual.

Wobstock always had "bills" on the brain when the slightest excuse offered itself, and he determined to make profit out of the storm and the delay it occasioned.

"How will this read?" he said, holding a sheet of paper, wet with ink, before Ben's eyes. "Wobstock's menagerie snowed up—caravans blown down—escape of all the animals—terrific encounters and recapture of the wild beasts—the gorilla discovered hunting an old man on crutches—the whole country in fits—Wobstock's men frozen stiff in their caravans after their exertions—gallant conduct of Mumbo the elephant, who kept the baby warm without hurting a hair of the darling's head."

Ben read this literary effort with some feelings of alarm.

"Of course you know best," he said; "but do the facts warrant such statements?"

"Ah! I see you are rather squeamish," Wobstock replied. "I used to be until I found that to make money nowadays you must take high flights of fancy. If Plum says that his soap will wash a nigger white, why shouldn't Wobstock have a go at gulling the public? That bit about Mumbo and the baby will draw the women like winking."

Ben laughed as he said he supposed it would, and went about his work, leaving Wobstock to correct the draft of the bill.

Scouts were sent out in all directions, and returned, reporting that the roads promised to be in a fair condition by the morning, and everything having been put in apple-pie order, all retired to rest with lighter hearts.

The caravan occupied by Ben and Tim was drawn up in the rear of the abode of Mumbo, the elephant, and between the vehicles a number of trusses of hay, covered with tarpaulin and corded down, were piled.

It was a fair and beautiful night.

The full moon shone so brightly that a newspaper could have been read by its light without difficulty, and all Nature lay sleeping peacefully, as if wearied with the struggle imposed by the late storm.

Hours passed away, but just as the moon was paling before the coming light in the eastern sky, Ben, who had been slumbering heavily, was aroused by a tremendous commotion.

Tim Toppem, with his hair on end and his eyes starting out of his head, was shouting, as he put on his clothes anyhow. Mumbo was trumpetting his loudest and trying to break the chains that manacled his feet. The animals and birds were roaring, screeching, and jabbering their loudest, and men, halloing and bellowing, were running about everywhere.

In a moment Ben was out of bed, and was in his clothes before Tim, who was in dire difficulties.

There was no need to tell our hero what was the matter, as he could see and hear for himself.

The trusses of hay were on fire, and huge, hissing tongues of flames leaped up to the sky and filled it with an angry glare.

Jack Wyatt was the only man who dared approach Mumbo now.

The huge animal, filled with wild paroxysms of fear, would have instantly killed any man but the one he was hourly accustomed to, and Wyatt, knowing his business, struck off the chains with an axe, and marched the elephant off as quietly as if he were on daily parade.

Meanwhile all hands were showering buckets of water on the burning mass.

It was a hopeless case, for the hay had caught on all sides, and the small supply of water only added to the fury of the flames.

It was consequently left to burn out, and strenuous exertions were made to move the caravans out of danger. This was done amid great excitement as the horses seemed powerless and utterly oblivious to words of encouragement or the whips which were applied without stint.

But at last Wobstock knew that his property was safe, and went to comfort the women and children of the establishment, who were huddled together at a safe distance.

"This is the work of some villain," the proprietor of the menagerie said. "The hay must have been set fire to in several different places."

At this moment Ted Barrett, black with smoke and his clothes almost scorched to tinder, strode up, and, dragging Wobstock aside, whispered something in his ear.

"What !" gasped Wobstock, "the lads run away— bolted. You are mad to say such a thing."

"I almost wish I could think so," the lion tamer replied. "The moment you turned away Ben Brierton said something to Tim, and they both raced away towards the hills."

William Wobstock's face grew as dark as a gathering thundercloud.

For some moments he was silent, and, then clenching his fists and speaking through his teeth, he said—

"Barrett, you are not going to tell me that you think those boys caused this mischief ?"

"I tell you nothing but facts," Ted Barrett responded, shrugging his shoulders. "They were the last to appear on the scene, and now they are off."

This completely knocked Wobstock out of time. His strength failed him, and he sought the support of a tree, against which he planted his back and gave himself up to reflection, which it is lucky he did not give utterance to.

He had a soft, pliable heart, but when roused he was a man of strong passions, and those hands which had been seldom closed to strike a foe, became as heavy and dangerous as sledge-hammers.

"Barrett," he said, hoarsely and slowly, as if he could not trust himself to speak too fast, "I hope for their sakes that you are mistaken. I hope so, because if I should ever meet either of them, be they young, old, rich, or poor, I'll— Pooh! I am raving. What cause had the lads to do such a dastardly deed?"

"It may have been an accident after all," Barrett suggested.

"It was not an accident," Wobstock declared, emphatically; "and I'll not believe that the lads are guilty until I have better proof. Think how Ben saved your life; think what a good lad Tim has been. Haven't we tried by our very kindness to show how we appreciate them?"

"Mind this," Barrett returned, uneasily; "I never said that the lads set fire to the hay. They may have got up earlier and fooled about with the lamps, or something of the sort, and seeing what they had done ran back in terror to the caravan."

"No," said Wobstock; "I won't have it at any price. We'll wait until the lads come back and hear what they have to say for themselves."

What really happened was of a very different character than that imagined by the lion-tamer.

Ben Brierton and Tim were engaged in dragging their caravan, scorched and blistered by the heat, to a safe distance, when our hero cried out, "Follow me, Tim!" and set off at the top of his speed.

Tim never asked questions when Ben commanded, but tore off on his track until they were fully a mile from the rescued menagerie.

"I have lost sight of him," Ben panted, as he came to a standstill.

"Lost sight of him!" Tim cried. "I saw nobody. Who was it?"

"I am not certain," Ben replied; "but I think it must have been the man you met. I happened to turn my head, and I saw him creeping away through the trees. He saw me, too, and started like a hare for the hills, and now—now he has vanished like a spectre."

Tim Toppem ran his fingers through his dishevelled hair, and an expression of doubt and alarm fell upon his face as he looked at Ben.

"I hope the fire hasn't upset you too much," he said.

"Are you sure that you were not mistaken? It is strange that I did not see this man."

"You were not looking with my eyes," Ben replied; "and I did not care to waste my breath just then. The rascal is lurking about, and cannot be far away, I am sure."

"Hadn't we better run back and get assistance?" queried Tim.

"No, that would be an easy way of permitting the fellow to escape," Ben replied. "We'll hunt him down, and take him back a prisoner. If the man had anything to do with the fire, we'll take the credit of capturing him, Tim."

"I wish I had half your pluck and strength," Tim replied, admiringly. "Well, I am with you. Lead the way, and I hope it will turn out all right."

"It will turn out very bad for him if he should be the the guilty party. Keep a sharp look-out now, and be prepared for a sudden rush. There may be more than one in this affair."

"That is exactly what I was thinking," Tim observed, rather uncomfortably convinced of the fact. "But my head is thick, and has borne a good deal in its time—a copper-stick and a brass candle-stick occasionally, to wit."

Ben Brierton was in too serious a mood even to smile at Tim's fond memories of the past.

He was satisfied in his mind that foul play had been at work, and that Sable Wallack the gipsy had had a hand in it.

Now, side by side, the lads wandered on until they came to a wild part of the country.

Their progress was checked by a rocky gulch, through which torrents of water were boiling and seething with a din that almost deafened them.

The sound increased as they advanced cautiously along the bank, and they found that the hubbub was accounted for by a waterfall of considerable dimensions.

Here an accident had formed a bridge from bank to bank, a large tree having been uprooted and fallen across.

"Going over?" Tim demanded.

"Yes," Ben replied; "the trunk looks slippery, and almost as dangerous as a tight-rope. I will go first, and tell you how to follow."

"For goodness sake! mind what you do," Tim said, glancing down at the churning water. "If you were to slip you would be killed to a certainty, and I should take a header after you."

"That would be as sensible as the man who, finding the medicine did him no good, choked himself with the bottle," Ben remarked. "Keep your eyes open while I try the experiment."

Tim trembled in spite of himself, as Ben, setting his feet firmly on the tree, began the somewhat perilous journey.

When about half-way, and our hero was about to shout—"All's well! come along," he was startled by a sharp cry, and, looking round, saw Tim on the ground, wrestling with a man who had him by the throat.

Ben was in the act of wheeling round and rushing to the rescue, when Sable Wallack leaped upon the tree from the opposite side, and advanced so quickly that almost before the lad could realise the gipsy's sudden appearance found himself locked in an embrace of iron.

"You'd better give in without a struggle, youngster," Sable Wallack hissed in Ben's ear. "I've got the strength of ten like you."

Bold Ben Brierton braced up every nerve to cope with the ruffian.

Heedless of the danger that threatened him, he exerted all his strength to gain the mastery.

Rocking to and fro, and writhing like a pair of giants at war, they struggled, now up, now down, now slipping and sliding, and often within an inch of being hurled to certain death.

"I tell you it is no use," Sable Wallack roared. "You are committing suicide."

"If I cannot get the better of you, I can drag you down with me," Ben replied, "and I'll do it."

"Then take your fate, as you have sought it," the ruffian cried.

Slipping his arms down, he caught Ben round the hips, and was in the very act of throwing him over his shoulder when his feet slipped forward.

Both fell, the back of Ben's head coming in contact with the tree, and stunning him.

"Whew!" whistled Sable Wallack; "it was a near shave for both of us. How are you getting on there, Rushmore?"

"Oh! this one is quiet enough," Rushmore said, grinning. "I crept up behind him unawares, and hit him when he wasn't looking. He only gave music once, and kicked a bit. What shall I do with him?"

"Pitch him into a clump of bushes, and leave him," Wallack replied. "Our business is with this boy; the other would only be in the way. Look alive! There isn't a moment to waste."

Rushmore did as he was requested with Tim, save that instead of pitching him into the bushes, he stood him on his head in the midst of them, and coolly left him to recover or die.

As Rushmore ran to Sable Wallack's assistance, Faro appeared.

CHAPTER XVI.

TIM'S RECEPTION AT THE MENAGERIE.

THE three rascals trotted with their unconscious burden along through the woods until they arrived at a hut.

Sable Wallack now ordered a halt, and tumbling Ben into Faro's arms, ran to the door and uttered a peculiar cry as he struck at it with his knuckles.

Instantly there came the sound of a chain being lowered and bolts drawn. Then, as the door opened a few inches, the sour visage of Ebeneezer Chipps peeped out.

"What news?" he asked.

"The best," Sable Wallack growled. "We've got him, with no more hurt done to him than a cracked head."

"A cracked head! Oh! dear me; it must be a very disagreeable thing to have," Chipps replied; "and a bad one costs money to mend, I suppose. Some winters ago I brought a piece of ice on my boots with me, and fell down twelve stairs into the cellar. I am almost sure Ben laughed on that occasion."

"Cease your chatter and open the door," Wallack said. "Has anything happened?"

"Nothing, only I've had a dreadful feeling all the time that somebody was looking at me through the keyhole."

"The same party who was looking over your shoulder last night?" the gipsy remarked, as Chipps opened the door.

"What party?" the miser demanded.

"Oh! he is an old friend of yours," Wallack replied, laughing, as he gave the signal to the others to bring Ben along. "Black all over, red eyes, and blessed with a tail and a pair of horns."

"Young man," Ebeneezer Chipps said, severely, "to a man of my age and disposition such remarks are very unbecoming."

As Ben Brierton was borne into the hut and laid at full length upon a bench, the miser forgot that he was an old man, and performed a dance entirely of his own invention, and expressive of the greatest delight, round the lad's unconscious form.

"To think that I should behold him again, and have him entirely in my power!" he cried. "Oh! Ben—Ben, you little thought when you ran away from your happy home that you would come to me with a cracked head."

"It's only a bump after all," Faro remarked.

"So much the better," Chipps chuckled. "It will save sticking-plaister. A bump? Ha, ha! What's a bump to a boy? Nature ordained that he should have bumps, but I hope this is a good one."

"Ain't he a nice sort of old gent?" said Sam Rushmore. "Here! get out of the way, you lover of brimstone, and let us see how much damage has been done."

"There isn't much now," Sable Wallack remarked; "but there will be plenty and to spare if he wakes up and catches us napping. I've wrestled with a few people in my life, but I never felt a pair of arms round me like his. He only wants a few lessons to be a champion. Faro, fetch that rope down from the wall, and we will make sure of him."

"I feel," said Chipps, who was in ecstacies of delight, "that I could take his boots off and tickle him into fits with a feather. Gentlemen," he added, "it's only natural that after all the time and care I have bestowed on him that I should think a little mild correction necessary."

"If he should ever get his liberty, which I don't think is likely," Sable Wallock remarked, "the correction you'd get from him wouldn't be mild, or with a feather. Your property would go into another channel it he set about you in right-down earnest."

Occasionally in the police reports we find a hardened being, when sentenced to durance vile for sundry months *à la* calendar, informing the magistrate that he is able and perfectly willing to pass the allotted period "on his head."

It is reasonably to be presumed that this individual with such a thorough ignorance with the regards to the rights of other people's property, and embued with virtuous notions as to his own, and strong acrobatic tendencies, and would probably have made his fortune had he been initiated into the mysteries of circus life.

Our gentle and faithful friend, Tim Toppem, was performing on his head very much against his will, and having been guilty of nothing to be ashamed of.

Luckily, as it happened, the bushes out of which his heels were gracefully sticking contained no brambles nor plants of a thorny nature, yet the attitude was not only sufficiently uncomfortable, but dangerous.

If Tim had been an ordinary boy it might have been our painful duty to bid him a fond farewell, and erase him from the story ; but Tim, as the rejected lover put it, was ' doomed to live."

By degrees his legs slid down, and his body collapsed and lay huddled up ; but in about half an hour the youth displayed certain unmistakable signs of coming round.

In the first place he indulged in a prodigious sneeze, which forced his eyes and mouth open, and then Tim sat up in his bower of evergreens and peeped wistfully out of it.

There was, to him, something very much like an Arabian Night Entertainment about the whole thing, and for some time he could make nothing whatever out of it.

In a confused way he mixed up runaway elephants, escaped monkeys, trusses of hay on fire, Ebeneezer Chipps, and Ben Brierton, and saw them pass before his vision as glass changes its shape and hue in a kaleidoscope.

There was, however, one thing that Tim Toppem was quite certain of.

The right side of his head, especially under the ear, was sore and swollen, as if he had suffered from toothache for a month.

All of a sudden the truth flashed upon him, and he started up and gazed wildly around.

" Ben—Ben !" he cried, staggering up and down, for he was still weak and giddy. " Where are you ?"

The echo of his own voice mocked him, and in utter despair he wrung his hands and burst into tears.

" I remember all now," he cried. " The brutes have either made him a prisoner or killed him. Oh ! Ben, if you are lost to me I have nothing to live for. If you don't come back I shall wish myself dead. I wish I may die if I don't !"

Poor Tim was very shaky on his legs, but he contrived to crawl on his hands and knees over the fallen tree ; but when on the other side he was as wise as ever.

What to do he did not know. The thought that Ben had been spirited away, or, worse still, had been hurled into the cataract, nearly drove him frantic ; but at last he wisely determined to hasten back to the menagerie and tell the doleful story.

It occurred to him that it would be worse than folly to continue the search single-handed, so, nursing his aching head with one hand, he retraced his steps, running and walking alternately, until he came within sight of the caravans.

At Cloisterville Tim had been famed for uttering cries calculated to startle people out of their senses.

He had been know to imitate the roaring of a mad bull to perfection, following it up with the harrowing shriek of an old lady in full retreat, and Tim now gave full power to this particular talent, and produced a yell that even silenced the lions, and made them wonder what addition had been suddenly made to the collection.

Wobstock and all the rest heard the fearful sound, and Ted Barrett, with wild cats in his mind, ran to the locker that contained his pistols and loaded them hastily.

But the mystery and consternation ended with the appearance of Tim Toppem.

Wobstock ran to meet him with an expression of mingled gladness, doubt, and alarm depicted on his face.

"Blue monkeys and pickled pelicans!" he gasped. "What's the meaning of this? Why, lad, your head is all on one side."

"It's a wonder it isn't off," Tim replied, with a groan. "Oh! Mr. Wobstock, Ben—Ben—Ben—"

"Where is he?" Wobstock demanded, seizing the distracted youth by the shoulders and shaking him up with as little ceremony as if he were a bottle of physic. "Speak out. Tell me everything in as few words as possible. Barrett, fetch a drop of brandy. This boy's eyes are working in a style enough to frighten a scarecrow."

"I don't want any brandy;" Tim replied, "it would only make me worse than I am now. Please let me sit down, and I will tell you all about it."

"Such," Wobstock murmured to himself, "is the difference between youth and age. When I'm put out, and want to say anything partic'ler, I must stand up or bust."

The strollers gathered round, and listened to what Tim had to say in silence.

"All this," said Wobstock, at the conclusion of the narrative, "comes about of two well meanin' boys doin' what they didn't orter. But youth is ever wild and skittish."

"Ah!" sighed Angelina. "I have heard what you were years ago."

Mr. Wobstock took a mental measurement of his nose as this remark was delivered.

"My love!" he replied, getting slightly mixed in his speech, "never mind what I were; you must take me for what I are. Never mind, Tim, we'll find Ben right enough, and punish the cowardly crew who kidnapped him."

"I wish they had kidnapped me, too," Tim observed, tearfully. "Why didn't they take me with him, instead of planting me in a bush as if they expected I would grow there?"

"As I said before," Wobstock observed, "all this trouble was caused by an excess of impecuniosity—I mean impetuosity—but we will look over it, and hope for better things.

"Once upon a time," he resumed, as if he were about to tell a fairy tale, "I was playing with another boy in a fishing punt, and by some means or other I fell out of the back of it into ten feet of water.

"Now, instead of that boy tryin' to help me out, he got ashore and went across the meadows like a steam-hengine to the house where I lived, and hammered in a manner that brought my father to the door pretty quick.

"'What's the matter?' says the dad.

"'Your boy's gone and tumbled out o' the punt and drowned hisself,' says my companion.

"My father," continued Wobstock, solemnly, "was very fond of me. First of all he put on his hat and coat, and then, walking slowly into the kitchen, said to my mother, who was crossin' with a b'iler full of Irish stew, 'If Will-i-am shouldn't come home to dinner don't you be surprised.'

"'Why not?' says my mother, turning white, and lowerin' the handle o' the b'iler. 'What's happened to him?'

"'Boys,' my father says, 'are very much alike all over the world; and if they will play down by the river-side, why—'

"Down went the b'iler, and my mother kickin' and screamin' in the Irish stew.

"Just then I arrived all mud, weeds, and water.

"'Father,' says I, 'I ain't drowned.'

"The dad wipes away the tears which had gathered in his eyes, and feels round the door for a stick.

"'Will-i-am,' he says, pointin' to the staircase, 'you'll go up slowly, and I'll keep time to your movements. I was just off for the drags; you've sent your mother into fits, you've spiled the dinner, and now you come to me and say you ain't drowned.'

"With which," said Wobstock, gazing sternly at Tim, "he laid on, until the lady as lived next door sent in word hopin' that there wouldn't be any beatin' of carpets until she had taken the linen in. And why was all this? Impetuosity."

"No doubt about it," Angelina remarked. "Let this be a lesson to you, Master Toppem."

"I was impetuous to fall out of the punt," Wobstock continued to moralise, "and my friend was impetuous in runnin' straight off to my father. And," he added, "if Ben and you hadn't run off without orders both of you would be here, and we should be on the road."

Tim Toppem, although much impressed with the story, could not see where the comparison came in.

"But let it all go," Wobstock went on, with the air of a martyr. "We must wait till night before we make a move. The sight of us would startle the quarry, and goodness only knows what mischief might not be done, which a little forethought and caution may save."

Tim Toppem was on thorns to think there was to be a moment's delay, but he was entirely in the hands of Wobstock, who evidently knew what was best to be done.

He found some little occupation for his mind in a mustard poultice which Angelina made, and insisted that he should wear and not remove until she gave consent.

The poultice was the hottest thing, next to a red-hot poker, that Tim had ever come in contact with.

It made his eyes water and his swollen cheek steam, and it caused him to go close behind the caravans like an Indian witch-finder.

It is quite probable that he would have disregarded Mrs. Wobstock's injunctions; but she had so tied and pinned the handkerchief containing the torturing mixture that Tim discovered that little short of decapitation would have removed it.

He bore his sufferings until the welcome time came for his release, and then Angelina, finding that she had been a little too lavish, bathed the side of Tim's head, and dredged it liberally with flour.

"I must look a pretty spectacle," he observed, ruefully, to Ted Barrett.

"You do," the lion-tamer replied, laughing; "but remember Wobstock's words—it's all through impetuosity."

"I feel," said Tim, leaning the cool side of his head against a tree, "as if one side of me had been half-stewed, and then roasted before a quick fire. But the pain is nothing to my misery about Ben."

"Take courage," Barrett replied. "If he is alive—and there is very little doubt about that—we will have him amongst us again before day dawns."

"Then," said Tim, "if you hear me grumble about anything again between now and the time we start, just kick me as hard as you can."

"I will," responded the lion-tamer, "and perhaps I had better put on my thickest boots, in case there is need to oblige you."

Though Tim pretended to be hopeful, and as cheerful as circumstances would allow, the day was full of terrible anxieties.

Every moment was an hour, and every hour an age.

But the sun performed its course, as it always does, alike over scenes of rejoicing and sorrow, and in due time dipped its glowing face into a bank of purple clouds to rouse the other half of the world to life and activity.

Wobstock and the lion-tamer had not been idle.

They had made their preparations for the coming event, in making torches, and fashioning into shape cudgels heavy enough to have floored a similar number of oxen.

The lion-tamer was not satisfied with being thus armed. He put a brace of pistols into his pocket and wound several yards of rope round his waist.

The search-party consisted of six, including Jack Wyatt and, of course, Tim Toppem.

Wobstock delayed the start until it was quite dark, and the night favoured them, for the moon was obscured by masses of dark clouds, threatening rain.

Acting as guide, Tim went forward with a dark-lantern

in his hand, the slide of which he kept discreetly closed, save when light was absolutely necessary.

This happened once, when Wobstock crashed wildly into a tree, and performing a precipitous backward journey, floored the man nearest to him, and then wildly requested that somebody would either take off his hat or pull his head out of the top of it.

When the tree forming a bridge was reached the real excitement of the adventure began.

Light was now a matter of sheer necessity, and Tim, holding the lantern down so that the small white disc illuminated the smallest possible space, crossed first and showed the others the way.

They all got safely over.

"I think I must have lost a pound of flesh crawling over that thing," Wobstock said, as he reached the other side, and wiped the perspiration from his face. "I've heard of the Bridge o' Sighs, but this has been the Bridge o' Groans to me."

Ted Barrett had now taken the lantern from Tim, and was wandering hither and thither, looking like a substantial Will-o'-the-Wisp.

"I have found the track, and something else," he said, as he regained the party. "Here is poor Ben's knife, which must have fallen from his pocket, and, as far as I can see, there is three in this game. Two wore boots and the other was bare-footed."

"Sable Wallack!" exclaimed Wobstock, smiting his battered hat; "by some means he must have fallen in with the other lot. We have our work cut out to run him to earth."

While Tim's heart sank at the words, it seemed to him that the injured side of his head grew as large as a toy-balloon.

"But we'll do it," Wobstock continued. "If we don't go back with Ben before daylight, I hope that Hangelina will set about us with a red'ot frying-pan! Forrard, Ted!"

"It's all very well to cry out 'Forrard!' Barrett replied; "but this place is like a jungle and the Rocky Mountains rolled into one. In spite of the lantern, I've

"In the name of wonder, how do you think they are to be got back to the cage again?"

done nothing but break my shins against all sorts of things."

"Shins !" Wobstock gasped; "I think I must have left mine on that dreadful tree. What do you say to more light ?"

"We must risk it," the lion-tamer replied. "I don't suppose we shall come upon any of the conspirators, unless they have placed a scout. Wherever they are, they are snug enough by this time—the boy drugged again, perhaps, and they sound asleep and snoring. Is there a man here who has been through this country before, or who knows anything about it ?"

Wobstock stopped as if he had suddenly ran up against another tree, and, in trying to smite his brow, knocked his hat off and sent it spinning into the air.

"Why," he said, "if I wern't a fool, with parched peas in my head instead of brains, I should have remembered that we are on the way to the Calderon-road. Now, let me think."

He tapped his head, pursed up his lips, and reflected so deeply that Barrett called out impatiently—

"Give those parched peas a shaking up! This isn't a Quaker's meeting, you know."

"Ted," Wobstock replied, "I was tryin' to think o' somethin'. Once a rabbit ran out of a bank, and nearly tripped me up, and I thought I would teach it a lesson. I ran, and ran, and hollered, just as huntsmen do; but the rabbit didn't stop, but suddenly disappeared behind somethin', which I discovered to be a hut. When I got back, somebody told me that a gamekeeper had committed suicide in that hut, and nobody cared to go near it."

[It is a popular, but fallacious, notion amongst people in the country that a pursued rabbit will stop all the sooner for being yelled at. It is no uncommon sight, especially in the eastern counties, when the crops are being cut, to see a score of men and boys in full cry, in both senses of the word. No wonder that poor bunny eventually surrenders.]

"That's something worth taking notice of, at all events," Barrett said. "We will find the hut, if possible. Wallack may have profited by the story, and taken possession of it.

"I was thinkin' the same," Wobstock returned. "White elephants and green porkypines! Light the torches. We must not miss a single haystack. Tim, my boy, keep cool ; you are swellin' all over with impatience."

"Only on one side !" Tim replied.

CHAPTER XVII.

THE PRISONER IN THE HUT—BOLD BEN'S DEFIANCE— THE RESCUE.

THE fall had stunned Ben so effectually that he showed no signs of returning consciousness, although Sable Wallack dashed water over his face and Sam Rushmore beat the palms of his hands.

"Let him come round in his own good time," Wallack said.

"It might end in brain fever," Chipps observed. "The boy was always of an excitable temperament, and as touchy as gunpowder. If he were to have a long illness we should be in a nice pickle, for what could we do with him ?"

"He might die," Sam Rushmore croaked, "and save a lot of trouble."

"He's worth a dozen dead 'uns yet," Wallack said, brutally. "As soon as I've settled matters with the swell you call Mr. Reginald, I'll pack the youngster off to the coast, and get him away, as I promised."

As he spoke, the dog called Fury crept out of a shadowy corner and sniffed at Chipps' legs.

"Tell that brute to lie down," the miser gasped, skipping behind Wallack. "I am sure he intends to bite me."

"Very likely," the gipsy replied, laughing, "and you're going just the right way to make him do it. If Fury took hold of you in earnest, half-a-dozen men wouldn't pull him off."

Ebeneezer Chipps turned pale with horror, and beads of clammy perspiration stood on his brow.

"I wouldn't be bitten by a dog for the best sovereign that was ever turned out of the Mint," he said. "My good friend, do take him away. There! He's showing the whites of his eyes and teeth at me again."

"The dog seems to be uneasy," Faro said. "Listen! I thought I heard voices shouting in the wood."

Sable Wallack ran to the window, which was covered with a wooden shutter, and placed his ear against it.

"I hear nothing but the wind," he said. "The menagerie people have enough to do to look after themselves. Sit down, Chipps. Don't stand there making faces at the dog, or he will fly at your throat. It's a way he has with strangers who pay him too much attention."

"Perhaps if Chipps would let the dog have one good nibble at him, he might be satisfied," Sam Rushmore remarked, with a grin.

At that moment Faro held up a hand warningly, and pointed with the other to Ben Brierton.

"Hist!" he whispered; "the boy is coming round. Stand back! It won't do to startle him too much at first."

Ben's lashes were quivering and his lips moving, and presently he drew a deep breath and opened his eyes.

"Tim!" he cried, faintly, "where are you?"

"Where you won't see him in a hurry," Rushmore muttered.

Ben now tried to rise, but he was bound hand-and-foot, and could not move a limb.

"Where am I?" he cried out. "Who has dared to make me a prisoner? Where is that cowardly scoundrel who attacked me like a wild beast?"

Sable Wallack made a sign to Ebeneezer Chipps, and the miser sidled across the hut so that Ben could see him.

"You here?" Ben exclaimed. "I understand it all now. Mean, pitiful wretch that you are, tell me why you persecute me?"

"Hear him!" Chipps rejoined, throwing up his hands. "This boy, whose board cost me fourpence a-day at the least, calls me a mean, pitiful wretch. Oh! Ben—Ben, I was always afraid that you would turn out a bad boy, but I never thought it would come to this."

"Why do you not let me go my own way?" Ben cried. "Times out of number you threatened to turn me out into the streets, but no sooner do I leave you and try to earn an honest living than you follow my footsteps, employ hirelings to hound me down. Mean and contemptible as I know you to be, I gave you the credit of having one spark of manhood left, and I call upon you to tell me the truth."

"The truth—the beautiful truth!" Chipps returned, squeezing his hands together, and rolling up his eyes. "Yes, Ben; you shall know the truth. You were a beggarly brat when I took you under my care, and I don't intend after all the care and training I have bestowed on you to let you have all your own way."

"Care and training!" Ben Brierton echoed. "You beat and starved me. You tried to teach me all the tricks of low cunning, tor which you are so deservedly hated, and it is no fault of yours that I did not become a vagabond and a gaol bird."

In his excitement Ben worked himself up to his feet; and then he saw the other members of the assembly.

"You keep nice company," he continued, bestowing a look of scorn upon Chipps, "and doubtless flatter yourself that I am in your power, but don't deceive yourself. For every suffering, for every insult you have inflicted on me, I will repay tenfold."

"Wait until you get the chance, my lad," said Sable Wallack, striding forward. "You crow too loud for a bantam."

"I can fight as well as crow," Ben retorted. "Cut these bonds and I will take my chance against you all. No! You are too cowardly to offer me even so slender an opportunity of regaining my liberty."

"You will have it soon enough," Wallack said. "I have bought you of your kind and considerate uncle, and you are already sold to a friend of mine."

"Sold to a friend of yours?" Ben cried, aghast.

"Yes; he asked me to find a likely lad to make up a troupe of acrobats bound for the East, and I fell in with Mr. Chipps just in time to make a comfortable arrangement about you."

"Is this true?" Ben demanded, furiously, as he turned to Ebeneezer Chipps.

"Well—ahem!—you are not quite sold; not a slave exactly, Ben; but I have lent you to this good man and his friends for a few years."

"You monster in human form!" Ben cried. "If at this moment I had my hands free I should be tempted to rid the world of you for ever. But I am dreaming! This is a hideous mockery, for such a thing must be impossible in these days."

"Not so impossible as you may think, youngster," Wallack said, "and you will find it so. You'll do no good by making a fuss, so take matters easy."

Ben Brierton, however, did not take this advice.

Suddenly exerting all his strength, he strained at his bonds until his face grew distorted and the veins upon his brow stood out like whipcord.

"Fury!" Wallack cried. "Fury! watch him, good dog!"

With a snarling growl the brute planted its fore paws on Ben's shoulders, and breathed hotly upon his face.

Overcome with horror, Ben recoiled, and, losing his balance, fell upon the floor.

"That's better," Ebeneezer Chipps chuckled. "I've taken quite a fancy to that dog, after all; he is a most sagacious animal. Don't move, Ben, unless you wish to lose your ears; I observe that the dog has his eyes upon them."

"Cease your prating," Sable Wallack cried, darting across the apartment. "I hear something more than the wind now."

A dead silence fell on all.

Ben would have shouted for help; but it would have been bad policy on his part, as Faro snatched up a cudgel, and stood over him, ready to strike at the first word uttered.

"There's somebody sneaking about," Wallack said, creeping back on tiptoe. "Come here, Fury, old fellow. A taste of your fangs will be sufficient to send the party home in a violent hurry."

"What are you going to do?" demanded Ebeneezer

Chipps, in a hurry. "You don't mean to say that you are going to be so rash as to open the door?"

Wallack made no reply, but his eyes flashed on the miser in a manner that told him that he had better mind his own business.

The ruffian seized the dog by the neck and led him to the door, and Fury, after sniffing at the bottom of it, lifted his head and gave forth a rumbling growl.

Wallack drew back the bolts softly, and, lifting the latch, opened the door just wide enough for the dog to pass through, and Fury, yelling, snarling, and snapping right and left, dashed out.

It was the last journey the brute was destined to take.

There was a flash, followed by a loud report, and Fury, bounding wildly into the air, fell dead at the feet of Ted Barrett, the lion-tamer.

Then the air rang with the voices of determined men, the door was smashed in, as if it was mere tinder, and Wallack, with a howl as savage as the last which Fury had indulged in, caught up a three-legged stool, and knocking Wobstock down, leaped over him and vanished into the darkness of the wood.

So sudden and violent were the means used by the ruffian that the band of rescuers were taken by surprise, and made no attempt to capture him.

Faro tore aside the wooden shutter, and contrived to scramble out of the window; but Ebeneezer Chipps and Sam Rushmore stood as if their feet had taken root to the floor, and only stood glaring in horror and dismay at the brave fellows who had snatched Ben from their clutches.

"Look to them, Jack Wyatt," the lion-tamer said. "you know what to do if they lift a hand or move a foot! Tim, take this knife and cut those cords. Courage, Ben; Don't look as if you didn't know us, lad."

"I know you all," Ben replied; "but I must confess that you took my breath away. Tim, old fellow, don't take my arms for pump-handles."

Tim Toppem had lost his voice, and was crying for very joy, but Ben's words brought him to himself.

"Ben—brave Ben" he said. "I have had such a

day of misery, but, thank Heaven! I see you safe and sound again. Have these brutes been ill-treating you?"

"They have not had much time," Ben replied. "I have been unconscious many hours, and my head is swimming now. What is that in the corner?"

The object was Mr. Wobstock, who sat exactly where he had fallen, with his legs sprawled out and his hat over his eyes.

Nobody, in their anxiety to relieve Ben from his uncomfortable position and to secure Chipps and Rushmore, had thought of going to the assistance of the menagerie proprietor, and it dawned into his confused mind that it would be just as well if he assisted himself.

"There's somethin' evil and unlucky about this hat," he said, as he tore it off and glared viciously at it; "it's constantly gettin' me into trouble. What did the wampire strike me with? Was it a scaffold-pole or a batterin'-ram? A stool, eh? Well, let it all go. Ben, my lad, I give you joy on your lucky escape. It has been a near squeeze for you."

The word squeeze seemed to suggest a brilliant idea to Mr. Wobstock.

Rushing at Ebeneezer Chipps, he seized his nose in a vice-like grip, and turned it almost round.

"That's for you, you old villain," Wobstock roared. "And as for you," he added, turning upon Rushmore, "take that!"

It was a blow that would have felled an ox, and Rushmore went down and lay like a log.

"This is the most painful thing I have ever experienced," Chipps whined, as tears of anguish rolled down his cheeks. "My dear sir, do you know that you have done a most unlawful thing? Probably you are not aware of the penalties for assault and battery?"

"I'd like to batter you with a wengeance," Wobstock hissed. "I'm only sorry that we ain't in the backwoods of Ameriky, where we could hang you out of hand. Oh! you precious pair of rascals, to treat a poor lad in this shameful way. I must have another squeeze! I can't stand lookin' at you without doing you some kind o' mischief."

Ebeneezer Chipps howled most unmelodiously at the second painful operation on his nasal organ, and Sam Rushmore joined in with a chorus of groans.

Ben Brierton stood with his arms folded and his eyes full of triumph, gazing at the discomfited pair, but he contented himself with looking on.

"I think we have had enough of this beastly den," Ted Barrett said; "so we had better march our prisoners off."

"Prisoners!" Chipps gasped; "you don't dare to say that you intend to kidnap *me?*"

"I mean to say that I intend to take great care of you," Wobstock cried; "and what is more, if you say another word I'll have such another squeeze as will leave your ugly face without a nose."

Jack Wyatt jerked Sam Rushmore to his feet in a most unceremonious manner, and in a trice secured him to Chipps with the very rope that had been used for Ben.

"I have another trifle of cord here," Ted Barrett said, "but that will come in to hurry up your movements, if necessary. Now, then, quick march! and, mind you, lift your feet up. If one falls, the other will go down with him."

"This is a nice pickle you have got me into," Rushmore moaned. "If they hand us over to the police we shall find ourselves in close quarters for a considerable time."

But Wobstock had no such intention.

"You are right, my lad," he said, after he and Ben had exchanged a few words; "there is some great mystery about all this, and we'll wring the truth from the old hunks. I'll make no bones about the beggar, Ben. I'll keep him, and use him so that his life shall become a misery. As for the other wretch, it wouldn't cost me many scruples to shove him in the way of Mumbo, when he is in one of his awkward moments, and flinging his trunk about like the lash of a whip."

Wobstock looked as if he really meant what he said, and every time he looked at Chipps he became violently agitated, and made short darts at the miser, uttering threats that made the wicked old man s blood run cold.

Tim led the way joyfully with a torch, giving every now and then a shout of exultation.

"Wobstock," Barrett said, when they reached the tree spanning the torrent, "how are we to get them over?"

"That is their look out," the proprietor of the menagerie replied, darkly. "If they should go over, why, they would go over, of course."

The lion-tamer, however, took the matter into his own hands, and clutching Chipps and Rushmore tightly by the collars of their coats, marched them safely across.

Soon after a shout rent the air, proclaiming that the menagerie was in sight, and Angelina, dragging the Wobstock olive-branches hand in hand after her, saluted Ben in a motherly fashion, and then threw her arms round her husband's neck.

"Will-i-am," she cried, hysterically, "I am proud of you. You've done a deed worthy of a hangel. Never again will I say a cross word to you."

"Don't you go and make any rash promises," Wobstock retorted; "it ain't in the nature of the best wife in the world to be all honey. We must have our bitters with our sweets, and that is the reason why winegar was inwented."

CHAPTER XVIII.

CHIPPS AND HIS FRIENDS ARE VISITED BY AN APPARITION.

EBENEEZER CHIPPS and Sam Rushmore were unbound, but only to be rebound back to back, and in such a style as to make every bone in their bodies ache.

Hobbling along, their movements being accelerated by Jack Wyatt and Ted Barrett, who did not scruple to tread on their heels, they reached an open space, in the centre of which a cauldron, depending from a tripod, gave forth an aroma suggestive of Irish stew.

"Now, look here, you fellows," said the lion-tamer, loading a pistol with small shot as he spoke, "you see this little article. Well, I shall have my eye upon you, and if you attempt to get away I'll pepper you until you dance like grasshoppers."

Ted Barrett and Wyatt left the prisoners in the most miserable condition.

Independent of the threat, which they felt sure would be carried out, there was but little chance of escape.

If they moved at all they tripped each other up, and every effort racked their arms.

"I shall be dead in an hour," Chipps groaned. "Oh! Rushmore, this is too dreadful to be true."

"It's true as well as dreadful," Rushmore returned. "I s'pose the whole b'ilin' lot of them will come 'ere presently and gorge themselves afore our starvin' eyes. The smell from that cauldron has made me feel quite hungry."

"So it has me," Chipps said. "In spite of all the agonies I am enduring I could eat a good supper, especially if it cost nothing."

Wobstock had taken Ben and Tim to his caravan, and regaled them sumptuously, and the captives could hear the sounds of merriment—sounds that only aggravated them.

"They can't mean to keep us like this long," Chipps gasped. "Though they deal with the lower order of brutes they are men after all."

"Hold your tongue!" Rushmore growled. "Somebody's comin' to alter this awful state o' things, and p'raps to give us some supper."

He had scarcely breathed the last words when a terrific yell caused Ebeneezer Chipps to start violently.

"What was that?" he asked, in a tone of abject terror.

"I don't know," Rushmore replied, lashing out with his feet; "but I know that if you skip like that again you'll put my shoulders out of joint.'

"I couldn't help it, Sam—really, I couldn't," Chipps replied. "I have a dreadful notion that they may have let some of the animals loose to devour us."

"Not likely," Rushmore said, with all the contempt he could throw into his quivering voice. "Wouldn't the animals go first for them, you fool?"

"I don't know," Chipps returned. "I am entirely ignorant of such matters, and glad to say that I have never been guilty of wasting a penny upon an entertainment."

"You're gettin' one for nothin' now," Rushmore

observed, grimly. "So am I, and it's likely to last me my lifetime. If ever I get out o' this muddle I think I shall make a clean bolt of it."

Again the terrific yell assailed their ears, and a shriek of terror burst from the lips of Ebeneezer Chipps.

Leaping, dancing, growling, and chattering, and coming straight at him, was the most enormous ape he had ever heard or dreamed of.

"We are lost, Rushmore!" he said, his teeth chattering and his eyes fit to start from his head. "I was right, after all. They have sent a gorilla to devour us."

"A what?" demanded the ruffian, who could not see the monster in consequence of his face being turned the other way. "You're getting light-headed, old man."

Chipps swung him round so that he might have optical demonstration of the fact, and Rushmore set up such a howl as to cause the gorilla to come to a standstill and glare at him.

"Help! Murder! Help!" Rushmore exclaimed. "Take the brute away! Oh, lor! Mur—der! If any of you've got a grain of pity don't let us be chawed up!"

In the meantime Ebeneezer Chipps was kicking and plunging wildly.

CHAPTER XIX.

THAT PLAYFUL GORILLA.

CHIPPS' antics seemed to please the gorilla mightily, and, strangely enough, the tyrant of the jungle, who was, of course, no other than Tim Toppem, had in one of his paws a long wooden spoon.

With this weapon he proceeded in the most playful manner imaginable to hammer Ebeneezer's hat until it was all out of shape, and then skipping round to Rushmore, tapped that individual so smartly over the bridge of the nose that he was treated to a brilliant display of coloured lights.

Chipps thought he must have died, and Rushmore yelled like a madman.

Tim lent a series of most appalling sound to the din,

and then, suddenly dashing the spoon into the cauldron, thrust some of the scalding stew between the men's lips.

This was too much even for the old man with a fondness or cheap suppers.

His legs gave way under him, and he went sprawling down, dragging Sam Rushmore with him.

With great relish Wobstock had watched the performance from behind a tree, and now came to the front.

"You've done enough, and done it well, Tim," he whispered. "Run back and get into your other togs, and I will join you directly. We shall sleep without fear of being disturbed to-night."

Then, stooping over the affrighted captives, he cut the cords, and bade them rise.

But Chipps was perfectly incapable of taking advantage of this invitation.

Paralysed with terror he lay clutching at the grass, and tearing up earth with his hooked and quivering fingers.

"I believe the old man has gone silly at last," Wobstock said, "but you aren't so bad. Come, get upon your hob-nails, or I'll find ways and means to make you look lively."

Rushmore obeyed him sullenly, and eyed him in a style that was at once cowed and malevolent.

"Well," the ruffian said, "I should think you are satisfied with what you have done."

"Not half," Wobstock replied, blandly; "I am going to put you into an empty cage next door to a hyena. You'll find him good company as he is always particularly lively at night time; but if you'll take my advice don't go too near to the bars, as you may get scratched a bit."

Wyatt, Barrett, and some of the other men now appeared on the scene.

Two of them raised Ebeneezer Chipps in their arms, while the lion-tamer and Wobstock gave their attention to Rushmore.

"Look 'ere," said the last named, "if you'll let me go I'll tell you somethin' about that mumbling old miser and the boy."

Wobstock was about to reply, when Chipps, who had

temporarily lost his reason, began to rave.

"What's he talking about?" demanded Wobstock.

"It's all mixed up," one of the men said, "but there's something about a cellar, a box, and some papers."

The proprietor of the menagerie laid his forefinger on the side of his nose.

"Oh! yes," he said, smiling. "I'm not going to be caught in such a trap. The old villain is only shamming after all, and trying a misleading dodge. It won't do."

"But s'pose he's speaking' the truth?" Rushmore said.

"He couldn't do it if he tried, and you either," Wobstock retorted. "I don't want to hear another word from you. Here's your lodging, and make the best of it. Come, hurry up, or down you go."

No sooner did Rushmore step into the cage than a wooden shutter was thrust before him, and Wobstock laughed as he heard him scramble into a corner, as far as possible from the hyena next door, who favoured him with a diabolical laugh, and an attempt to convert the two cages into one.

"What are we to do with the old 'un?" Wyatt asked. "If he is shamming it is wonderfully like the real article."

"Put him into my van and leave him to me," Wobstock replied. "I want to have a few words with the old gent, when he can talk sensibly."

Mrs. Wobstock, although fully aware that her husband was sailing very close to the wind of the law in detaining Ben's enemies, also knew that he was acting in a just and manly spirit, and was sufficiently discreet to keep out of the way while her own Will-i-am was doing his best to "pump" Ebeneezer Chipps.

The old miser was in a state bordering on madness.

When laid upon the bed he threw his arms about wildly and rolled his head from side to side after the fashion of a man in the delirium of a virulent fever.

"Steady, old boy," said Wobstock, "or you will bang your head against the bed-post. You know me, don't you?"

"Yes, you are Mr. Reginald."

"Mr. Reginald, eh!" rejoined the showman. "Well,

I've got another name, so you may as well out with it."

Ebeneezer Chipps hesitated, and turned a pair of glassy eyes upon his interrogator.

"That's a secret between us, I know," Wobstock said, bending over the miser, and speaking in a low tone of voice; "but we are alone now, and can talk as freely as if we were at the bottom of an empty coal-mine."

"You made me swear that I would never write, or breathe your real name, and you are not going to catch me in a trap now," Chipps replied, struggling with his scattered faculties.

"Humph! the old 'un is artful," Wobstock said to himself. "I'll try him on another tack. I say, what about them deeds in the cellar?"

This question acted like an electric shock on Chipps. He uttered a wild cry, and, starting up, stretched out his arms as if to ward off a blow.

"The cellar! What cellar?" he demanded, glaring round the caravan. "I said nothing about any cellar."

"Who said you did?" Wobstock returned, cautiously. "I made a remark about your smeller, which is rather red from being pulled. Perhaps another tug or two might bring it back to its natural colour. Keep still! I'm going to keep you with me until I know why you hunt Ben Brierton as if he was a mad dog."

"He is my nephew, and I am his lawful guardian until he comes of age," Chipps retorted.

"Wery good," Wobstock said; "but that answer won't do for me. Just sleep over it, and perhaps by the morning you'll be in a better frame of mind."

"This is a free country, and you have no right to detain me," Chipps responded. "Mark me, you shall suffer for this."

"Bring along your sufferin's," the showman said; "I know sufficient to convince me that you daren't say a word or hold up a finger to do me harm. You unnatural old villain, your great desire is to smuggle Ben out of the country, but not to suit all your own purposes. There's another and a richer man in this plot, and I'll unearth him if it takes me twenty years to do it."

"You'd better give in," Sable Wallack hissed.

"What has put such an idle story into your mind?" Chipps gasped.

"Suppose the man we caught with you has made a clean breast of everything," Wobstock rejoined; "or s'pose—and that may be nearer the truth—while you've been here waggin' your head about as if you wanted somebody to play crab-apple with it, that I've heard a neat little story from your own mouth?"

"It is a lie!" Chipps cried, fiercely. "I have said nothing, for the simple reason that I have nothing to say. Beware how you attempt to put a falsehood into my lips. I tell you again that you will be held answerable for this monstrous treatment."

"Now that's what I call plucky," Wobstock said, taking a key from his pocket and rising, "and I didn't expect so much from an old man who may die in a fit at any moment. I'm goin' to leave you here for a time, but I hope to get rid of you by to-morrow night. Don't so much as put your head out of the window, or you'll get it cracked; I shall be about, and so will my men. Why, you antiquated old sinner," he added, with sudden animation, "I should like to serve you as Ben did the lion, and tickle you with a red-hot iron."

Ebeneezer Chipps looked as if he had not the slightest doubt that the showman's wish was nearest his heart, but the miser deemed it wise not to argue the question, and Wobstock left him, doubly locking the caravan door.

"If you want to write a full confession of your misdeeds you'll find pen, ink, and paper in a locker above your head," the showman said through the keyhole.

Chipps growled out some uncomplimentary reply, and then, burying his face in the pillow, smothered the groans which were wrung from his tortured heart and brain.

CHAPTER XX.

HOW TOPPEM SENIOR KEPT HIS TRUST, AND WHAT BECAME OF HIM WHEN THE CANDLE WENT OUT.

WILL-I-AM WOBSTOCK was abroad and very lively when the sun rose.

First of all he paid a short visit to each of the prisoners, and finding that they were safe, knocked up Ben, who looked little the worse for his adventure.

"My lad," said Wobstock, "the menagerie will go on in Barrett's charge, but you and me will take a journey another way."

Ben repeated the words in amazement, wondering what they could portend.

"Yes," Wobstock continued, jerking his hat on to the side of his head and thrusting his hands into his pockets, "we are going to make a trip to Cloisterville. I s'pose you would find your way into Chipps' house without much trouble?"

Ben Brierton could not help smiling at the suggestion.

"It would be no trouble at all," he replied; "but for the life of me I cannot understand why you should desire to see inside of the miserable old dwelling."

"I've got a strong fancy to do so," Wobstock returned. "With a fast horse we shall reach Cloisterville by night. I rather fancy, Ben, I am going to astonish you."

"You are keeping me in suspense now," our hero said.

"And there I must keep you for a few hours," Wobstock said. "I suppose there is no fear of tumbling across the police near Chipps' house?"

"Never saw one there in my life," Ben replied. "It is too dark and gruesome a place for a man to prowl about in the dead of the night; but there are neighbours, and they may be on the watch."

"Blow the neighbours!" Wobstock returned, laughing. "They wouldn't think anything of your going home to—ha! ha!—your uncle's own house, and if they did, why, let them. I'll be off to arrange matters with Barrett, and you be ready to start at a moment's notice. We'll breakfast and dine on the road, for I'm inclined to be merry and to make a day of it."

The lion-tamer answered to Wobstock's call, and stood chatting with him for a few minutes.

"You'll feed them prisoners like the other animals," Wobstock said. "Pick out a few o' the best pieces of shin of beef, for you know, Ted, that though I'd shoot the dog that bit me, I wouldn't starve him. As for the rest, mum's the word."

"I understand," Barrett said, nodding his head. "Good luck to you, and the lad, too!"

"Thankee!" Wobstock said. "I'm as sure of success as I wants a new hat. I pretended to believe that the old 'un was shammin', but he was speakin' his mind right enough. Just one word more, and then I'm off. Keep your eye on Tim. It would be the death o' me if I heard there was a cartload o' monkeys about again."

The lion-tamer promised that he would take Tim completely under his wing, and Wobstock looked much relieved.

"After Ben and my own children," he said, "I like him best; but a boy who has stood upon his head for half-an-hour in a clump of bushes is likely to be a little dazed for a time. Treat him kindly, Ted, and when I come back I shall expect to find you doing a roaring business. Whatever you do, don't forget to have them new bills struck off, and get them well about."

Bold Ben and Wobstock were soon on the road, where we will leave them to complete their journey and take a peep at Toppem senior.

He was a man who could adapt himself to most circumstances, providing that he had sufficient to eat and drink (the latter for choice), but for once in his life he felt uncomfortable and ill at ease.

The miser's house was old and rambling, and at night the spacious and almost bare rooms were filled with uncanny noises; but Mr. Toppem heard little of these, as he was a sound sleeper, and by the morning forgot everything, save that he had a headache and a yearning desire to drink out of a pail.

"Still," to use the saying of a few years ago, "he was not happy," and, not hearing anything of Ebeneezer Chipps, he began to feel anxious on his own account, as he had attempted to do nothing for himself, money had run short, and the small tradesmen of the neighbourhood had refused to trust him a penny.

He had confined himself principally to the rooms in which the miser had lived, the rest being kinds of Bluebeard's cupboards to him, into which he scarcely dare peep.

At times the tumbled masses of rubbish—some in bales, some in boxes—and all kinds of stuff littered about assumed ghostly shapes, and seemed to be endowed with the power of motion ; and Mr. Toppem would shiver and shake as he scuttled down the stairs that led to the more congenial room overlooking the court.

One evening, as he was sitting disconsolately at the window, " thirsting for a pint," like Eccles in the famed play of " Caste," he saw the postman coming along, and his eyes gleamed for very joy.

But the letter was for the shoemaker next-door, and as there was twopence to pay the champion of the last told the Government official to keep the missive, and hoped it would do him good.

Mr. Toppem's spirits went down to zero, and icy winter reigned again in his heart.

" I ain't going to stand this," he said, aloud. " If Chipps thinks I can live on chips he's jolly well mistaken. There's a score as long as a scaffold-pole agin me at the Briton's Arms ; Mrs. Garrison, as keeps the general shop, won't give me tick for a rushlight ; and there's nothin' but rags, bones, sacks, and old boxes to comfort me. If I was Dr. Tanner, as fasted a matter o' five weeks, I might put up with it—but, as I ain't, I can't. I wonder what's in the cellar ?"

Now, strange to say, Mr. Toppem had never paid a visit to the lower regions of the house.

He had expected to find nothing there worth looking at, but it suddenly dawned into his mind that Ebeneezer Chipps being a miser, he might have hidden treasure in this place, where it would be less likely to be looked for.

Lighting the only piece of candle left to him in the wide, wide world, Mr. Toppem tried the cellar door, and finding it was locked, and the key absent, his suspicions and hopes were at once aroused.

" It's only fair," said he, " that if he don't send me money I should sell somethin', or take a trifle to keep me goin'. This 'ere lock is one o' the old sort, and easily opened."

A wrench or two from the blade of a clasp-knife performed the necessary work, and Mr. Toppem, holding the light over his head, descended the rickety staircase, very much after the fashion of a cat paying a nefarious visit to a pantry.

The cellar was, like most of the rooms above, lumber, lumber everywhere, but nothing that, to Mr. Toppem's mind, would fetch a meal.

Suddenly his eyes were attracted by an object, harmless in itself, and such a one as he had often used in palmier days. It was nothing more than a common spade, but near to where it leaned against the wall the earth seemed to have been disturbed at a no great distant date.

" Ho ! ho !" cried Mr. Toppem, " this is where the old willain has hidden his gold. I'll just take a suv'rin, and when he sends what is doo to me, I'll let him know that I'm as hartful—" here he looked down his nose.

It struck him that the act he meditated might end in the visit of a gentleman whose costume is invariably blue of colour, ornamented with plated buttons ; but necessity knows no law, and seizing the spade, he went to work.

Accustomed to the task in hand, he soon dug down to the lid of the box, which, as the reader knows, Ebeneezer Chipps had been so anxious about.

" 'Ere's a find," he gasped, hauling it out. " 'Ere's temptation put suddenly in a man's way. If my 'eart wasn't 'onest as virgin gold, I might— What's that ?"

He thought he heard a noise overhead, and for a moment his flesh crept upon his bones.

" Bah !" he said, as he tore the lid of the box open. " It's nothin' but a rat. There's any number of 'em about. They has there Derbies and run races every hour of the day. Hullo ! 'ere's a disappointment ; nothin' but mouldy papers."

Tossing out a number in his rage and chagrin, he clutched one, and held it up to the light of the candle.

A sharp cry broke from his lips as he read the first words on the parchment : " This is the last Will and Testament of—" And then a sharper cry as the candle was struck from his grasp, and a pair of hands caught his throat in a grip of iron.

"Mister Chip—Chippy—Chipps!" he gurgled. "Take your 'an—ands off. Be—believe me, as I'm a ma—ma—man, that I didn't me—mean to r—r—rob you. Oh lor! I'm a dyin'."

"And you've got to die if you are not quiet," growled a ferocious voice in his ear. "Say but one word more—utter a cry for help, and the hole you made in the earth will be your grave."

Toppem senior heard these words as in a dream. He was drifting fast into unconsciousness, and, as the threat was completed, he fell limp and senseless on the floor.

"You may light that candle again," said the voice of William Wobstock. "He will be all right for some time."

"I hope you have not hurt him," Ben returned, as he complied.

"I only shook him up a bit and fright did the rest," Wobstock said. "Thanks to the old flint walls it was easy enough to reach the fust window; but only fancy finding him—him that I employed to keep his eye on Chipps—here."

Meanwhile Wobstock was coolly stowing away the documents in his capacious pockets without even troubling himself to glance at their contents.

"I was almost afraid," Ben observed, glancing at Toppem, who lay spread out as flat as if he had dropped fifty feet, "that he would see us as we stood on the staircase. If he had only turned his head he must have caught sight of us."

"But as he didn't," Wobstock replied, disposing at once of past probabilities, "why you see he didn't, and a good job too. Here's some old newspapers lying about; stuff them into the box, and drop it back where it came from, and fill the earth in."

"What then?" Ben demanded.

"Why, we will carry Toppem upstairs, and put him in his bed," Wobstock replied, chuckling. "When he comes to himself he will ponder on the wonderful dream he has had."

Toppem senior was as limp as any of the rags that Ebeneezer Chipps dealt in, and showed no signs of returning consciousness during the journey to his couch.

"He seems to be in a dreadful faint," Ben said, anxiously. "I hope that no harm will come of this strange adventure."

"Not an atom," Wobstock replied. "He will be himself again in less than half an hour. Now we'll be off, and by the way we came, to keep up the mystery. Come along, my lad; he is coming round already. His nose is twitching as if he was goin' to wake himself up with a sneeze fit to blow the top of his head off."

"There is only one thing that really troubles my mind," Ben said. "What can I say to my old friend, Tim, about all this?"

"I think you are the sensible lad I take you for," Wobstock replied, "so you will say nothing at all. If he asks you questions, give him amphibious—I mean ambiguous—answers."

It so happened that ingress to the miser's house proved a less difficult matter to Wobstock than departing from it.

Ben Brierton went first and was soon on his feet outside, but the proprietor of the circus was a bulky man, and by some means he got fixed in the region of the armpits.

The more he wriggled the more complicated his situation became; but a sudden wrench disposed of the matter, and he came down into the court with a bang suggesting that he had been hurled bodily from the window.

CHAPTER XXI.

BOLD BEN AGAIN PROVES HIMSELF WORTHY OF HIS TITLE—RUNNING THE GAUNTLET—RIGHT IS MIGHT—A COAT TO MEND.

"BEN!" Wobstock gasped, "get to the right end of me and lift me up, for I'll be bothered if I know which is my head and which are my heels. I'm all over alike —one mortial bump!"

While Ben was engaged in this merciful office the shoemaker and his wife next door were engaged in a little domestic strife.

The good lady was absent when the postman called, and, hearing on her return that her husband had refused to take in an underpaid letter, it occurred to her that it might have come from her son, who was serving his Queen and country as a soldier, and perhaps contained a remittance.

From words they came to something worse.

Having been called a born fool some few score of times, the irate shoemaker returned the compliment by politely heaving a hammer used in his trade at the woman whom he had sworn to "love, honour, and cherish."

The retaliation was prompt and effective in the form of an ironing-box, and just as the uproar was at its height the dull thud following Wobstock's involuntary descent was heard.

"What was that," demanded the shoemaker's wife, ceasing her shrill clamour. "I thought I heard a bang at the door."

"P'raps it's the postman come back ag'in," her husband said, hopefully. "I'll go and see."

He required no light, as the ironing-box had created sufficient illumination to his eyes, and, running downstairs, opened the door, and looked out.

The instant he did so five knuckles came into collision with his head, causing him to withdraw it as swiftly as if he had accidentally put it through the lunette of a guillotine.

"Mary-iar!" he roared up the staircase, "I'm bein' attacked by a pack o' murderers. Will you stand and see your lawfully wedded 'usband torn to bits afore your eyes?"

The shoemakers wife thrust the window open, or rather, removed a neat arrangement of brown paper with which half the casement was covered, in the absence of glass, with her head, and made the air ring with heart-rending screams.

In an instant there were a dozen people at the upper end of the court, shoutin, "Fire!" and "Police."

"We've made a pretty mess of it, Ben," said Wobstock, pulling himself together, "and I don't see how we are to get out of it. Hark at the doors and windows flying open. "And, oh lor'! here comes the mob like a swarm of bees."

In the meantime, the shoemaker, smarting under his

wrongs, had armed himself with the leg of a chair, and brandishing the weapon made or the first human figure he saw in the gloom.

It happened to be Ben Brierton, who floored his antagonist in such a manner that he retired precipitately to the sacred precincts of his own home, and remained there rolled up at the foot of the staircase.

The next to appear on the scene was a valiant man who had grown stout and lusty on the profits accruing from the sale of boiled pork, cold plum-pudding, peg-tops, gun-caps, and a circulating library, all dispensed from one evil-smelling little shop.

Dark as it was, Ben knew him in a moment, and went for the bellicose gentleman so vigorously that he performed the postman's knock with the back of his head, and cried out, as if addressing somebody at his establishment—

"The whole stock o' gun-caps is busted !"

"Keep 'em at bay for a moment while I get this right shoulder of mine in working order," Wobstock said. "We've got to run the gauntlet, Ben, and we'll do it like Britons, or fall like our forefathers did when the Rummons attacked 'em."

Ben was now engaged with half-a-dozen people of all sorts and sizes, who bit, kicked, and clutched at him with the impartiality the rag, tag, and bobtail of society set upon a weaker foe.

Our hero kept his back against the wall, and lunging out right and left continued to keep the foe at arms' length until Wobstock took up the cudgels.

Then those who had attacked Ben went down like dominoes, sprawling and stumbling over each other, and creating such a hullabulloo as surely was never heard within the space of one courtyard.

"Stick to me, Ben !" cried Wobstock, as they fought their way towards the street. "Somebody's made ribbons of my coat, but never mind. We've made it a case of bellows to mend with a dozen or so of the cowards. Hullo ! what's this ?"

It was the flash of a policeman's bull's-eye, and for a moment it staggered Wobstock and took away his breath, but he regained his self-control as quickly.

The proprietor of the menagerie had heard that it is a good thing to take a bull by the horns, and he took that bull's-eye with his fist, flattening it against the officers belt, causing its bearer to join the majority of strollers.

"Follow me!" cried Ben. "I am acquainted with a lot of byeways and turnings where we can defy pursuit.'

"I—don't—think—that—Chipps—would—give—nine-pence—for—my—coat," Wobstock panted, as his feet skimmed over the stones. "Bless—these—cobble-stones! Oh! my toes—oh! my corns."

"We can take breath now," said Ben, as he darted under a dark archway, with passages to the right and left of it; "only listen at them. There goes the policeman's whistle."

"I thought there were no police about this part. You told me so, at least," Wobstock rejoined, reproachfully, as he gathered the rags of his coat round him. "Here's a nice garment to appear in public in. I'll exhibit it as a patent ventilator, warranted to keep a man cool, and to give him a free shower-bath when it rains. Never mind, Ben, you fought like a giant, and I don't care a pin for the rest."

"But I do," our hero responded. "I fear you have suffered more to night than you'll get over in a hurry."

"Don't you trouble yourself about me," said Wobstock; "the only thing that worries me is what the people will say at the inn when we put up the horse and trap. You had better settle the bill, and meet me at the cathedral gates. It's dark then, and if I attract attention I shall be taken for a tramp. I've got my wind again, so forrard."

Bold Ben knew every inch of the locality, and could have found his way blindfolded, acting as guide, giving forth at intervals such warnings as—"Mind this corner," "Stoop low, there's a huge wooden beam just above your head," "Catch hold of me, and let me lead you down this flight of steps," until Wobstock wondered whether he had not drifted into some deserted city which had been jumbled together by a volcanic eruption.

"Here we are!" said Ben, as the gleam of a gas-lamp appeared at the end of a long passage.

"It's like looking down the wrong end of a telescope,"

Wobstock remarked. "But we must be thankful for small mercies. Oh! I see where we are, now; there is the gate opening into the close."

"Yes, and I will be with you in a quarter of an hour."

Ben Brierton was as good as his word, and better.

He had made a hasty purchase of a rug from the ostler at the inn, and also a flask containing something to warm Wobstock on the journey.

"This is kind of you, Ben," he said, with emotion. "Stimylant is good if taken at the proper time, and I'm as cold as hice, Ben—as cold as hice. Drive on a bit, my lad, while I stimylate."

Ben gave the horse his head, and the animal, refreshed with rest and a double feed of corn, clattered through the narrow streets, and once more Cloisterville died away and became a mere, dull glow, relieving a sky as black as a wall of jet.

———

CHAPTER XXII.

A SAD AWAKENING—ASTONISHING NEWS AT THE MENAGERIE—WOBSTOCK GIVES SAM RUSHMORE A LIFT IN THE WORLD BEFORE PARTING WITH HIM.

MR. TOPPEM'S swoon continued all through the hubbub attending upon the fight in the court, or it may be that he returned to semi-consciousness, and finding himself in bed went to sleep.

When at last he awoke to sense and reason, he sat up, and made hay of his hair with his fingers.

"If I've been dreamin'," he said, "it's the most wonderful dream that a mortial man ever had. Let me think it hout. I went down to that there cellar, and I dug a hole; in that hole was a box, and in—

Here Mr. Toppem's memory failed him, and he performed upon his hair again in the most distracted style.

The grey dawn of morning was climbing the sky, and Toppem, taking the hint, climbed out of bed, and stole downstairs as far as the cellar-door.

To his surprise it was secured. Ben having accomplished the feat by slipping the lock back into its place, with

Toppem's own knife, which was carefully restored to its owner's pocket.

When the bewildered man discovered this fact, his face turned the colour of the dingy wall, and making his way to the front door, he threw it open, and literally fell into the courtyard.

"There's been a fight," he murmured; "'eres two buttons, a sixpence, a farden, the tail of a coat, and a boot. Wonderful and more wonderful. Blamed if I ain't stunned with these rewelations. Shall I stay and make henquiries? No! I've done with this place o' dreams and wisions," and the latter part of his adventures floated into his brain; "it's the fust time that I hever heard of a wision layin' hold of a man's throat."

Looking round his eyes alighted on a piece of chalk, and taking it in his hand he wrote—

"TO HEBENEEZER CHIPPS.—*I'm horf. I've chucked the key in the river so as nobody can burst in. Adoo.—Yures trooly,* T. T.

And then diving his hands into his pockets, he slouched away, muttering—

"I'll find that menagerie chap, and do a bit of romancin'. He promised to be my friend, and he looked like a man of his word. Besides I shall be with Tim again, and that will be a comfort."

It was soon after that Toppem had left Chipps' house to take care of itself that Ben Brierton and Will-i-am Wobstock were well on their way to the menagerie.

When once well clear of Cloisterville, and there was no longer fear of pursuit, the horse was allowed to go his own pace.

Dawn still found the travellers jogging on their journey, and a halt of two hours duration was made at an inn at which breakfast was partaken of, and the willing gee-gee carefully attended to.

It was nearly noon before the menagerie was sighted, and to his great delight Wobstock saw that the establishment was in full swing, and the place crowded almost to suffocation.

"Barrett didn't forget them bills, and they've done the

Coming straight at him was the most fearful ape he had ever heard or dreamed of.

trick," Wobstock said. And then a sudden thought occurred to him, "I wonder how they have managed to keep the prisoners from the people's notice. I forgot to tell Ted to jog them if they give any trouble ; but perhaps he's done it on his own responsibility."

At that moment the sharp crack of a pistol was heard, followed by a shout of applause.

"Ted is givin' his mornin' performance," Wobstock said, leaping out of the the trap, and giving the reins to one of the men. "Well, Phil, how goes it ?".

"You'd better ask, Barrett," the man replied, with an uneasy look in his eyes. "He'll be out o' the den in five minutes."

Wobstock knew that something was wrong, and beckoning to Ben Brierton to follow him dashed up the steps, and confronted the gentle Angelina, who was arguing with a fat man about the genuineness of a sixpence just tended for payment.

"Will-i-am," she said, dropping the doubtful coin, and permitting the corpulent party to sidle into the show unawares, "if hever I was glad to see you it is at this moment. Don't blame me—I say agin, don't blame your wedded wife, Will-i-am."

"What is there to blame you about, my girl ?" Wobstock asked, pressing his hand to his head in bewilderment. "What has happened ?"

"You'd better ask Barrett."

"Dash it !" cried Wobstock ; "that's what Phil Munrow said. "Come along, Ben ; we'll soon know what's o'clock."

The lion-tamer had just emerged from the cage, and was bowing his acknowledgments to the plaudits, when Wobstock made his presence known by elevating his white hat in the air.

Barrett pressed his way through the crowd, and taking the proprietor of the menagerie by the shoulders, whispered a word in his ear—

"Bolted !"

Had it not been for Ben Brierton, Wobstock would have taken a seat upon one of the braziers filled with red-hot coke.

"Bolted?" he gasped. "What! both of 'em?'

"No, only one—the old 'un," Ted Barrett replied. "He managed to crawl out of the trap at the top of the van—the trap used for ventilation in fine weather, you know."

"And I was fool enough to forget all about it!" Wobstock groaned. "Hah! hass that I am. What about t'other one?"

"I gave him something to drink and he went to sleep as comfortable as a dustman at a bean-feast," Barrett returned. "I don't think he'd grumble about staying on the same terms for a month."

"Ben,' said Wobstock gazing at our hero, "I've lived nearly fifty years, and since the days of my youth flattered myself that I could not be taken in; but now I've been sold like a horse-buyer at Barnet Fair. If you was to take it into your head to tickle me with one of them red-hot irons, I should deserve it."

"Pray, do not take the matter so much to heart," Ben rejoined, as he followed the proprietor of the menagerie into the caravan.

"But I do," said Wobstock, "and all the more be cause I thought I was so clever. I'd swap Mumbo away just to have the old man here for an hour now. Here comes Tim after you, Ben; but mind, not a word about his parient. I've got a little readin' to do, and want to be alone."

CHAPTER XXIII.

NEWS OF EBENEEZER CHIPPS—A NEW KIND OF EXTINGUISHER.

WHEN the menagerie was cleared, and the people connected with it were at dinner, Bostock paid a visit to Sam Rushmore.

That refined and classical-featured individual was just waking up from a heavy slumber, and had his lodging been concealed from the public view his yawns and grunts might have been put down to the expostulation of some fresh addition to the menagerie unsafe to be exhibited until better accustomed to its quarters.

"Well," said Wobstock, "how do you like it?"

"Mostly neat, but never with too much water," Rushmore replied, vaguely, rubbing his bleared eyes. "Hullo! Where am I?"

"That remark," said Wobstock, "shows that you have a bad memory. I suppose that you are a trifle thirsty, now?"

"Thirsty!" Rushmore echoed, hoarsely. "I dreamed that a wat in a brewery busted, and that I was doin' of my level best to drink the lot."

"What have they been giving you?"

"I think's it was whisky, but it don't matter what it is, so long as it's wet," Rushmore responded, smacking his lips. "How long am I to be cooped up 'ere?"

"Until I think proper to let you go," Wobstock replied. "Now then, just one or two questions."

"I can't talk with a throat like a lime kiln." Rushmore said.

"Not another drop," Wobstock rejoined, sternly; "but if you tell me the truth I'll treat you well."

"Then fire away."

"Who is this Mr. Reginald that Chipps is in league with."

"He's a gent with means, but I think he gets 'em by his wits," Rushmore replied.

"Where does he live?"

"That's mor'n I can tell. You'd better ask Chipps, but I expect he hangs somewhere about London."

"That's a nice address, certainly," said Wobstock, sneeringly, "why didn't you say South Ameriky?"

"Well, I've told you all I know," Rushmore said; "of course, he's got another name, but he always kept it dark with me. I give you my word, though p'raps you won't think it worth anything, that I don't know why he is so anxious to get hold of the boy.

"P'raps I do," Wobstock returned; "but, come, you haven't told me all yet. You are keepin' back somethin'. How came you to appear on the scene?"

"It was like this," Rushmore replied; "Chipps came to me and says, 'I've got a boy as 'angs 'eavy on my hands; will you 'ake him orf if I guarantee a good round sum down ?' Says I, 'I will, and bring him up to a nice light sort o' business.' "

"What may the nature of that business be ?"

Rushmore took his stubbly chin between his fingers and looked as if he had accidentally swallowed a fish-bone.

"Look 'ere," he said, after a pause, "don't you ask too many questions. I've told you the truth up to now, but if you go on worryin' of me I shall be compelled to prewaricate."

"P'raps," observed Wobstock, "the police are as anxious to know what the business is as I am ?"

"P'raps they are and p'raps they ain't," said the ruffian, turning deadly pale ; "howsomdever, you'll get no more out o' me."

"Very well," said Wobstock, as he refixed the shutter. "I shall know how to deal with you after this. Barrett," he added, in a whisper, as the lion-tamer strolled up, "let this beast have something to drink, and we'll get rid of him when we are on the road to-night."

Naturally enough, Tim Toppem was inquisitive as to Ben's journey, but as our hero would give nothing but ambiguous replies, Tim saw that his questions found no favour.

"Well," he said, "I see that I only bother you, so I will say no more about it."

"That's right," Ben replied, clapping him heartily on the shoulder. "There are two very good reasons why I cannot answer you. Firstly, Wobstock made me promise that I would not tell anybody why we went away, and, secondly, that I am as much in the dark as I was at starting."

This was a poser to Tim, who laid hold of his hair and tugged at it violently ; but before he could make any reply the orchestra struck up for the afternoon perform-ance, and he was called away to become once more a gorilla.

"Ben," he said, "much as I respect Wobstock, it was in a weak moment that I consented to put on that beastly skin. I think I'd rather be one of those Spartans I've heard you talk about."

"Why, what is the matter now?" Ben asked. "I thought you were getting along so well?"

"So I should if I was left alone," Tim moaned; "but I suffer agonies in that case. Yesterday a boy threw an apple at me with such force that it nearly knocked my head-piece off, and a man almost as vicious as old Chipps—I think he must be some relation to him—poked a hot cinder from the fire-basket into the cage when I wasn't looking, and I sat on it."

"Poor Tim!" said Ben, laughing in spite of himself. "Never mind, your sufferings only last half an hour at a time."

"And that's an age," Tim replied, gloomily. "This morning I looked at my upper lip, where the moustache will grow. Well, you can see for yourself, there's a white hair on each side, and it's all through the gorilla trick."

At last the day, with Tim's martyrdom, came to an end, and by eleven o'clock the menagerie was on its way to the next pitch, a town named Hantley, boasting of a railway-station and a station-master, who combined the light duties of porter, ticket-clerk, and an agent for a patent sewing-machine.

But long before Hantley was reached Rushmore was disposed of.

In the darkness of the night, and by the fitful gleam of a lantern, Wobstock and Ted Barrett removed him, snoring like a hog, and having pinned an inscription on his breast bearing this inscription—"This man is a scoundrel, and as venomous as an adder," laid him gently in a dry ditch containing a fair selection of nettles.

It was fair time at Hantley, and the menagerie prolonged its stay from the Tuesday to the Saturday.

On the morning of the last-named day when Tim and Ben were taking a walk out of the town they came upon an old-fashioned roadside inn.

"There should be some fine rooms in that house," Ben said, glancing from the porch to the upper windows. "What do you say, Tim, shall we make an inspection of the interior?"

"The landlady might object," Tim observed.

"Two bottles of lemonade shall be our 'open Sesame,'" Ben replied.

He led the way, Tim following somewhat doubtfully, under a porch, through a passage that echoed with their footsteps like the aisle of a church, and up a broad staircase into a room used by the neighbouring farmers.

A pallid young man, who looked as if melancholy had marked him for its own, and was engaged in the exhilarating task of cleaning windows, took the order, observing at the same time—

"Why couldn't you drink the lemingnade down stairs?".

"Because," Ben replied, sharply, "we prefer to drink it here."

The young man sighed as he tucked one corner of a green baize apron under the string, and departed on his errand, and, having executed it, again went his way, leaving a pail of water behind him.

"Ben," said Tim, "can you tell me why it is that waiters are always pale?"

"Perhaps it is because they are a race of men who have been blighted in love and never survive the blow."

"It may be so," Tim said, as he walked to the window, "but—"

To Ben's alarm, his friend staggered back on his heels.

"What's the matter?" Ben demanded. "Are you ill?"

"Eb-en-eezer Chipps!" Tim gasped.

"Nonsense! You are dreaming."

"Look for yourself," Tim replied

And sure enough there was the miser, glancing furtively to the right and left out of his ferrety eyes.

He dodged round the horse-trough and slunk up to the porch, at which the landlord was standing.

"Bring me a glass of ale," Chipps said; "the mildest and cheapest. If it is a little sour I don't mind, providing you make a reduction. I have just come off the train, and the villainous fare has almost ruined me."

"I thought you might have escaped from the menagerie at Hantley," the landlord retorted. "If you want some beer you won't find it here, Lucifer."

"Lucifer!" Chipps gasped. "Oh! yes. Ha—ha! I suppose there is something striking about me."

"There is; and it ain't pleasant," the host of the inn replied. "Tuppence is the price of a glass of ale, and you may either take it or leave it."

"Oh! dear me," Ebeneezer Chipps groaned, "couldn't you put a pennyworth into a large glass and fill it up with water? And, my friend—ah! I know when I see a benevolent man—if you should have a few stray bits of cheese and a crust to give away I will think of you as long as I live."

"I'd rather you didn't," the landlord retorted; "it might give me bad dreams, and make me smell brimstone. If you can't afford the beer, go and have a pull at the horse-trough."

It was destined that Ebeneezer Chipps was to make the acquaintance of the horse-trough quicker than he expected.

The window at which the boys stood listening opened directly over the porch, and, slipping lightly out, they lay concealed on the top, Tim taking the pail of water with him.

"What is that for?" Ben demanded.

"You will see," Tim chuckled. "I think I have hit upon a new kind of extinguisher."

Ben understood him now, and stifled a laugh with his hand.

"Well, bring the ale," Chipps continued; "but as it is so expensive mind it is the best. Don't try to deceive me, for—"

The landlord's blood was now up.

He gave Ebeneezer Chipps a slight push, and as the miser receded from the porch, Tim, with excellent aim, tilted up the pail, and dropped it clean over his head.

A muffled howl came from the utensil, and the next moment Ebenezer Chipps deposited himself in the horse trough, to the great terror of a number of ducks and geese engaged in their usual avocation in picking up unconsidered trifles.

CHAPTER XXIV.

IS IT A GHOST?

BEFORE the roar of laughter the yokels had indulged in, the astonishment of the landlord, and the invectives of Chipps had died away, the boys scrambled unseen into the room.

"We must hide somewhere," Tim said. "The room will be full of people in a minute."

"Perhaps it will be as well," Ben assented, "as Wobstock must know that Chipps is in the locality before I interfere with him. Here's a cupboard big enough to hold us. Slip in, or we shall be caught. I can hear them coming upstairs."

Tim had the forethought to remove the key of the cupboard and turn it on the inner side.

"We mustn't move about," Tim said, "for there's an awful lot of glass things in here, and the slightest accident might produce an awful smash."

Before Ben had time to make any comment on this timely warning the landlord, Chipps, and a crowd at their heels, entered the room.

"I can't understand it," said the host. "I never heard of a pail jumping out of a window before. Where's Bill?"

"Here I am," replied the pallid man. "I'm lookin' for them two boys as were here just now. They ain't here."

"Perhaps they went out with the pail," said a voice.

"Boys!" screeched Chipps. "What sort of boys?"

"There's a question for you," said the landlord, contemptuously. "Well, I can't make this out, so you'd better go and have a dry in the kitchen. If you keep turning round and round before the fire you'll be all right in about an hour."

"I'll have something else, and that's compensation," the miser spluttered, shaking his fist. "I am a gentleman by birth and education, although I may not look like it."

"You don't," the landlord retorted; "but as the aristocracy don't patronise this place it can't be good enough for you. Bill, assist this gent downstairs, and be very careful that you don't rub him against the wall paper, or it will come off in strips."

"If you think that you will get out of your responsibility in this way you are mistaken," Chipps said, as the waiter took him by the arm. "You will hear from my solicitor in a few days, and—"

The rest of the words were drowned by the rattling of heels descending a flight of stairs, and then the pallid young man came back more pallid than ever.

"Which way has he gone?" the landlord demanded.

"Towards Hantley," Bill replied, "and you could track him by the water as is running out of his boots."

"I don't like mysteries, and this is one," said the proprietor of the establishment. "Have you been cleaning the porch?"

"Yes, I tidied it up."

"Then, you villain!" roared the landlord, seizing him by the ears; "you left that pail on the edge, and it overbalanced itself."

"I—I—if," said the waiter, as plainly as his chattering teeth would permit, "my head was to be cut off this wery moment, I'd swear—"

"Oh! you'd swear to anything," his master interposed. "I don't suppose that old man will give any more trouble, as he looked as if he was running away from somebody, but if he does you may say farewell to your wages for a few months—perhaps years."

The irate landlord skirmished all out of the room, and banged the door behind him.

"This is nice," Ben said, laughing softly, "and it would interest me very much to know how we are going to get out. I wish you and I had the power of rendering ourselves invisible."

"So do I," Tim returned. "There, now! I've done a nice trick. There goes the key."

"And by the sound it made it has dropped among some glass dishes or something of the sort."

"And," Tim rejoined, with a deep drawn groan, "we haven't such a thing as a match to bless ourselves with. There's nothing to be done but to feel about for it."

"Don't stoop too low," Ben said. "I think I noticed a pile of dishes just behind you. Steady, Tim, steady—there goes something down. Oh! mercy, they will hear us below and then what a pickle we shall be in."

"There's all kinds of things everywhere," Tim moaned. "I've just run my nose into the neck of a decanter, and it's a wonder it didn't stick fast. Confound it, Ben! I can't find the key. What on earth are we going to do?"

"It seems to me that we must wait until somebody comes to let us out," our hero replied. "Hullo! I've picked up something like a table cloth. I've got an idea, Tim; keep up the search for the key, and don't lose your head."

"Hush!" Tim whispered, "somebody has come back to the room."

It was the distracted Bill, who had returned to his window-cleaning.

"I'd rather suffer the tortures of the hinquisition than pay a arden," he said, aloud. "Them boys chucked the pail out and then bolted by the back way. I'd give a trifle to have an up and downer with them imps."

Bill dabbed the whiting in lumps over the window as he remembered the wrongful accusation under which he suffered.

"I might as well be a badger drawed and worried by terriers," he said, aloud. "If it wasn't for the wittles which is good, I—"

At that moment a hollow blood-curdling groan broke upon his ear.

The waiter was a nervous young man, and the sound caused him to relax his hold of the sash, and he had the narrowest escape of falling out of the window.

Descending from his elevated position he peered round the room, under the tables and chairs, under an old-fashioned piano, with keys yellow with age, and the wires all out of tune, up the chimney, and, in fact, everywhere but the right place.

"This 'ere's a kind o' deloosion," he murmured, as he turned paler and paler; "I'll say nothin' to the guvnor about it, or he will say that I am mad and insist on my goin' to the nearest loonatic asylum."

in fear and trembling he went on with his work, but soon desisted.

A second groan more harrowing than the first gave him such a shock that he lurched forward and broke a window with his nose.

" I can't stand it," he gasped, as his hair rose slowly on end, " it's more than flesh and blood can bear. I'll put the things away, and go on with the knives and forks downstairs. The cook is a wicious party, but she's better company than none."

Now it so happened that the materials used for cleaning the windows were kept in the cupboard where Ben Brierton and Tim Toppem were imprisoned.

Little dreaming what was in store for him the waiter walked or rather tottered up to the door, and made a dead stop before it.

" Where's the key gone to ?" he said. " It I didn't leave it in the lock I had it in my hand when the guv'nor rounded on me. I hope I didn't swaller it in my fright."

Remembering that there was a duplicate key some-where in the lower regions of the house he ran to fetch it, and returning quickly threw the door open.

Then as Ben pushed up the table-cloth with his hands and favoured him with a whoop which a Comanche on the war trail might be proud of, the unhappy young man threw himself out of the room and headlong down the staircase.

In his descent he met a damsel connected with the inn coming up with a tray full of glass ware, and the result was of a character better imagined than described.

The landlord thinking that something had gone wrong with the roof, tore out of the bar to the foot of the stair-case just in time to receive the waiter's head in his waist-coat.

He was driven along a passage terminating in three steps, with a small landing beyond.

Here, in the words of Bret Harte—

" He smiled a kind of sickly smile, and curled up on the floor,
And the subsequent proceedings interested him no more.'

Meanwhile Ben Brierton and Tim Toppem were running for their lives, taking no notice of anybody or anything, save the way back to the menagerie.

Breathlessly they arrived at that haven of society, and told Will-i-am Wobstock their adventures.

" More impecuniosity—I mean impetuosity," he cried. " But Chipps—Chipps, where is he ? Fix my hat firmly on my head and I'll find him."

" I am afraid he is far away by this time," our hero rejoined. " There was nothing about his appearance denoting that he intended to stay."

" Never mind that," said Wobstock ; "he isn't a pantomime sprite, and the earth isn't full of stage traps. You leave it to me, my lad, and I'll bring him back by his ears."

But Wobstock's excitement and enthusiasm received a sudden check.

The man who had charge of a cage containing a brown American bear rushed up.

" I say," he said, wildly, "has anyone seen Grizzlyback walking about ?"

" Seen what ?" Wobstock shrieked.

" Grizzlyback," the man replied. " He's managed to unfasten the door at the back of the caravan, and slope."

CHAPTER XXV.

A BEAR HUNT—THE BEADLE AND THE PUMP—·BEN TO THE RESCUE AGAIN—A NEW WAY TO CATCH A TRUANT.

WILLIAM WOBSTOCK did not require any assistance in the fixing of his hat.

He gave the top of it such a blow with his fist that the rim came down over the bridge of his nose, and obscured the sunlight from his eyes.

" This beats Mumbo, and the confectioner's shop," he said. " If that brute isn't caught before he has time to do mischief there will be a hole in somebody's ribs to mend."

Without waiting to hear another word Ben Brierton snatched up a pitchfork.

"Come along, Tim," he shouted, "and bring something with you."

Tim cast a hasty glance round for a weapon, but he could see nothing more formidable than a mop, so he took that. Ben and Tim had not taken many strides before all connected with the menagerie were up in arms.

Ted Barret contented himself with pocketing a brace of pistols and throwing a wire net over his arm, but Wobstock having come to light again lingered to load a blunderbus.

It went off suddenly, blowing a hole through a painted representation of the lion-tamer seated calmly in a den filled with every known man-devouring animal, and a slug severing a rope brought the whole pictorial display down with a run.

Wobstock hurled the blunderbus from him, and followed in the wake of Ted Barret, who took an opposite direction to that chosen by Ben and Tim.

"What's the matter?" demanded a meek-eyed and pensive policeman.

"A bear loose," the lion-tamer replied. "You had better warn everybody you see to stand clear."

The officer seemed to think that the advice applied principally to him, and stood clear himself by climbing into the back of a passing coal waggon and burying himself under a pile of sacks.

"What's this?" roared the driver.

The constable repeated the information he had received from Ted Barrett.

"Then I'm off,' said the sable visaged teamster. "You can take the reins and drive if you like. I ain't so unhappy as to wish to be chawed up by a bear."

And down he dropped and up a narrow turning he went, leaving his horses at a standstill and to settle with bruin if he should come that way.

The first intimation Ben had that he was on the right track was a tramp, who had suddenly dispensed with a pair of crutches and was beating the record of his tribe hollow by actually running.

He was quickly followed by a stout but genteel retired colonel, making a dead heat of it with a ponderous lady, who occasionally thumped him in the chest, and a doctor's boy with a basketful of broken bottles.

A little further on there was conclusive evidence that the bear was not far away.

People of all sorts and sizes were making hurried entrances into any door that stood open or could be opened by human hands.

Dodging round the town pump in full dress was a beadle, and gathering his official coat above his knees, and with every expression of abject horror upon his face.

And gazing hungrily at the bogey of charity children and little boys who fall asleep under the influence of fifty minutes' sermons, was Grizzlyback, apparently making up his mind to make short work of the relic of Bumbledom as soon as he could get him in the open and give him the hug of death.

"Don't move!" Ben shouted, as he and Tim dashed up. "Keep quite still and I will save you."

Ben faced the bear, and gave him one taste of the pitchfork, causing Grizzlyback to sit up and paw the air, and growl in a manner that lifted the beadle's cocked hat off his head.

"Tim," said our hero, "thrust that mop into the bear's jaws, and I'll try and roll him over."

Tim Toppem dashed forward as valiantly as a soldier at the call of his superior officer, and bruin received the head of the mop in his capacious mouth as clean and clever as an artillery gunner ramming home a charge.

Ben drove at the bear again with all his force, and Grizzlyback went down with a thud.

"Now run," our hero cried to the beadle, "and make the best of your way to the nearest place of safety."

"There's nary a one," gasped the beadle; "every 'ouse in the town is locked up by this time."

"Run—run," Ben shouted, "you are only in my way. Tim, you go too; find some of the others and tell them to hurry up. The brute is getting vicious, and I may have the worst of the struggle."

And our hero feared the worst, for the brute, with a

A sharp cry broke from his lips as he read the words on the
parchment.

hide as impenetrable as the thickest leather that was ever tanned was now on his feet again, and slouching round Ben.

Grizzlyback seemed to have suffered as little from the prods of the pitchfork as if he had been tickled by a straw, and his ferocious growling, perhaps at having been deprived of making a meal of a gentleman clad in a yellow braided gown, and a laced hat, indicated that he meant to put up with Ben as a substitute.

Tim tore off as if he had wings on his heels, and he was lucky enough to tumble across Ted Barrett and the distracted keeper of the bear.

"Ben is in danger," Tim cried. "He's keeping Grizzlyback at bay with a pitchfork, and the exertion is tiring him out."

"All right," Barrett replied. "I have my pistols with me, and I'll give the brute a couple of pills which will disagree with him."

"Don't shoot!" pleaded the keeper, as all three raced away towards the scene of the unequal conflict. "I've got something in my pocket which will quiet Grizzlyback in a moment."

"What's that?" Tim demanded.

"Apples.'

Tim Toppem made no comment on this astounding reply, as he thought that the man had taken leave of his senses.

In less than a minute they reinforced Ben Brierton, and it was lucky they did so.

The brave lad was growing exhausted, while the bear as if knowing that his strength was failing redoubled his exertions to bring the matter to an end.

Seizing one of the pistols by the barrel Ted Barrett struck the savage beast a tremendous blow behind the ear, and as Grizzlyback shook his head as if deprecating the kind of treatment, his keeper rolled a couple of apples at his feet.

The bait acted like a charm.

Grizzlyback lowered his head to seize the delicacy and in an instant the net was over him, and he was dragged helpless over on his side and secured to the town pump which for once did a real public service.

"What's to be done now?" said the keeper. "We can't carry the bear to the menagerie on our backs and we must have some kind of conveyance."

"I noticed an empty coal waggon in one of the streets," Ted Barrett replied. "Keep your eye on that kicking brute and I'll be back as quickly as possible,"

The lion-tamer was as good as his word.

He found nobody with the waggon, and did not stop to make enquiries; but he was considerably astonished at seeing a black and blue policeman crawl out from under the sacks, and asking him where he was going to.

"To fetch the bear," Ted Barrett said, and then, contemptuously, "I must say you are a nice sort of man to look after the public safety."

"Show me the Hact of Parlyment which says that I am to run a bear in, and I'll do it," the officer replied, as he picked himself up, and vanished out of the back of the waggon.

The lion-tamer drove the horses as swiftly as if they were attached to a fire engine, and as other men connected with the menagerie had now come up the truant was finally safely replaced in his cage, and regaled with something more pungent and lasting than apples by his keeper, who looked ten years older than when he had gone to bed on the previous night.

Wobstock, with an ominous red streak on the bridge of his nose, walked about gnawing his knuckles and consigning all the bear tribe to a region never mentioned, save with bated breath, in public circles, and requesting that somebody would put down a trifle and cart Grizzly-back in particular away on skewers, and make legions of cats happy.

But at last he calmed down and began to laugh.

"It's a pity that I went another way," he said, "or I would have given a trifle to see that beadle. Bravo! Ben, and bravo! Tim, as well, and—"

He stopped, stared, and gasped, for sneaking round a corner was Toppem senior, looking as if he had been somewhere where his presence was not required, and had been ejected at the earliest opportunity.

"My bo—o—boy," he sobbed, making a rush at Tim.

"You're a chip o' the old block. When I see you wielding that mop like a knight a layin' about him with a seven pound chopper, I thought I should ha' bu'sted with delight.

"Don't, father, don't," Tim cried; "you are squeezing my nose against the top button of your coat."

"Tim," said Wobstock, kindly and firmly, "if you wish to speak to your father you had better remove him a little distance. When," he added, under his breath, "when I get excited as I am to-day, I can't hold myself responsible for where my boots get to."

"What are you doing here, father?" Tim demanded, in astonishment, as he took his loving parent aside. "If anybody had told me that I should see you in this place I should have taken it as a joke."

"A father is never a joke," Toppem senior replied.

"That's a fact," said Tim, "especially when he's got a strap and uses the buckle end of it."

"Oh! Tim—Tim," returned the author of his being, preparing to sob again, "why look back. What says the immortial bard, 'Let a father be never so wicious when trade is bad and beer short, he's a father for all that.'"

Tim screwed up his lips, made his eyes round, and rubbed his nose in a perplexed manner.

"Well," he said, after a pause, "you have not answered my question. Are you at work here?"

CHAPTER XXVI.

TOPPEM SENIOR HAS ANOTHER START IN LIFE.

"WORK!" cried Toppem senior. "I've been workin' on my feet for forty miles with a shillin' which I lured Bob Pinkley on to lend me. I heerd from a gipsy where the margarine—"

"Menagerie," Tim corrected.

"Margarine is good enough for a man of my time of life," his father said. "I heerd where it was likely to be, and I came on to pay you a visit."

"But why?" Tim demanded. "I sent you a registered

letter, enclosing a sovereign, from the last place we stopped at."

"You did?" Toppem senior gasped, recoiling on what was left of his hob-nailed boots. "Where did you send it to?"

"To the old address, of course."

Mr. Toppem took a deep breath and struck his brow in a manner that left it red and produced a report like a pistol shot.

"Just my luck," he cried. "I left the old house some time ago; but if I was a bloated haristocrat, with a carridge and a quarter of a 'undred of servants to bow me hin and hout o' a mansion, I should have the post-office people running all over the world after me; but as I'm only a poor man, why—"

"Don't talk nonsense," Tim interposed. "The letter will be returned to me as I put this address on it."

"Will the suv'rin come back, too?"

"Of course it will."

"Then there's some hope," said Toppem, brightening up. "But, Tim, my boy, a suv'rin in these days don't go far."

"Some people would look upon a sovereign as a little fortune," Tim returned. "But, father, there is something more you want to say to me. What is it?"

"I was wonderin'," said Toppem, senior, with a far-away expression in his eyes, "whether Mister Wobstock would take me on."

"Take you on?" Tim gasped. "What do you mean by that?"

"Give me a job," responded his parent. "I'm a handy sort of man, Tim, as you know."

"You are," Tim murmured, as his mind reverted back to the painful past; "but I dare not put such a subject before my master."

"But suppose I do it myself?"

"I am afraid," Tim replied, as gently as possible, "that you would not think the answer quite satisfactory."

"Then," said Mr. Toppem, in a tone of despair bordering upon frenzy, "there's nothin' but the workus left for your poor old father. Tim—Tim! I did not expect this of you. Doesn't it break your 'eart to think o' me in corduroys and pewter buttons? Doesn't the wision o' me pickin' hoakum with a labour-master standin' over me cut you to the quick? No! Blow up, ye winds, thou art not so unkind as the boy who smiles at the thought of his haged parient in the union."

This speech was delivered in so high a pitch that Will-i-am Wobstock strolled up.

"Well," he said, turning the eye of wrath upon Tim's father, "have you said all you have to say?"

"You seems to forget that this boy is my son," Toppem said.

"And you appear to forget that your son is my apprentice," Wobstock retorted; "and, moreover, that as long as I treat him well, and do my duty by him as a master, you play second fiddle in the show. But I want to speak to you, Mr. Toppem—excuse us for a minute, Tim."

"Now," he said, as he led the long-suffering one away, "I want the truth, and nothing but it, from you."

"Tim is my boy, and he's the essence of truth," Toppem observed; "therefore, wherefore and why do you suspect me of prewarication?"

"I don't want to offend you more than I can help," Wobstock replied; "but I'm afraid you pull the longbow at times when it suits your purpose. When did you see Chipps last?"

"I haven't set eyes on him since I saw you."

"Nor heard of him?"

"Nor heard of him," Mr. Toppem repeated.

This was perfectly true, but it flavoured so much of falsehood that Wili-i-am Wobstock doubled his fists and turned very red in the face.

"Do you mean to tell me that to my teeth?" he demanded.

"Yes; and to your heyes, nose, and chin, too," replied Toppem senior, who was getting exasperated under the cross-examination. "What are you gettin' at? Do you think that I would wear a marsk and play a double part?"

"I am so sure of it," Wobstock responded, "that if

your son wasn't here, I'd do my best to leave your shoulders without a head."

Like a flash of light the strange occurrence at the house of Ebeneezer Chipps rushed into Mr. Toppem's mind.

"You've put a good many questions to me," he said, "and now I'll put one to you. When was you last at Cloisterville?"

"That is my own business," Wobstock replied; "but if I were you I would be silent on that subject. Those who dig often find less than they expect, and sometimes more. I once heard of man who went prying and digging about another's property, and he got six months for it. You monstrous villain, I mistrusted and I unmasked you. I employed you to look after Chipps, and at the same time you were in his pay."

Mr. Toppem's face was now ashey grey, and his teeth chattering in his head.

"Wha—what about the cove as—as comes upon a man and lays hold on him like a lion in the lungle '—which, I meantersay, like a lion in the lungle?" he stammered.

"Perhaps it was a detective," Wobstock replied. "Whoever it was you may think yourself lucky that you got off so easy. Now go and find Chipps, and when you have found him tell him what you did, and how you were nicely trapped."

The proprietor of the menagerie guessed that if Toppem senior should set eyes on Ebeneezer Chipps he would take to his heels, and satisfied that he had made a hit, began to laugh again.

"Mr. Toppem," he said, "let this be a lesson to you; and remember that you can't come the double trick with a man of the world. I weighed you in the balance and found you wanting, so—"

"Do Tim know anything of this?" the baffled individual asked.

"No, and never will from my lips. You had better go and say good-bye to him, as he must soon return to his work."

"I wish I had some to do myself," Toppem, senior, groaned. "I'm without a penny in my pocket or a shelter for my head."

Wobstock, though angry, gazed at him with a pitying eye, and the hard lines he had drawn into his face softened.

"I wonder," he said, speaking more to himself than Toppem, "whether, if I gave you another chance, I could trust you?"

"Try it," Toppem cried. "I'll turn teetotaller and—"

"Honest and trustworthy?"

"All of 'em, and as many more as you like to throw in."

"Go away now, but come back and ask for me in an hour's time," Wobstock said.

And Timothy Toppem the elder went his way rejoicing.

"I s'pose," he murmured, "that if he gives me a start in life he will chuck in a suit of clothes. Them as I've not on ain't fit for a scarecrow to wear.'

CHAPTER XXVII.

THE MEETING IN PALL MALL—RETURN TO CLOISTER-VILLE—SAM RUSHMORE APPEARS ON THE SCENE BUT TAKES NO PART IN AN INTERESTING CONVERSATION —THE BOX OF DEEDS.

IT was one of those nights which the atmosphere of London seem to rejoice in, even when spring is weaving her garland of flowers round the earth—muggy, murky, rainy, and hopelessly disagreeable.

Those unfortunate beings, young and old, who earn the hardest of crusts by selling boxes of vestas, penny novelties, and "speshul heditions," had given up their avocations in despair, and crouched under any place that afforded them shelter.

Even the Strand, usually so full of life an 1 animation, was almost deserted by pedestrians ; but the theatres were full to overflowing, and would soon disgorge thousands of people, and send them adrift, longing for the sight of comfortable homes, supper over a cosy fire, and hours of rest in warm beds.

Just as the hour of eleven was struck by the myriads of clocks of the vast metropolis there emerged from a fashionable club in Pall Mall a man who was well, so far as his clothing went, prepared to defy the weather.

An inverness cape descended to the heels of his polished boots, and an umbrella of the best silk, mounted on an onyx-handled stick, saved his head and shoulders from the downpour.

For a moment he lingered on the lower step looking right and left for a passing hansom, and then turned to say good-night to some member standing in the vestibule.

"Not the sign of a cab," he muttered, "but I daresay that I shall pick one up in Piccadilly. What a night; it is not fit for a dog to be out in."

As he spoke the bent figure of a man hobbled across the road, and stood in the gentleman's path, but in the shadow so that he could not see his features.

"Go away," said the gentleman, "I have plenty of vestas, and don't want to be bothered. Yet, stay; I suppose a sixpence will not come amiss to you."

"Won't you give my boy one?" whined the other.

"Where is he?"

"With Wobstock's menagerie."

The gentleman started, and Ebeneezer Chipps chuckled as he pulled off his hat, and made a profound bow.

"Mr. Reginald," he said, "I hope you won't be angry with me for waiting outside to speak to you. Things have come to a pretty pass. Rushmore is caged up with a hyena, and I was captured too, but I gave that villain the slip. Oh! what I have suffered. I've more aches in my body than a hundred people taken into a chemist's shop after Boxing-day."

"How dare you come sneaking after me here?" Mr. Reginald hissed. "Haven't I told you over and over again that if you wished to see me, you were to make an appointment by writing to Brook-street?"

"That is true enough," Ebeneezer Chipps replied, humbly, "but you see I only arrived in London an hour ago."

"You have not been to my house?"

"Oh! no," the miser rejoined, with a sly grin; "I know my place and station better than that. I knew you generally spent your evenings here, so I thought I would wait like the faithful servant I am to you."

Mr. Reginald set his teeth, and the whites of his eyes glittered in the lamplight.

"You knew!" he exclaimed. "How did you know that I was a member of this club?"

"By the merest accident," Chipps replied, in an oily tone of voice. "One night, when according to your instructions I was waiting under the archway of the mews, two gentlemen passed, and I heard one say that you were here, and—"

"Yes, go on."

"And losing heavy sums of money in the card-room."

"Well," said Mr. Reginald, biting his lip, "I suppose I must believe you. We will walk through the park and I will hear what you have to say. Hush! Stand back, somebody is coming out. Walk on as far as Marlborough House, and I will meet you there."

In a few minutes Mr. Reginald, whose face had grown as white as a sheet, was at the miser's side.

"Keep your distance," the first-named said. "I don't want people to think that you are in my company."

Cringing, fawning, and vile of nature as Chipps was, these words stung him like the lash of a whip.

"You are a little too hard on me, considering what I have done, and—and what I know," he said, blurting out the last words, though he seemed to try to hold them in check. "You don't treat me quite fairly, upon my word you don't!"

"Because you are a muddler!" the other retorted. "What has become of those gipsy fellows Rushmore made such a fuss of, and who cost me so much?"

"Bolted, I suppose!" Chipps responded.

"Exactly, and that is the way my money is fooled away."

"Your money might have gone in a different channel," the miser said. "Now, Mr. Reginald, will you listen patiently to me?"

"I will try."

"Do you remember," Ebeneezer Chipps continued, "that I told you that the only chance of discovery was that of a certain document turning up, and that tne rest were destroyed by the fire at Holtham Grange ?"

"I am not likely to forget any scrap of conversation I have ever had with you on the subject," Mr. Reginald replied.

"Then," said Ebeneezer Chipps, "I regret to say that I told you a lie, for I happen to know where, not only that particular document is, but where the whole of them are."

Mr. Reginald relaxed his hold on the umbrella, and paid no attention to it as it was whirled away like a badly-constructed parachute by the wind.

"You hound ! never to tell me of this before," he said, hoarsely.

"The time is just ripe that I should do so," Chipps rejoined, coolly. "I am tired of being chased about like a wolf. Give me some money. Run down to my place at Cloisterville to-morrow, and we will strike a bargain."

Mr. Reginald made no reply.

He stood staring at the old man as if about to spring at him, and Chipps remained at a safe distance.

"I don't see what you have to grumble about," the miser continued. "You and I have been playing at the game of diamond cut diamond, and although I have held the trump cards, yet you may take them from my hand if you will."

"If ever a man was tempted to kill another I am tempted to put an end to your base and miserable existence," Mr. Reginald said. "But it shall be as you say. Expect me at your frowsy den to-morrow night at nine."

"I will not fail," Ebeneezer Chipps replied ; "but money—money, I must have money. Oh ! Mr. Reginald, when I think of that beautiful umbrella, which I am sure must have cost at least fifty shillings, flying away like a ha'-penny kite, I could weep. If you had given it to me, I could have sold it for—"

"Hold your tongue," the other interposed. "Here take these sovereigns. If I thought that the food and drink they will buy would choke you I should have some consolation."

"Ha! ha! a capital joke," Chipps sniggled as he snatched at the money much after the fashion that a starving dog snaps at a bone. "Good-night, my dear— dear patron. By this time to-morrow you and I will have parted."

"Perhaps for ever," Mr. Reginald muttered, as he turned away. "Well, I have been taught a severe lesson but I must make the best of it. The weapon that cuts me is of my own making, and it is too late to think of flinching at the smart."

Twilight was settling on the ancient city of Cloisterville when Ebeneezer Chipps arrived at his quarters and received an ovation.

It consisted principally of his old enemies, who having chased him into the court hurled anything and everything that came handy at him.

The miser charged into his foes, and at last succeeded in clearing the mob, but at the loss of his hat, and suffering to such an extent that it was well for the sportive youths that his claw-like hands did not come into actual contact with any of them.

When Chipps had time to breathe he made two discoveries. Mr. Toppem had deserted him, and the services of the blacksmith were an absolute necessity to open the door.

There was the usual wrangle over the charge, Chipps declaring that a man who charged a shilling for a rusty key should be drawn on a hurdle and executed before a delighted assembly of impoverished and down-trodden people.

"So," he snarled, as he went up the echoing stairs, "the villain has run away, but if he hasn't taken anything with him there is reason for congratulation. He cannot claim any wages now."

The miser rubbed his hands as he thought of this, and made a tour from the upper rooms down to the cellar.

"Everything is just the same as I left it," he chuckled; "the rags and bones smell a little worse, and there's more dust. So much the better, for dirt and money often go together, and to-night I shall have plenty of money. I hear it jingling in my ears, and what a sweet sound it has. They talk about the music of church bells, but give me the melody made by gold—precious gold—shining gold !"

As it was now growing dark Ebeneezer Chipps made a short excursion to the general shop, and returned with two candles and an equal number of bundles of firewood.

"We must be gay to-night, and light the place up like a palace," he said. "Ho—ho ! Mr. Reginald, you shall pay through the nose for all your slights and insults. I'll be as keen as a lancet, and I'll cut deep."

Just then he heard somebody pounding at the door, and thinking that some of his inveterate foes had returned he snatched up a billet of wood, and glided downstairs.

Wild with fury he flung the door open suddenly, and then started back.

Before him stood Sam Rushmore with all the signs of a long journey on foot upon him.

"Give me something to drink, if you have nothing to eat," he said. "I am famished."

Almost beside himself, Chipps produced a shilling, which Sam Rushmore tossed back.

"I want half-a-sovereign," he said, "so out with it, or you'll go out of this house only once more, and then not on your feet."

Chipps saw mischief in the ruffian's eyes, and gave way.

"You—you might stay away until the morning," he stammered.

"No," Rushmore replied ; "I am coming back again in ten minutes. Don't attempt to lock me out, or I'll smash the door in and every window out."

While Rushmore was away Chipps stood raving and mouthing in the passage.

"Where can I put him ? What shall I do with him ?" he gasped. "Just when I thought of having Mr. Reginald all to myself the rascal turns up. Where can I stow the brute, so that he is out of the way ?"

The brute settled the question for himself. He came back with a bottle of brandy and a jug somewhat the

A muffled howl was heard, and the next moment Chipps deposited himself in the horse-trough.

worse for wear full of beer, and marching straight upstairs into the miser's living-room, prepared to recruit his failing strength.

In half an hour he had drunk the brandy and the beer, and was sound asleep on the floor.

Chipps was about to drag him from the room by his heels, when Mr. Reginald arrived.

His summons at the door admitted of no delay, and the miser, on admitting him, spoke of Rushmore's presence.

"I suppose," Mr. Reginald said, "that this is a part of your precious plot?"

"No," Chipps replied, "I swear that such is not the case. The pig lies sound asleep on the floor, and snoring like one."

By this time Mr. Reginald was in the room, and he cast a malevolent glance at the unconscious ruffian.

"He is safe," he said. "Where are the deeds?"

"Where is the money?" Chipps demanded. "Five hundred pounds in gold, or Bank of England notes. I'll take no cheques."

"I have it here," the other replied. "The deeds—the deeds! Light a fire, for they must be burnt before my eyes."

"Patience," Chipps said. "I will fetch them in a quarter of an hour. Stay here; don't move, or I may repent of parting with them."

Down into the cellar he went, and commenced digging at the earth, which had settled down since it had been disturbed, and presently he came up hugging the box in his arms.

"Here are the deeds," he said. "Look at them. Feast your eyes on them, and then tell me if they are not worth five hundred times the money I ask for them."

In his anxiety Mr. Reginald over-turned the box, and snatching out the first thing that his hand came in contact with, held up an old newspaper.

"Do you call this a deed?" he thundered. "Is this the thing you ask me to feast my eyes on?"

Chipps uttered a fearful cry as he started back.

"I have been robbed," he yelled, "and that villain Toppem is the thief."

CHAPTER XXVIII.

TOPPEM SENIOR STARTS IN A NEW LINE OF BUSINESS,
AND ENDEAVOURS TO MAKE HIMSELF PERFECT IN IT
—BEN RECOGNISES SABLE WALLACK—THE STRUGGLE
IN THE FAIR.

"TIM," said Will-i-am Wobstock, "that precious father
of yours has developed hisself into a white elephant, and
it seems to me that I'm the man who's got to pervide for
him."

Tim Toppem's face was aflame with anger and dismay.

"It is I who really imposed this burden on you," he
replied. "I think you had better cancel my indentures
and let me go my own way. Find what fault you like
with me, and I'll give you just cause to complain rather
than have it said that I asked you to support my father,
who is quite able to work for himself."

"My lad," Wobstock replied, "I have lived a good
many years in the world without doin' a shabby trick, and
I'm not going to begin now. There's a man who wants to
get rid of a shooting-gallery, and I'll buy it and put your
father in charge of it."

"If you do," Tim said, "he will either shoot somebody
or himself."

"There's a risk in everything, even in loading a gun
when you ain't used to it," Wobstock returned, as the
light of humour stole into his eyes; "but I daresay your
dad will soon get used to it. The rifles only carry a pinch
of powder and small bullets."

Tim absolutely trembled, and seemed likely to assume
his favourite attitude on the ground, when suddenly he
started.

"Have—have you spoken to him about it?" he faltered.

"No; but here he comes, and we'll settle the matter
offhand."

Toppem senior expressed himself delighted with the
arrangement.

"I fired a gun when peace was proclaimed between
England and Rooshia and it busted and it went nobody
knows where," he said, "and I holds it that a man as has

fired a busted gun and lives to tell the tale ain't got no cause to fear anythink. Tim, you don't seem to take kindly to your poor father's new start in life."

"No, I don't," Tim replied, "and that's a fact. I shall never know a moment's peace, for I am sure that some dreadful catastrophe will happen."

At this moment Ben Brierton came up and greeted Mr. Toppem coldly.

"It's the way with boys in this age," he said, shedding a silent tear ; "my own son wishes to take the bread out of my mouth, and his friend—his friend as has set with his legs under my deal kitchen table, many a time and hoft—casts a heye of hice upon me."

"Well," said Wobstock, "you couldn't expect either of them to fly into your arms. Come with me, and Jem Henfold will put you in the way of loading the rifles, cleaning the target, and building up and taking to pieces the gallery."

"Perhaps," he added, "you might have a little practice at the bull's-eye yourself?"

"Of course," Toppem replied, "the man as has a bull's-eye orter to know how to hit it. Wot's the rest of the conditions, Mister Wobstock ?"

"Half profits and total abstinence for you," replied the proprietor of the menagerie.

At this generous announcement Toppem broke down.

He covered his eyes with the remnant of a red handkerchief, and not seeing where he was going plunged into a stall stocked with penny toys.

The proprietor rewarded him for this feat by giving him such a dig in the ribs that he forgot all about his good fortune, and manifested a desire to become acquainted with the interior workings of the striker's anatomy.

Wobstock put the matter right by seizing Mr. Toppem by the nape of his neck and marching him off to a more peaceful clime.

The shooting gallery soon changed hands, Wobstock paying money down.

"I'll leave this man in your hands, Henfold," he said. "Keep your eye on him and put him straight, as he wasn't born at Woolwich Arsenal."

"Right you are!" Henfold replied. "Now, then, to commence. 'Ere's a flask of powder, a bowl of bullets, and some gun-caps. Which would you use to begin with?"

"I should put the cap on first," Toppem replied, promptly.

"And blow your fingers off to a certainty," said Henfold, loading the rifle as he spoke. "Now it's ready. Hold it so that the barrel ain't in a line with people's brains, and call out—'Try a shot, sir! A penny a shot!'"

Toppem senior tried a shot himself by striking the rifle against his knee, and causing it to explode.

The bullet went clean through Wobstock's white hat, causing its owner to turn white with terror, and then purple with rage.

"What do you mean by it?" he roared. "Do you want to start by killing me?"

"How should I know that it was going off like that?" Toppem cried, wildly. "There orter to be some safety check inside it to perwent haccidents."

"Take the rifle from him," Wobstock gasped. "Here comes his son and Ben Brierton. Those boys will show him how to load and shoot, too."

"I'm always gettin' these boys thrown in my teeth," Toppem murmured, sadly; "but it were hever so with me. Perhaps the gipsy woman was right when I paid her tuppence for tellin' me that I were born under an unlucky star, and was doomed to die by falling through an open cellar-flap."

Tim and Ben engaged in a friendly shooting-match, and the ringing of the bell as the bullets went home into the centre of the bull's-eye soon attracted a crowd.

In the midst of the people stood a man, whose swarthy face was in strange and remarkable contrast with his white beard and eyebrows.

He seemed to be very much taken up with Ben's performance, and applauded each successful shot.

"You have good eyesight," he whispered, tapping the lad on the shoulder as he stepped back to make room for Tim.

"I have," our hero replied. "My eyesight is so good

that I can see through the disguise you are wearing, Sable Wallack."

At the mention of the gipsy's name Wobstock turned quickly, and just in time to see Ben tear off the false beard and make an attempt to detain Sable Wallack.

The gipsy raised one of his brawny fists, and struck Ben such a blow that he dropped upon his knees; but in an instant he was on his feet again, and wrestling with the man who had sought to do him so much wrong.

"I have you now," Ben cried, "and I'll make sure of you, you monster in human form!"

"Look out!" somebody cried; "he has a knife in his hand."

Ben Brierton saw the glimmer of the steel, and, relaxing his hold, started back just in time to escape an ugly, if not a mortal, wound.

Tim and Wobstock made a rush at Sable Wallack, as also did Toppem senior, who, clubbing one of the happily empty rifles, rushed into the fray.

He brought the butt-end of the weapon down—not upon the head of Sable Wallack, but with crushing force upon the long-suffering and much-enduring white hat surmounting Will-i-am Wobstock's manly brow.

The proprietor of the menagerie staggered under the shock and fell into Ben's arms, and commenced a series of frantic kicks and plunges, indicative of agony.

"Tim," Ben cried, "catch hold of him. Sable Wallack must not escape. Surround the villain, good people, and let me deal with him."

Knife in hand Sable Wallack stood at bay.

"You had better beware of me," he cried, menacingly; "when I strike I strike deep."

The people instantly made a lane for him, and he dashed through it.

Then the gaping yokels closed in again, and before Ben Brierton could release himself from Will-i-am Wobstock, who embraced him blindly, the gipsy had vanished.

Let it be said to the credit of Tim Toppem that he did his best to force his way through the crowd and follow the gipsy.

But fat farmers and agricultural labourers are solid

persons, and Tim, after being thrown about like a shuttle-cock for some seconds, gave up the attempt in despair.

His fond parent, aghast at what he had done, took a harlequin dive into the rival gallery, and crawled down until he stuck fast in the iron tubing.

"This is a sore disappointment," Ben Brierton said. "Giant as the villain is, if I had got him firmly in my grip I would have held him."

"It seems to me," Wobstock observed, as he struggled out of his hat, "that I am fated to be made a mark of. Where's that villain Toppem?"

"Father has retired into seclusion," Tim replied, laughng in spite of himself.

"Oh! he's there, is he?" cried Wobstock, glaring down the gallery. "Hand me a loaded rifle!—No, I'll be satis-fied with a fishing-rod, with a spike at the end of it to stir him up."

The instrument of recreation not being forthcoming Wobstock contented himself with bellowing down the tun-nel.

"Come out, and put your fists up to me, you useless vagabond—you good-for-nothing impostor!"

"It's all very well to say come out," Toppem senior moaned, "but it ain't in my power. I'm a reg'lar fixter.'

His voice sounded as if it came from a vault, and was so melancholy in expression that even Wobstock relented.

"I suppose we shall have to take the blessed machine to pieces," he said. "Fool as he is we can't allow him to choke down there."

"I'm chokin' now," Mr. Toppem gurgled; "I feel as if I was in a lemming-squeezer."

They went to work and soon fetched him out.

"And now," said Wobstock, glaring at the delinquent, "I should like to know what you have to say for your-self?"

"What can a man say, when he makes a mistake, more than he is sorry?" Toppem replied.

"You look it," Wobstock said, savagely. "It's my belief that the moment I've turned my back you'll think you've done something very funny, and laugh fit to split your sides."

"That's a fearful thing to say before my own son," Toppem said. "And how Tim could stand with dry eyes and see his father dragged out of a hiron drain-pipe is one o' them straws as breaks the camel's back!"

Scarcely knowing whether to smile or frown, Wobstock turned away, and at the same time Ted Barrett came up and put a telegram into his hand.

Wobstock read and reread it, spelling out each word in an audible tone of voice.

"Ben," he said, calling our hero to his side, "we are in luck. There's a mighty ig show coming off in London, and the promoters want my menagerie to take part in it. We'll show the cockneys something worth seeing. Ted, send a wire back at once to say that I agree to the terms."

Toppem senior turned pale as he heard these words.

"What about the rifle-gallery?" he asked.

"Oh! I suppose that must be thrown in," Wobstock replied.

"I think," Tim put in, "that father might do better if he travelled the country with it."

"Down on me agin!" cried his parent. "My own flesh and blood loathes the wery ground I walk upon. What could I do with this think without 'orses and a wan? Do you think I can carry it about on my back?'

Albeit that this argument was good, Wobstock had no intention of losing sight of Mr. Toppem.

"P'raps," observed the proprietor ot the menagerie, "your own flesh and blood thinks it may come to his turn to have a bullet within an inch of his brain, and to be whacked over the head afterwards. Come, lads, bustle, all of you. One more show here, and then heigho for London!'

CHAPTER XXIX.

THE MISER FOILED—THE MEETING IN BOND-STREET— BEN, WOBSTOCK, AND TIM TOPPEM GET INTO SORE TROUBLE.

MR. REGINALD shook the newspaper again in the face of Ebeneezer Chipps.

"You have brought me here on a fool's errand, or for something worse!" he hissed. "How am I to tell that Rushmore is feigning sleep, and that there is not some plot between you to force money out of me by threats or actual violence? You see that walking-cane I brought with me?"

"I see nothing very distinctly," Chipps groaned, pressing his hand to his brow, which was covered with beads of perspiration as cold as ice.

"Then let me tell you that there are two feet of the finest steel encased in it," Mr. Reginald returned, "and you may depend that, if needs be, I shall not scruple to use it. Come, out with the truth! What is the meaning of the trick you have played me?"

"Trick! It is I who have been tricked!" Chipps gasped. "When, years ago, I brought the box away, I brought the deeds too. I buried them in that box, and before I placed my house in the hands of that outrageous villain, Toppem, they were safe enough!"

No living man could have acted the earnestness of the miser.

He trembled and shook as if palsy had suddenly seized him, and every word was panted out as if it stuck in his throat and gave him intense pain.

"This is worse than all!" Mr. Reginald said. "If Toppem has stolen the deeds, and has sense enough to make use of them, it means ruin—utter ruin! Do you know anything of this man's haunts?"

"He was generally inside a public-house when he had any money," Chipps replied.

"He must be found if in Cloisterville," Mr. Reginald said.

"I fear he isn't," Chipps responded. "If—if—oh! lor', how can I speak the words—he understands the deeds, and has started in search of Ben, it is all up!"

It was Mr. Reginald's turn to change colour now.

Every muscle of his face quivered, and so strong were the paroxysms caused by the conflicting emotions surging through his brain, that he clutched at the table to keep himself from falling.

"I never thought of that," he said, hoarsely.

"Ah ! more idiot you to leave such a man in charge of your house. What was more natural than he should go prying about ?"

"And I thought he would, amongst the rubbish," Chipps returned ; "but I never dreamed that he would take to digging in the cellar."

"At all events, this man must be found, and if he has the deeds, and not parted with them, bribed to do so," Mr. Reginald said.

"But, on the other hand—"

"I must sell and realise everything I can get hold of, and leave the country," Mr. Reginald interposed.

"And I am to be left in the lurch, I suppose ?" said Ebeneezer Chipps, with a peculiar glitter in his eyes.

"No ; I must coax and feed you, as I would a dog I am compelled to keep."

"Thanks ; you are very complimentary," the miser said, sneering. "Suppose I made up my mind to leave England with you ?"

"With the greatest of pleasure," said Mr. Reginald. "If the worst comes, I intend to take flight to Mexico, and there I am told that a man's life is not held as being of so much value as a horse."

"I understand you !" Chipps gasped. "You mean to infer that if you got me into a quiet place in an almost lawless land, you would shoot me."

"And bury you, with as little compunction as I would put a snake under the ground," Mr. Reginald replied, calmly. "But now to find this man Toppem. I will go to London and get a solicitor to advertise for him in the morning papers. A notice something to this effect will fetch him, I think—' If Timothy Toppem, late of Cloisterville, will call at Messrs. So-and-So, solicitors, he will hear of something greatly to his advantage."

Ebeneezer Chipps forgot the threats which had been hurled at his head, and laughed gleefully.

"The bait will take," he said. "But in the meantime, what shall I do ?"

"Stay here."

"With him ?" pointing to Rushmore, who was still in the land of dreams.

"Yes, and take care you do not lose sight of him," Mr. Reginald replied. "Here is some money to go on with."

He pushed some sovereigns across the table, and put on his hat.

"There is just time for me to catch the mail-train," he said. "Look out for the advertisement, and if Toppem walks into the trap, I will send you the result."

Chipps lighted him downstairs and out of the house.

"If it weren't for my love of money and my hatred of the boy and the whole of his race," he muttered, as he retraced his footsteps, "I should laugh at the way he has been taken in. What a villain he is. How calmly he talked about shooting me. Ugh!"

The miser stopped as if his legs had become fixed in the springs of a man-trap.

Throughout the house there had rumbled a curious sound.

It was not unlike the sullen gust of wind that proceeds a thunderstorm, but the night was clear and the air still.

"Strange," Chipps said, "I never heard a noise like that. What can it be?"

There was another rumble, and the walls of the house seemed to shiver.

"An earthquake!" the miser gasped.

He rushed into the court, but neither saw nor heard any signs of alarm.

The shoemaker next door was hammering away and singing a song, and a small boy was just lounging back from an errand, trifling nefariously with some fried fish intended for his parents' supper.

"It must have been my nerves shaking and not the house," Chipps said, as he returned. "Bah! I thought I was made of iron, but now I know I am as weak as a child."

By way of consolation for his fright he kicked Sam Rushmore in the ribs, and finding that even such gentle attentions failed to awaken the ruffian, he threw a pile of old greasy sacks over him and went to bed.

.   .   .   .

Just before noontide the following morning three distinguished persons in our story were strolling down New Bond street.

Will-i-am Wobstock had brought Ben and Tim up to London, and was showing them the wonders of the West End.

Ben took the sights pretty calmly; but it was not so with Tim, whose eyes grew rounder and rounder, as he gazed into the windows of every shop window.

He ran against everything and everybody, and at last Wobstock and Ben had to wedge him in between them to keep him from coming into actual danger.

"I don't wonder," said Tim, as he stared amazed at a jeweller's establishment, "that Dick Whittington thought that the streets of London were paved with gold. Oh! I say, Ben, look at that snake with diamonds for eyes, and rings of rubies all down his body. I shouldn't wonder now if that thing was worth at least ten pounds."

"Multiply ten by a hundred, and you'll get nearer the figger," Wobstock remarked. "Ah! Tim, it's a wonderful sight, and yet it is strange that not far from all this wealth and show there are men wringing their hands in despair; lonely women weeping over hard tasks set by the sweater, and children crying for bread."

Tim's face fell in an instant.

"I'll look no more then," he said, as his eyes filled with tears. "I thought the rich looked after the poor."

"And so they do in many instances," Wobstock replied; "but all they give, and all the riches you have seen would be no more than a drop of water in the ocean to help the poverty of cruel, and mighty London. I'll show you what brings about more misery than anything in the world."

He pointed to the sign of a public-house, and shook his head until his hat fell off—the same white hat, neatly repaired, and the bullet holes artfully stopped up.

"Come along," he said, "such matters are for wiser heads than ours to settle. We'll find our way into Oxford-street, and have something to eat in a quiet place."

At that moment a gentleman walked out of a fashion-able hosiery shop and stepped into a brougham.

Bold Ben Brierton caught Wobstock by the arm and brought him up with such a jerk that for some moments he performed a series of totterings upon his heels and toes.

"Don't do that again, my lad," he said; "unless you want to see me go bang through a plate-glass window."

"That man," cried Ben, "is the one who was with Chipps and Rushmore when they attempted to capture me at the old water mill."

These words had such an effect on Will-i-am Wobstock that it looked as if the smashing of the nearest window would become an established fact.

He lost his balance, recovered it, and then tore madly after the brougham.

"Stop that vehicle," he bellowed, as he puffed and panted. "I've got a few words to say to the gent inside."

The coachman looked round, and seeing Wobstock, with Ben and Tim close upon his heels, came to the con-clusion that a street row was brewing, and fearing that the horses might bolt, whipped them up and dashed into Brooke-street.

"Sto-o-op thief !" Wobstock yelled. "A pound to the man who will stop that carriage."

It stopped of its own accord and Mr. Reginald alighted.

He gave one glance at those who were following him, and shouting out something to the coachman, which caused him to drive off in a violent hurry, hurried into his house.

As a matter of fact, a crowd instantly collected, and judging by Wobstock's ravings and gesticulations that he was mad gave him a wide berth.

"I'll have him out !" cried the proprietor of the menagerie. "If he won't come of his own accord, I'll drag him out by hair of his head. Stand back all. Don't touch me anybody, or in five minutes there won't be a spare bed in St. George's hospital. You monster—you hound, living on money that doesn't belong to you, come out !"

He rushed up the steps, and plied bell and knocker in a style that made the street resound.

"Now then, what's all this about," cried the stentorian voice of a policeman.

The "minion" of the law found an easy passage through the crowd, as most people have corns and object to have them turned red hot by stout official boots.

"There's one of 'em," cried a man, pointing Ben out : "they've been hunting the gentleman who lives in this house, and he had to run indoors for his life."

As the constable seized Ben, and twisted his arms behind him, Tim took a strong fancy to the officer's coat-tails and pulled away at them as if he were engaged in a tug-of-war, and at the same moment the door flew open, and two stalwart footmen proceeded to assault Will-i-am Wobstock most grievously.

One drove his fist down upon that fatal white hat while the other hit away with all his might.

Dazed, and almost helpless under the sudden attack Wobstock could only expostulate feebly, but they turned a deaf ear to him, and twisting him round like a pair of scales shot him down the steps, and skipped back into the house banging the door behind them.

Meanwhile, the struggle between Ben, Tim, and the constable was going on.

"You've got the wrong party," Wobstock shouted. "If you must take somebody take me. Let this boy go."

"Yes, let the boy go," cried a chorus of voices.

"Ha ! you monster," screamed a woman ; "if the boy was my son, I'd make ribbings of you."

It began to dawn upon the constable that there was a mistake somewhere, and he released Ben, and went for Wobstock, the self-accused.

"Take me away !" said Will-i-am, "but don't make a bigger wreck of me than I am. I'll go quietly, and be thankful if only I can get the thing as calls himself a gentleman to appear at the police-court."

"What is the charge against this man ?" demanded the constable locking hopelessly up at the windows of the house.

"I charge myself!" Wobstock roared. "I charge my-self with coming here and demanding to see the owner of this house."

"I can't take that charge unless the gentleman wishes," said the constable; "but I can run you in for creating an obstruction, and I'll do it pretty quickly if you don't take yourself off."

Wobstock began to see that under these circumstances he would get the worst of the bargain.

"Oh! for a brickbat to shy through the winder and bring him out," he groaned. "Ask him if he knows a villain named Ebeneezer Chipps; ask him if he didn't try to kidnap an innocent boy; ask him if he knows what was found in the miser's cellar!"

The crowd, now perfectly assured in their own minds that the man with the battered white hat was out of his mind, cheered derisively, and the policeman, thinking it time that he did something effectual to clear the path, began to trot Wobstock up the street.

"Don't shove me about!" cried the excited man.

"But I will shove you about," said the constable. "If you have a grievance against the gent, why don't you go the proper way to work to settle it, instead of making a fool of yourself in the public streets?"

"You're right," Wobstock replied. "Hold on a minute while I get at my weskit pockets; there should be a stray half-crown floatin' about in one of them."

The constable's wrath was appeased in a moment.

He danced Wobstock up a narrow turning, and in a moment came back smiling.

"Ben," said Wil-i-am, as they turned into Oxford-street, "I've often lectured you on the folly of impetu-osity, and here I'm the first to run my head against a brick wall. What I ought to have done was to follow the carridge quietly, marked where the villain got out, and set a watch on his movements. Let us hope it ain't too late to do so now."

"I am almost sorry that I pointed the man out," Ben returned; "for see what trouble I have got you into!"

Will-i-am Wobstock threw his head back, and laughed.

"Don't bother your head about that," he said. "The

Two stalwart footmen assaulted Will-i-am Wobstock grievously.

only thing I regret is that my hat has come to grief again, and I'm afeard it won't hold out much longer. I wonder," he added, musingly, "if I bought a new hat whether I should get any allowance for the old one ?"

CHAPTER XXX.

SOMETHING TO HIS ADVANTAGE—TOPPEM SENIOR GETS UPON HIS DIGNITY AND EXPERIENCES A GREAT FALL.

A FEW years ago it was the custom to hold a public carnival on Wormwood Scrubbs at holiday time, and it was there that Wobstock's menagerie was pitched, the promoters of the affair taking all risks and paying well for the show.

There was also a circus in the open air, pony racing, running matches, chariot-racing, and a host of other attractions that brought the people of London to the great stretch of green sward in their thousands.

Westbourne-park was then a rural suburb, Acton a village, and Harrow-on-the-Hill a health resort recommended by the medical faculty ; but that gentle-minded creature, the jerry-builder, who is so innocent that he does not know mud from mortar, has blotted out most of the pleasant spots with rows of hideous houses. Wormwood Scrubbs is now a training-ground for the military, and has been favoured with the unpleasant adjunct of a convict prison.

It was early on the second day of the show that Mr. Toppem senior having nothing particular to do, purchased a newspaper and sat down to read.

More by accident than design he came upon the advertisement, and read with, as it were, the earth sliding away from him—

"If Timothy Toppem, late of Cloisterville, and now supposed to be in the Eastern Counties, will call upon Messrs. Parch and Serritt, solicitors, 99, Thavies' Inn, Holborn, he will hear of something to his advantage. The sum of one pound will be paid to any person supplying the said Timothy Toppem's address."

Mr. Toppem closed his eyes and opened his mouth, then he closed his mouth and opened his eyes, and stared again with all his might at the advertisement.

"I always thought there was money in my family," he said ; "but who can have left it now ? It can't be Aunt Jane, for they had to get up a friendly lead to buy her a mangle ; and Uncle Joe had nothin', unless he saved a fortune out of the half-crown a-week the parish allowed him."

Mr. Toppem suddenly became an important member of the community.

He adjusted his shirt collar, brushed his hat carefully, and threw his chin up.

"I'll say nothin' about this to any of this lot," he muttered, with a contemptuous wave of his hand towards the caravans, "unless they find it out for themselves, which ain't likely, as the hagony column is hout o' their line."

How to get away without creating special attention was his next thought.

It was almost time for him to get the shooting gallery into proper order, but he despised such low things now.

"Let 'em look after it themselves," he said. "I've done with it for ever. When I get my ortune I s'pose I must give Wobstock a little and there's Tim—he must go to school, of course."

And yet with all his great expectations he sneaked away like a coward, as it seemed very much like biting the hand that fed him to keep the good news to himself, and creep out of the sight of the people who had been so kind to him.

After becoming the victim of several pirate busses, each of which took him the wrong way, he reached Holborn and found Thavies Inn without much difficulty.

The offices of Messrs. Parch and Serritt consisted of the ground floor of a grimy old house, and a grimy boy, with a pen in his mouth and another behind his ear, asked the visitor's name.

No sooner did the child of fortune give it, than the boy became active and polite.

He bustled off his stool, and in the blandest of tones asked Mr. Toppem to follow him.

"I ll not forget you, my lad,' said Toppem, "you know your place you do."

Mr. Serritt was out, but Mr. Parch was in.

"Sit down, my dear sir," he said, rubbing his hands softly. "I am very glad our advertisement was so successful."

"So am I," Toppem replied.

"I presume," said Mr. Parch, looking him straight in the eyes, "that there is no mistake about your identity. To begin with, you are the man who had charge of a house in the occupation of Ebeneezer Chipps."

Toppem started, and turned a little pale! What on earth connection could there be between his fortune and the miser!

"I did look after his house, it is true," he faltered, "but I left it in disgust. But look 'ere," he blurted out, "what's this somethin' to my adwantage?"

"You shall know presently," the lawyer said. "I expect our client, in fact, the gentleman who instructed us to advertise, to be-- Ah! here he is."

As he spoke the door opened and Mr. Reginald entered, and was forthwith introduced to Toppem, whose castles in the air were beginning to dwindle away.

"Now," said the lawyer, "we can get to business without delay. Mr. Toppem, I am going to put a plain question to you, and I hope you will be as straightforward with me. Have you parted with any papers lately?"

"No," Toppem replied. "What sort o' papers do you think I should part with?"

Mr. Parch thought that his amazement was assumed, and smiled and nodded knowingly at Mr. Reginald.

"That means," said the lawyer, "you still have the documents in your possession."

Toppem senior brushed his hair on end, and drew his feet close to the rail of his chair.

"I should like to know what this game means?" he said.

"It means," responded the lawyer, "that while acting as caretaker in the house of Ebeneezer Chipps you dug up a box containing certain valuable documents, which you took possession of, and replaced some old newspapers in their place."

"What a whopper !" cried Mr. Toppem, starting to his feet. " I never did nothin' of the kind."

"It seems to me," observed Mr. Reginald, "that this case is one that needs the calling in of a policeman."

Toppem bade farewell to his fortune which was now extremely visonary.

He went white and trembling as the lawyer ocussed him with his keen eyes.

" I'll tell you the truth, gentlemen," he groaned ; "it's true that I found a box and there was papers in it. I took up the first one, but I'd no sooner read : ' This is the last will and testament,' than somebody put out the light and nearly choked me. I swooned away and—and bolted the next mornin'."

"And who do you suppose assailed you in this remarkable fashion ?" demanded the lawyer.

" I put it down to Ebeneezer Chipps," Toppem replied ; " but whoever it was knew how to use his hands. But the most mysterious thing is, I found myself in bed, and I've often thought that p'raps it were all a dream."

"And do you expect me to believe this story?" said Mr. Parch.

" That's your own look out.'

"Where are you now ?'

"With Wobstock the menagerie man."

"That settles the question at once," cried Mr. Reginald, darting to the door, and placing his back against it ; " this scoundrel has concocted this pack of lies to deceive us. Mr. Parch, will you kindly telegraph to Chipps, who of course must act in the capacity of prosecutor, as the felony was committed in his house ?"

" Prosecutor—felony !" Toppem gasped. " I'm innocent of doin' any harm. Chipps owes me money, but left me to starve, and I was lookin' about for somethin' to raise a trifle an when—"

" You had better keep any further explanation for the jury," said the lawyer ; " but I'm willing to give you one chance. Come, Mr. Toppem," he added, in a wheedling tone, "don't let us beat about the bush any longer. Put the documents into my hands and I will put a hundred guineas into yours."

"I tell you," Toppem almost shrieked, "that I never took 'em! I hadn't the chance."

"Shall I tell your clerk to fetch a policeman?" Mr. Reginald demanded.

"I fear we must have recourse to stern measures," the attorney said.

"Then do it," said Toppem, doggedly; "bring the whole force if you like."

Mr. Parch drummed his fingers upon the table, and looked askance at his client.

The case was assuming a complicated complexion, and the cute lawyer began to think that Toppem had been telling the truth.

Suddenly Mr. Reginald moved from the door, and approaching the lawyer whispered something in his ear.

"Yes," returned the lawyer under his breath. "I will put the question, but I fear it is almost a hopeless one. Now, Mr. Toppem," he said, aloud, "you tell us that you are with Mr. Wobstock; do you happen to know if he has paid a visit to Cloisterville recently?"

"No I don't; but I heard a word dropped that he and Ben Brierton—Chipps' nevvy, you know—had been on a mysterious journey."

Mr. Parch and Mr. Reginald exchanged glances.

"I suppose," said the former, after a pause, "that you are going back to the menagerie?"

"I ham," Toppem responded, emphatically, "unless somebody makes it worth my while to keep away."

"And I suppose," continued the lawyer, "that if you do go back you will not forget to repeat what has passed between us?"

"You never got nearer the mark in your life," said Toppem, becoming suddenly defiant; "you've lured me 'ere under the pretence that there was somethin' to my advantage; but what do I find? Why you rounds on me with a conspiracy! You wants to make me hout a thief. Bah! that for you and your prosecutions, and that for Chipps."

He snapped his fingers contemptuously, and rising to his feet made a show of leaving the room ; but he turned on hearing the crisp rustle of paper.

" Will this silence you?" demanded Mr. Parch, holding up a Bank of England note.

"How much is it worth?"

" Ten pounds.'

" Then," said Toppem, "it will keep me quiet or ten weeks."

" More than time enough," said Mr. Reginald.

" Ample," added the lawyer. "·Mr. Toppem, do you know the nature of an oath? I am a commissioner, and about to swear you to keep this business secret and sacred. If you break the oath you will be liable to a term of penal servitude."

This was of course shallow nonsense, but it sufficed to frighten Toppem.

He took the oath, and what was more agreeable, the ten pound note, and breathed more freely when he was outside the stuffy office.

" What a mix up it is !" he said. "There's some plot goin' on ; the only thing I can make of it all is that Chipps stole the papers, somebody knocked me on the head when I was lookin' at 'em, and now these pair o' sharps want to know where they are gone to. I s'pose there'll be a jolly row when I get back, but ten pound is worth it.'

CHAPTER XXXI.

TELLS HOW WILL-I-AM WOBSTOCK TOOK A BATH WITH HIS CLOTHES ON.

IF Toppem senior did not intend to break the oath he had taken he certainly broke the pledge.

It was very late when he reached Wormwood Scrubbs ; the people were coming away, and the showmen closing for the night.

Wobstock met him at the gate, and instead of asking him why he had absented himself, knocked him down.

A quantity of gold, silver, and copper coins flew out of

Toppem's pockets, and the roughs attracted to the spot by the scrimmage, scrambled wildly for them.

Driven to fury, Toppem fought like a tiger and contrived to secure about half his "fortune," with the addition of a pair of neat black eyes, and a nose modelled in the form of a prize tomato.

"Very well," he said, glaring at Wobstock. "I'll remember this agin you. Keep your shooting gallery— keep my boy, but I'll make it hot for you at the first opportunity. I'm orf, and when you see me again, the hour of reckonin' will have come."

"Go away, or I'll pound you to a jelly !" Wobstock roared. "Go back to Chipps, you deceitful scoundrel, and tell him that you took a double job on. Tell him you've been between two stools and have come to the ground."

As the proprietor of the menagerie stepped forward, evidently with the intention of flooring Toppem a second time, a man stepped from the crowd, and seized him by the arm.

"Let him go," the stranger whispered. "I have news for you."

Wobstock suffered himself to be led away to a quiet place, where the private detective, for such the man was, could talk freely.

"In the first place," he said, "I tracked Toppem to a lawyer's office in Thavies Inn, when he was in the company of the man who calls himself Mr. Reginald, but whose real name is—"

"Reginald Brierly."

"Exactly," returned the detective; "Brierton and Brierly are very similar, and I wonder that the villain Chipps did not find a different name for the boy. I let Toppem go his own sweet way, and then I followed Reginald Brierly to the Grecian Club, where I left him, and then went off to the house in Brooke-street, which is empty and the blinds down. All I could learn there is that the servants had been suddenly paid off, and the tradesmen in the neighbourhood hastily settled with. The bird intends to fly."

"He can't," Wobstock said ; "the wires of his cage are

too strong for him to break. At the very moment that he thinks about taking to wing I will checkmate him."

" Does the boy know nothing about the good fortune awaiting him ?"

" Nothing ; absolutely nothing," Wobstock replied. " All he knows is that he is no relation to Ebeneezer Chipps, and that he has been surrounded by enemies ; but does not dream of the real reason. Keep a good watch on Reginald Brierly, Mr. Herry."

" You may depend on me. If Holtham Grange goes to the hammer we can stop the sale in five minutes ; but as to the timber I fear that the axe has been laid to the root of many a good old tree."

" I can't help that," Wobstock said ; " trees will grow again, but it isn't every day that a youngster who was half starved by a miser finds himself with an estate enough to make a man's mouth water to think of.'

They parted, Wobstock chuckling as he tapped his breast pocket, and murmuring—

" Will-i-am, you never did, and never will do, such a night's work as when you climbed through the window of the miser's house."

The proprietor of the menagerie was abroad early the next morning, and accosted Ben Brierton and Tim who had risen with the sun and were busy looking after the animals.

" Lads," said Wobstock, with an air of mystery, " you may stop work, for I've made up my mind that you and me shall retire into private life for a time. Tim, I—I suppose you have heard about your father ?"

" Yes, I have." Tim replied, demurely, " and I am heartily sorry for it."

" It's no fault of yours," Wobstock said. " Let the old man go his own way for a time, and, mark me, he will see the error of his ways and settle down to a changed and better life."

" I see you have a gun under your arm," said Ben, who was as anxious as the others to change the subject.

" Why, yes," Wobstock responded. " I've made an arrangement with a man down Ealing Dean way to let us see if we can knock any young rooks over, so I thought we'd take a walk across the fields, and brace ourselves up for coming events."

"For coming events?" Ben repeated.

"Well, you see," said Wobstock, vaguely, "we never know what may happen. Put on your hats and let us be off at once."

In a few minutes they started, leaving the old farm which still exists at the western end of the Scrubbs on their right, and striking almost immediately into picturesque and beautiful country.

The Grand Junction Canal lay on their left and a little way beyond a narrow stream flowed swiftly.

"Plenty of fish in here, I should think," said Tim, casting a critical eye on the water. "Do you remember how the roach used to bite near the granaries of Cloisterville, Ben?"

Our hero nodded and smiled, for he also remembered how Tim had invariably hooked anybody who stood in his way.

They followed the course of the stream until they came to a rustic footbridge.

Wobstock crossed it, observing as he put the gun into Ben's hands—

"I'm a bit blown, and will take a spell of rest. You two youngsters amuse yourselves as you like. When I'm ready to start again I will call you."

Tim also crossed the bridge with some notion that if he searched very hard in the long grass he might discover a lark'snest. Ben continued to pace the brink of the stream.

The boy was full of thought, for during the previous night his slumbers had been disturbed by a strange and vivid dream.

Ha had fancied himself to be back again in the ruinous old house at Cloisterville, waiting, as was usual, hungry and disheartened, for the miser's return, when lo! the crumbling walls vanished, and stately and beautifully-decorated ones took their place.

The frowsy furniture disappeared, and in their stead was the luxurious appointments of a mansion.

But one thing remained, and that was Wobstock's white hat.

It seemed to be endowed with a kind of butterfly life, hovering from a richly-inlaid table to a soft, yielding couch; and when Ben seized it in desperation he found that it's weight was more than he could well support, for the wonderful hat was full to the brim with gold.

Absurd as the dream was it disturbed Ben's mind.

Meanwhile Wobstock, with the real and invincible hat over his eyes, was stretched at full length upon the grass, apparently dozing, but in point of fact his brain was active.

Suddenly he heard the sound of approaching footsteps, and looking up saw Tim running at headlong speed.

"What's the matter?" Wobstock demanded, lazily.

"A b-b-bull!" Tim shrieked. "Look out, the brute's coming straight at you!"

In a moment Wobstock was on his feet, and in another saw his danger.

The bull came thundering on with tail erect and head close to the ground.

Tim just contrived to dodge sixty stone of living and infuriated beef, but Wobstock, not being so active, looked about for some haven of safety.

He rushed towards the bridge, but in that moment of agony it occurred to him that the bull was quite as capable of reaching it as himself, and acting under a sudden impulse he floundered up to his neck in the stream.

"Keep afloat!" he heard Tim shout. "I've got hold of the bull's tail, and he's going round and round with me. Ben—help—Ben!"

Our hero was fully two hundred yards away from the scene of the catastrophe, but taking it in at a glance he ran up and reached the foot of the bridge just as Wobstock grasped at it convulsively.

"Hold on, Tim!" Ben cried. "I'm coming!"

"Then make haste—oh! make haste," Tim gasped, "for I'm as giddy as a kite in a hurricane."

Ben's first thought was to put a charge of shot into the bull's head, but he changed the idea for a better one.

Dashing across the bridge he favoured the beast with a staggering blow between the horns with the butt-end of the gun.

The bull stopped to reflect.

Probably he wondered where the blow came from, and whether there were any more like it in the vicinity, and it is just as likely as not that he discovered the mistake of attempting an assault on a peaceable party.

At all events, Toro did not wait for a second attack.

CHAPTER XXXII.

THE DENUNCIATION.

BELLOWING loudly to keep up his dignity, though defeated, the bull trotted away, leaving Tim nearly exhausted, and Ben to assist Wobstock out of his uncomfortable predicament.

"The man," said Wobstock, as he crawled out and lay upon the bridge, not unlike a stranded turtle, "who keeps a bull to worry other people ought to be tossed in a blanket every morning before breakfast for a month, and then handed over to his own brute to trample on."

He was, though not to his own taste, prettily festooned with weeds, and had left one boot in the mud.

"I'd like to know how I am to get back in this state?" he groaned. "Look about you, lads, and see if you can't see some signs of a house.

"No, but I see a man," Tim replied; "and he looks as if he meant to say something to us."

"Perhaps," said Wobstock, "we are trespassers."

"No," Ben returned; "this is evidently a public foot path."

"Then," said Wobstock, "that man will do well to keep out of the reach of my arm."

The man, a neighbouring farmer, came up with a dog at his heels.

"Rather damp, ain't it?" he said, with a grin.

Words failed Wobstock for fully a minute.

"Is that mad animal yours?" he gasped.

"It is," the farmer replied, "and if you had gone a little further on you would have seen a board with 'Beware of the bull,' on it. But you're in a bad plight, so come up to my house, and go to bed for an hour or two while we dry your clothes."

This was an invitation not to be declined.

Wobstock was cold and shivering, but after a short rest he was himself again.

"Ben," he said, as he returned to Wormwood Scrubbs in borrowed boots and clothes, "the next time you hear me talk about rook shooting, or catch me napping in the hay stir me up with a pitchfork."

    .   .   .   .

On the evening following William Wobstock's adventure with the bull, a cab stopped at the eastern end of Pall Mall, and Ben and the proprietor of the menagerie alighted. Wobstock looked about as if he expected to see somebody, and presently the detective he had employed to watch Reginald Brierly tapped him on the shoulder with one hand and pointed to the club with the other.

"Just gone in," he said.

"That's lucky," Wobstock said. "I don't think I shall require your services again after to-night. There's going to be a general settling up of accounts."

"At all events," responded the detective, smiling, as he lifted his hat, "you have settled handsomely with me."

"Now, Ben," said Wobstock, "we are going into that swell place, and you'll hear a neat little story, mostly about yourself. Come on, I'm ready for the battle."

"The longer I live the more I am mystified," Ben said. "Mr. Wobstock, tell me before I go into this place the meaning of all that has passed since I had the good luck to find a friend in you."

"You will know soon enough. Here we are. All you have to do is to keep up your pecker and leave the rest to me."

They went up the splendid flight of steps leading to the vestibule of the club, where they were challenged by the hall porter.

"I want to see Mr. Reginald Brierly," Wobstock said.

"You had better send your card in," the porter said, eyeing the visitors suspiciously.

"Card!" Wobstock echoed. "Do I look like a man who would go to the expense of having cards with my name printed on 'em?"

"Well, then, give your name, and I'll send that in."

Acting under a sudden im:ulse ... d up to his neck in the stream

"My name is my own business," Wobstock retorted. "I have come to see Mr. Reginald Brierly, and see him I will."

Just then a door opened and the subject of the conversation appeared.

"Stop!" cried Wobstock. "I have run you to earth at last, and I mean to have my say out to you."

Reginald Brierly went white to his very lips.

For a moment he stood as if undecided whether to retreat or advance.

"Edwards," he said, hoarsely, "put these people out."

"Put us out, will you?" Wobstock roared. "Twenty of you might."

Reginald Brierly entered a room on the left, and Wobstock, fairly dragging Ben after him, followed.

"The first man who attempts to stop me will pay dearly for the luxury," he cried, flourishing his fists.

The hall-porter took him at his word, and Wobstock performed his promise in the most unmistakable manner.

The blow would have felled an ox, and the rash porter turned a complete somersault, and then, scrambling to his feet, stood holding his head and groaning.

Reginald Brierly had taken refuge in the card-room.

Several gentlemen were present, and the incident was of so novel a character that they sat staring from Wobstock and Ben to Reginald Brierly in speechless amazement.

"Gents," said Wobstock, "I beg your pardon for coming so hastily into your company, but you'll own that I had good grounds for so doing. Do you know the character of that man?"

He pointed to Reginald Brierly, who stood on the other side of the table, livid, trembling, and grinding his teeth with passion.

Nobody vouchsafed a reply to Wobstock's question.

"Then I'll tell you," he said, snapping his fingers. "He is an impostor, a rascal, and a thief—worse than a thief, for he has lived on this lad's money. Ben, I am sorry to tell you that that man is your dead father's brother."

" What ?" our hero cried.

" Yes," said Wobstock ; " that man standing there is your uncle. Look at him and watch him well. He knows that I am telling the truth. Bad as he is, he will not have the villainy to deny it against such proofs as I have."

" What are your proofs ?" Brierly demanded.

" Your brother's will, leaving you a thousand pounds, and Holtham Grange and the estates to his only child, Ben Brierly, better known as Bold Ben Brierton."

" Bah !" said Reginald Brierly ; " this is some neat conspiracy to extort money from me, but it will not do. My brother made no will, and his child died at the age of three, within a month of his mother's decease."

" Oh ! he did, did he," Wobstock returned. " Well, first of all, here is the will, and, secondly, here are some precious documents in your handwriting to Ebeneezer Chipps. What was this Chipps before he settled down at Cloisterville ? Come, you need not leave me to tell the whole story."

Reginald Brierly twisted his fingers. His lips moved, but no sound came from them.

" Well, I'll tell you who he was," Wobstock continued. "He was the man you employed to steal your brother's child, and he succeeded. He took the youngster to his vile den, and brought him up as his nephew."

" All false," said Reginald Brierly.

" So false that you have been trying to get the boy into your hands, and smuggle him out of the country," Wobstock responded. " Now look here, my fine bird in borrowed plumes, you had better own up at once and tell the truth, or you will march out of this place with a pair of handcuffs on your wrists. It was I took the deeds from Toppem, and I have them now."

He struck his breast pocket and crowed like a child with glee.

Reginald Brierly found that he was beaten.

" I must have time to frame a proper answer," he said.

" I mean to have it in writing, or before witnesses," Wobstock said.

" You shall have the whole truth and nothing but it, it

you will meet me to-morrow night, at this time, at the house of Ebeneezer Chipps."

"Very well," Wobstock said ; "but, mind, don't you try to give me the slip. I look upon myself as Ben's guardian, and I intend to see justice done. If you try to bolt I'll follow you round the world and back again, and what's more, I'll advertise your name as a scoundrel at every street corner."

A mist gathered before Reginald Brierly's eyes.

"Bring the boy with you," he said, walking unsteadily towards the door.

"Not if I know it," Wobstock replied. "You are such an old hand at foul play you may have some new scheme in your mind. You may try to kidnap me, if you like ; but Ben has had enough of it te 'ast him a life-time."

There was something so unique in the idea of kidnapping Will-i-am Wobstock that even our hero, confused and dumfounded at the revelations unfolded to him, laughed.

Reginald Brierly left the room and club, never to return to it again.

"Good night ! gents," said Wobstock, affably. "I'm glad that it didn't come to a police case. That rascal has nearly run to the end of his tether ; but it's strong enough to hold him until I like to let him go."

Proud of his success, Wobstock led Ben away into the busy street.

"What do you think of it ?" he asked.

"I cannot think," our hero replied. "My brain is in a whirl, and nothing seems to be real to me."

"It will be real enough by-and-bye," Wobstock said. "There's a cartload of sovereigns waiting for you, Ben, a house fit for a prince, and good, broad lands, too. There's our cab ; jump in and go home, and don't move an inch until you hear from me."

Wobstock stood alone on the pavement, his round face lit up with smiles and his eyes flashing with triumph.

Suddenly, to the astonishment of a policeman, he lifted up his feet and began to dance.

"What sort o' game do you call that ?" the officer demanded.

" My safety-walve," Wobstock replied. "I'm afraid of getting too jubilant, so I work it off with my feet. Ha —ha !"

He passed on, the constable looking wonderingly at him.

" That's a curiosity," he said. " I hope it isn't a case of drink ; for he looks a good-hearted sort of fellow.

Will-i-am Wobstock went down to Cloisterville that very night, and reached the cathedral city just as day was dawning.

He walked down to the old house, and stood gazing at it.

" I've come early and I've come prepared," he said. " I wonder what old Chipps would say if he knew I was here. I could hug myself when I think of the face you will pull to-night."

Wobstock walked back to the silent streets, and as soon as the houses were open he put up at a small inn near the railway station.

All day long he sat at the window watching the passengers coming and going.

At last his long vigil was rewarded.

Late in the afternoon Reginald Brierly arrived, and paced slowly on his way without looking either to the right or left.

" Still thinking," Wobstock murmured, rubbing his hands softly. " Perhaps he is wondering how he is to live, or perhaps— No, he is too fond of himself to commit suicide.

Punctually to the moment, and apparently in his happiest mood, he presented himself at the door of the miser's house, and bestowed a series of thundering raps upon it.

Ebeneezer Chipps replied to the noisy summons, and holding the door open snarled at the proprietor of the menagerie like a surly dog.

" So you know what I've come about," Wobstock said. " Well, that will save a deal of trouble. It's a pity you didn't take that box away with you when you went in search of Ben, isn't it ?"

" Come in," Chipps returned. " Reginald Brierly has

written out his confession, and I have put my name to my share of it."

"That's satisfactory," Wobstock said, "and now I suppose you both mean going abroad? It's wiser than staying here, and risking ending your days in penal servitude."

By this time he was half way up the staircase.

"I feel quite at home here," he said. "Ah! that is the room where we put poor old Toppem, and— Ah! would you?"

Sam Rushmore had dashed from a niche in the wall, and swinging a formidable cudgel aloft, brought it down with tremendous force.

Wobstock saved his face by throwing up his arms, but the blow made him reel and stagger.

Chipps now came to the ruffian's aid, and Wobstock, attacked on both sides, struck out madly, but a sudden blow on the temple brought him down.

"Now for the deeds," cried Chipps, tearing open the wounded man's coat? "Where are they? Surely he brought them with him? Ah! here they are at last."

But his cry of triumph changed to one of disappointment and dismay.

"These are not the originals," he cried. "They are copies. Mr. Reginald, we have been too clever again."

The prime mover of the conspiracy peeped out of the room Wobstock had intended to enter.

His face was ghastly pale, and he trembled in every limb with the fear he could not conceal.

"Is—is it over?" he demanded.

"He's quiet enough, if that's what you mean," Sam Rushmore returned. "Shall I give him the finishing-stroke?"

"He deserves it for cheating us," Chipps said. "The cunning fellow has made copies of the deeds which are here, but the originals are—he only knows where."

Keeping his eye upon Reginald Brierly, Rushmore moistened his palm and grasped the cudgel.

"What are you doing?" the coward gasped. "There must be no murder on our hands. The boy knows that he is coming here."

"Then all our work has been done or nothing," Chipps said, malignantly. "Let me think of the best course to pursue. There is the landing-stage at the bottom of the court, and a man might walk in by accident."

"We'll make the accident," Rushmore said, savagely. "It's time that the whole of us bolted, and left this beastly place."

"I tell you I will have no hand in such a crime," said Reginald Brierly, clinging to the door-post for support.

"And yet you talked boldly enough about shooting me," Ebeneezer Chipps returned, sneering. "What was that?"

His own face grew livid as a sound broke upon his ears.

It was a step, the careful step of a man feeling his way in the dark, then silence, and again a step that came down heavy and echoed through the old house.

"Is it possible that I left the front door unfastened?" said the miser, panting for breath.

The question was answered by the sound of a man's voice.

"Show a light." he cried. "I've done nothing but kick my shins against these break-neck stairs."

"Sable Wallack or I'm a Dutchman," cried Rushmore; but," he added, turning fiercely upon Chipps, "it is no ault of yours that a policeman's bull's-eye is not turned upon this pretty scene."

It was Sable Wallack and more like a demon than a man, he looked by the light of a candle, which the miser procured.

"Our gang has been broken up in a poaching affray," he said. "We made a good fight of it with the keepers, but they proved the masters. Faro, he's at the Hawthorne hospital with a couple of charges of shot in his ribs, and there is no hope for him. The police are on my track, and you must hide me for a time, and then find me the means to get away."

The miser's hand shook to such an extent that the hot tallow from the guttering candle rolled down and blistered his fingers.

"Look there," he said, pointing to the insensible body of Wobstock; "didn't you see him before?"

"No! I received some grains of powder in my eyes and I see everything as through a mist. Ah! now I see him—the menagerie man."

"If you wish to be sheltered here," Chipps said, "even for a night, and it will not be safe to stay here after, you must earn the price of it."

"How?"

"He," said Chipps, still meaning Wobstock, "must be got out of the way."

The miser drew Wallack aside and whispered something in his ear.

"No," he said, "I'll stain my hands no more. All I want to do is to get off where I can breathe freely and forget the whole business."

"What, squeamish!" cried Rushmore. "You turn white-livered—you who boasted a hundred times that you would as soon kill a man as knock a pheasant over? Bah! You shall help me to carry him down to the river at midnight."

"I'll not stay to see it done," Reginald Brierly cried.

"Then get away and come back in the morning," Chipps snarled. "You can settle with us, then, for I am sure you have not forgotten to realise a large sum of money.'

"Take your shares now,' Reginald Brierly said, flinging a pocket-book down as if it had stung him. "You will find more than will satisfy you."

He thrust his hat upon his head, and rushed downstairs, fancying that mocking laughter was ringing in his ears. Once outside he stood and reflected.

He had robbed his nephew, and left the lad's best friend to the mercy of the three of the greatest scoundrels that ever escaped the rope.

He knew that a hue and cry would soon be raised after Wobstock. What, therefore, was to be done?

There was just time to catch the last train to London, from there he could slip off to Liverpool, and noontide of the next day would see him on board a vessel bound for America.

Like the cur he was, he sneaked up the dark and lone-some court, and once in the street fairly bolted.

Before him seemed to dance the figure of the man doomed to death.

His own plan had been to overcome Wobstock, seize the deeds, and, deprive Ben, if possible, of what he could not enjoy himself; but now he found that Chipps and Rushmore had made up their minds to carry the matter out to a terrible ending.

He reached the station just as the train was starting, and, selecting an empty carriage, leaped in.

.   .   .   .

The cathedral-clock struck the hour of twelve, and the riverside houses frowned darkly upon the river.

In the distance, where a few lights gleamed, there were a few spectral-looking objects—barges with long, taper-ing masts, and heavy, lumbering boats, moored to a quay-side.

But for the flickering lamps showing that human hands had been at work, Cloisterville might have been taken for a city of the dead.

There was not a living creature abroad to awake the echoes of the silent streets.

A solitary policeman, leaning against a church-wall, half asleep and dreaming fitfully, awoke with a start, thinking he heard a shout.

But he put it down to fancy, and dozed again, for he was a pointsman, and as the sergeant would not visit him for an hour or more, he could afford to take matters easy.

At the very moment that the heavy-eyed constable thought his ears had deceived him the body of a man was shot into the river by two miscreants, a third keeping watch.

"It is done," Rushmore whispered, hoarsely; "the tide will carry him clean away in a couple of hours. Let us get back."

And back they went, with no human eye, full of horror and rage, upon them, and no human voice to denounce them as murderers.

Wobstock was a heavy man, and for fully half a minute he continued under the surface of the water.

Rushmore had given him (according to the villain's notion) a second quieting tap over the head, but cold and deadly as was the night-blackened river, it was kind for once.

The immersion revived Wobstock, and brought him to his senses just at the moment when it promised to extinguish his life, for the water was pouring through his parted lips and into his expanded nostrils.

CHAPTER XXXIII.

TELLS HOW WOBSTOCK PROVES UP TO THE HILT THAT A STOUT MAN SWIMS BETTER THAN A THIN ONE.

As Wobstock's head rose above the surface he took in the position in a moment, so far that he was in deep and swift-flowing water, and likely to drown.

Will-i-am Wobstock was no great swimmer, but he was a corpulent man, and a corpulent man will float where a lean man sinks.

Still dazed, and certain of nothing but that his life was in danger, he looked up at the dark vault of night through which no star gleamed, and then to the left and right.

It appeared to him that he was in some fearsome tunnel of running water—a terrible floating chamber of death.

He tried to cry for help, but his tongue refused its office, and therefore he was compelled to be content to lie upon his back and keep his hands and feet moving.

"If I keep on like this," he thought, "I shall either be carried to the sea, or run into something which will settle the question for ever. I am not afraid to die, but I have a wife and children who love me, and will miss me very much. Heaven spare my life for their sakes!"

Just then he came into violent contact with something.

In the conflict with Rushmore and Ebeneezer Chipps, he had jammed his hat firmly over his brow, and the blows he had received were delivered on the sides of his head.

His hat, the same immortal white one still remained in its wonted place, and probably saved his life.

Wobstock thrust out the arm nearest to the object he had floated into, and grasped what he knew to be the gunwale of a boat.

He turned himself round and clung to it—ah! how he clung to it—filling his lungs with air, and breathing as it were a new life.

But he was very weak and benumbed.

The rushing water made strange and awful music in his ears, and he felt that, unless he could drag himself into the boat soon, his hands, which were as cold as ice, would soon give way.

With the means of rescue so close at hand, it would be hard to perish; and, making one superhuman effort, he drew himself up breast high, and throwing himself forward, rested upon the boat.

It was a diminutive craft, the kind of one used for small pleasure parties—and it rocked ominously, as if trying to resist any attempt at intrusion.

But Wobstock could afford to be patient and careful now.

He remained still, with his legs still dangling in the water, until he felt a little stronger, and then, drawing up one knee, he rolled himself over, and falling plump on the flooring of the boat, laid as supine as a turbot in a fishmonger's shop.

Now that he had cheated the river of its prey, he felt a strong desire to go to sleep; but he roused himself and felt about, creeping on his hands and knees, searching for a pole or oars, which he thought might have been left.

He was not mistaken.

He found a pair of sculls, and then, unfastening the rope that moored the boat, he pulled out into the stream.

His head was now throbbing with a racking pain, that threatened to unhinge his brain and drive him mad.

"I'll not have it!" he muttered, shaking himself; "I'll bear up. Hangelina, your husband is worth a dozen dead men yet. Ben, my boy, I'm still alive to settle with that pack o' rascals. Oh! how they did hammer into me. Never—no, never !—did I get such busters. Bear up, Will-i-am—no impetuosity !"

Just then he saw a glimmer of light, and heard a splash.

A man attending upon some horses, which were being got ready for an early journey, was getting some water in a pail attached to a rope.

"Ahoy there !" Wobstock shouted.

The man, startled by a cry from the river at such an unearthly hour, dropped the pail, and held the lantern over his head.

"Who—who's there ?" he stammered.

He was a nervous man, and had some belief in the report that the ghost of a certain dealer in aërated waters, who, despising his own harmless liquids and taking to something stronger, had dropped himself out of the second floor window of a riverside house because his wife had forgotten to fry some onions with a beef steak.

Wobstock having shouted once, felt compelled to rest before he could repeat the performance.

The ostler was about to bolt when the midnight river wanderer gave music again.

"I ain't quite sure who I am yet," Wobstock cried. "Just lend a hand here, old fellow. I'm in a awful pickle, and feel almost as dead as a flat bottle of soda-water."

This was enough for the superstitious individual ; he relinquished his hold on the lantern, and was flying, howling, when Wobstock roared—

"What's the matter with you ! Are you afraid of a man who has met with an haccident ?"

The words reassured the ostler ; he returned to the landing-stage, although somewhat dubiously, and having reassured himself that Wobstock was real flesh and blood, and not a shadow, with a smell of brimstone hovering about it, helped him out.

"Where do you live ?" Wobstock demanded.

"Close at hand."

"Then take me home and put me to bed. I'll pay you well."

The ostler was a good fellow at heart, and lost no time in complying with his request.

"You'll find some money in my clothes," Wobstock moaned as he was being tucked up between the blankets. "Don't breathe a word of this to any living creature. I've made a fool of myself, and have paid the penalty."

"But who are you?" the ostler asked.

"I'll tell you when I wake up."

It was a long time before Will-i-am Wobstock did wake up to his proper self, for within an hour he was in a high fever.

CHAPTER XXXIV.

BEN'S DESPAIR—THE SEARCH FOR THE MISSING ONE—THE DISTRESSED PARENT.

HANGELINA waited for her husband's return all the next day in vain.

Will-i-am had promised faithfully to come back to the bosom of his family within four-and-twenty hours, and had ordered his wife to prepare a feast on a grand scale.

"For, my dear," said he, with a knowing wink, "the greatest day of our lives is at hand, and if any of the men do kick a bit over the traces we must excuse 'em."

Ben Brierton was very uneasy.

He could find no rest, but walked up and down, not caring to speak to anybody, even to Tim.

The last-named youth's hair manifested a tendency to rise on end as the day closed.

No letter or telegram came; the suspense was terrible.

The hours of the night dragged themselves slowly on finding no closed eyes, save those of the animals within the menagerie.

Dawn brought hope.

A letter might arrive, and the postman was eagerly watched for, but he passed by whistling, carrying his small but significant cargo of news that brought joy and sorrow to many hearts, wealth to some, and poverty to others.

Hangelina bore up wonderfully, but her swimming eyes and haggard face told what she was suffering.

"My Will-i-am—oh! my Will-i-am," she moaned to

Ted Barrett, the lion-tamer. "I am sure that something dreadful must have happened to him."

"Wait until noon," he said. "A train comes in at eleven, and it would not take Wobstock more than an hour to get here."

Noon came, but brought no Wobstock.

Ben Brierton could stand it no longer.

He had a short interview with the absent one's wife, and declared his intention of going in search of Wobstock without another moment's delay.

"He announced his intention of going to Cloisterville," he said, "and I am sure he went. If he is not there I shall know—"

"What—what ?" Hangelina screamed.

"Well," Ben replied, hesitatingly, "perhaps, after all, some important business detained him in London."

"What business should detain him ?" Mrs. Wobstock cried, wringing her hands. "If he had stayed, he would have stayed here, or sent me word where he was."

"I will take Tim with me and take the four o'clock train to Cloisterville," Ben said, "and I will keep you posted with every item of intelligence I can possibly get hold of."

Mrs. Wobstock pressed a well-filled purse into Ben's hand, but he pushed it gently back.

"Thanks to your husband's kindness," he said, "I have plenty of money of my own."

"But I insist," she returned. "You never know what you may require, and this is a poor world to travel in without money. Good-bye, my boy."

She kissed him in a motherly style, and Ben's heart went out to the despairing wife as he returned the embrace.

He and Tim dressed themselves in their best clothes, and rode in a hansom to the terminus.

"Spare no expense," Mrs. Wobstock had cried, after them, "and while you are away live in the best of style."

Tim was still all amazement, and even a cup of tea and a plentiful supply of sandwiches, dispensed by a disdainful young lady in the gilded saloon (which the public have to pay outrageously for) at the railway station failed to bring his mind round into a settled state.

Ben, thinking to inspire him with confidence, sent him to fetch two second-class tickets, and Tim performed his mission by bringing slips of pasteboard entitling them to ride first.

It was a waste of money, but there was no help for it.

They had a compartment to themselves, and Tim, after sitting down as if he were afraid of hurting the cushions, drew a long breath and looked anxiously at our hero.

"Put your hat on straight, Tim," Ben said. "You look as if you were trying to think of half-a-dozen things at the same time.

"I was thinking—wondering," Tim replied, in a voice like an echo of his own, "whether it is possible that Wobstock has committed suicide?"

Absurd as the suggestion was, Ben started.

"Certainly not; he is the last man to think of such a thing. Besides, why should he?"

"I don't know," Tim returned, despairingly; "men do strange things sometimes. My father once threatened to kill himself one Sunday morning because there was nothing but cold water in the house."

"I can't help saying," Ben rejoined, "that Wobstock and your father are entirely at variance in their nature and disposition.

"I own it," said Tim, sighing; "and what will become of my poor old dad—for, with all his faults, he is my father after all—I hardly dare think."

Ben Brierton did not care to pursue the subject, as he could see it was a painful one to Tim.

"I am a little tired," he said, "and will try to get a few minutes rest. Look out of the window, Tim; you will find plenty to amuse you."

But rest was out of the question. He closed his eyes that he might ponder the better on the situation.

Tim's notion of suicide had set him thinking.

"What if he should have fallen into some trap, and lie murdered somewhere?" he thought. "Great Heaven! if such should be the case, I will never forgive myself."

Although they were travelling by express, with but few

"*I aint dead yet,' cried Webstock.*

stoppages, the journey seemed as if it would never come to an end.

Once, when they were tearing through a station, Tim cried out that he had seen a man with a white hat standing on the platform ; but in the same breath he informed Ben that it could not be Wobstock, unless he had been passed through a mangle.

The sun was going down in a glory of crimson, purple, and gold, and the shadows were gathering when the pinnacles and towers of Cloisterville Cathedral reared above the distant city, and stood, set in bold relief, against the sky of as lovely a summer evening as ever delighted mortal eyes. There was life and hope in everything.

Even the inspector who took the tickets at a little station within a mile of the beautiful city had a flower in his coat, and hummed the snatch of a song between his polite "Thank you, sir," or "Thank you, madam."

And it was even excusable that he should keep the train waiting a minute while he argued with the guard the one and only proper method of keeping the birds away from certain rows of ne plus ultra peas, these fully podded within view and begging to be taken down in their prime of life and boiled with mint.

Cloisterville at last. Clad as the boys were nobody recognised them, and they passed unnoticed from the station.

Outside they were beset by the conductors of the busses attached to the principal hotels.

"Royal, sir !" cried one, pressing a card into Ben's hand.

"Cathedral Hotel, sir !" shouted another, almost making a capture of Tim. "Best accommodation in the city, sir. All the quality stay at the Cathedral, sir."

Tim could not help laughing, in spite of his sadness, for the selfsame, red-nosed conductor, about whom there always floated an atmosphere of rum and lemons, had on several occasions threatened to exterminate himself with apoplexy on catching Tim "riding behind" when he was engaged sorting the luggage on the roof.

Ben elected to go to the Cathedral Hotel, and that having been settled the rival conductors challenged each other to mortal combat there and then.

The conflict might have become an established and painful fact but for the prompt interference of an official, armed with the authority of the law, who hit the " Royal " violently in the waistcoat, and digging his knuckles violently into the neck of the expostulatory but eminently triumphant "Cathedral."

As soon as the lads were fairly settled within the comfortable and luxurious walls of the hotel Ben ordered dinner.

Within an hour they sallied out and made direct for the region so well known to both of them.

It looked more squalid, and the houses more grim, lopsided, and threatening than ever.

The neighbourhood seemed to have changed even in so short a time, the people, men and women, more forlorn, and the children flitting about like bats, more pinched of face, ragged, and poverty-stricken.

The lamp near the top of the court had either been blown out or extinguished by some high-spirited youth, the latter most likely, for a post surmounted by a ginger-beer bottle suggested that urchin sport had received a sudden check.

A little further on they came upon a full-bodied boy hanging over an iron rail, and staring with all his might through an iron grating into a cellar containing nothing but dirt and red-eyed rats.

Behind him, describing vicious circles with a strap, stood a man bent on serious business.

Both man and boy were so wrapped up in their pursuits that they gave no heed to Ben and Tim.

They had not taken twenty paces when a loud crack and a louder bawl proclaimed that the fell deed of parental vengeance had been done, and the full-bodied boy racing past hurled himself down three steps into a house, and went to cover under the kitchen table.

In another moment Ben Brierton and Tim Toppem stood before the house of Ebeneezer Chipps.

It was plunged in darkness, but the miser, as has been pointed out before, preferred gloom to light, and he might be at home nursing himself in some shadowy corner, like an aged spider with a sharp look out for flies.

Ben walked steadily up to the door and knocked vigorously at it, but the noisy summons brought no response.

Our hero knocked again, and then the shoemaker next door thrust his head out of a window and said that "When they had done with that musical box, he would like to go to sleep."

"Where is Chipps?" Ben demanded, altering his voice.

"Don't know, and don't care," came his reply. "I should think it very likely that the party as he sold hisself to long ago has walked off with him. "There was a mighty thunderstorm last night and p'raps that accounted for it."

Having fired off this sally the man of leather announced that there was plenty of water on the premises, and that it would be liberally distributed if the knocking went on, he banged the window and went growling to bed.

"It is no use staying here it seems," Ben said. "Chipps and Brierly have flown, but where is Wobstock?"

"Perhaps they did not meet him here, and he may have gone on their track," Tim replied. "Oh! I say, suppose they have bolted to America, and Wobstock has gone after them?"

Ben shook his head, and, taking Tim's arm, they went despondingly back to their hotel.

CHAPTER XXXV.

A SURPRISE AS STARTLING AS IT WAS PLEASANT.

FOR four days the boys roamed the city and its surroundings, and scores of telegrams passed between them and Mrs. Wobstock, whose husband had vanished as suddenly as if he had taken a header into the crater of a volcano.

Advertisements appeared in all the papers, the police were communicated with, but all in vain.

Chipps had not been seen, nor had anybody observed a person answering the description of Reginald Brierly in the neighbourhood of the miser's house.

The whole affair was wrapped in profound mystery, and for the simple reason that Wobstock in his semi-delirium assured Button the ostler and his wife with whom he was staying that he was a retired tinker, and that his name was Potts.

The truth of the matter is that when Wobstock came round and was on the fair way to recovery, he was under the impression that he had had nothing more than a long refreshing sleep, and the people of the house did not take the trouble to undeceive him.

The self-named Mr. Potts arose on the fifth evening, and, having paid Mr. Button in a way that made him stare, he went forth, bent on vengeance.

The soreness of his head had passed away, but his spirit was sore and angry within him.

He felt that he had been duped and taken in in a manner that he thought he could never have allowed himself to be.

But, on the other hand, the real purpose of his mission held as good as ever, and it was with pardonable pride that he reflected on his artfulness in copying the deeds.

It now occurred to him that it would be useless to go to the miser's house direct.   He must purchase some sort disguise, and dodge about all over the country in search of the villains.

"And I'll find 'em," he said, clenching his fists, "it I have to sell every blessed monkey in the show."

He went to the hotel he had previously occupied near the railway-station, and wrote off at once to his wife, and sent the letter direct to the post-office.

Then, ordering something to stimulate his nerves, he took up a newspaper and began to read.

"Why, what's this?" he cried.   "There's a mistake here.   I arrived on the nineteenth of June, and this paper is dated for the twenty-fourth.   Hi! waiter—what is the date?"

"Twenty-fourth, sir."

Will-i-am Wobstock experienced a strange eeling creep through him.

"Hang it!" he gasped; "here's a nice state of things. I say, young man, has anybody inquired for me?"

"No, sir," the waiter replied; "you never left your name."

"My name is Will-i-am Wobstock."

The waiter rushed frantically across the room, snatched up the newspaper which Wobstock had thrown down, and pointed to a paragraph.

"Blue snakes and boiled helephants!" Wobstock shrieked. "Where's my hat?"

Like a madman he rushed to the Cathedral Hotel, and, having ascertained the number of the sitting-room occupied by Ben and Tim, he dashed into the presence of the surprised lads.

"My lads!" he cried, flourishing his arms about, "don't be frightened. I ain't dead. Your old friend Will-i-am is hisself again."

CHAPTER XXXVI.

TOPPEM SENIOR REPENTS OF HIS EVIL WAYS, AND GETS HIS REWARD—THE NEWS HE BROUGHT TO THE ROYAL HOTEL.

IT was all very well to tell our hero and Tim not to be frightened.

Wobstock had come upon them like a substantial will-o'-the-wisp, and the boys gazed at him as if they could not believe their eyes.

But the fact that Will-i-am was alive and well required but little proof, especially when after holding Ben in his arms, he rushed at Tim Toppem and favoured him with a bear-like hug, a display of affection that caused the afflicted youth to howl most unmelodiously.

"Where—where have you been?" demanded Ben, who could not recover from his astonishment.

"My lad," Wobstock replied, sinking down into a chair, and ringing the bell with a view to refreshment, "I went for so long a swim that I felt compelled to take a rest afterwards."

This led Ben and Tim to think that the proprietor of the menagerie should be put to bed again without delay; they fully believing that some untoward excitement had unhinged his brain.

This notion attained further evidence when Wobstock laughed and cried at the same time, thumped his chest, coughed, choked, and ran to the window for air.

But soon his story was told, and Ben rushing up to him clasped both his hands.

"And you have suffered all this for me?" he cried. "I shall never be able to forgive myself unless you are fully avenged without delay. The truth must be told to the police at once."

"Steady—steady!" Wobstock returned. "Let us have no impetuosity. We will keep our own counsel for a time for your own sake, Ben; for to go to the police with such a story would ensure your uncle standing in a felon's dock. If I had only Ebeneezer Chipps to deal with, I wouldn't give a snap of the fingers to save him; but bad as your blood relation is, the disgrace would be too great to know that he was dragging trucks of stone about at Portland."

Ben hung his head and a mist gathered before his eyes.

"Look here," said Wobstock, after he had partaken of a little weak brandy and water; "we will go for a stroll, and talk the matter over. It's a bad job at the best, but the worst of misfortunes are to be got over with patience and perseverance. If I can have proof that Reginald Brierly is out of the country well and good, for then we'll produce our documents and appeal to the Court of Chancery which will set us right. Come on! Ah!" he added, gazing at his white hat, "I little thought you and I would have such adventures. When you are quite worn out you shall rest under a glass-case."

With a dream-like sensation upon him, Ben suffered Wobstock to take him by the arm and lead him out of the hotel.

Tim Toppem brought up the rear, and did nothing but stumble over his own feet and stare hard at Wobstock's extensive back.

"If he hadn't squeezed my nose all out of shape," he murmured, "I wouldn't believe that he was alive now. Oh! the murderous villains to drop him into that horrible river."

Meanwhile Wobstock was talking earnestly to Ben, and so they reached the market-place.

The wooden stalls used by the vendors of the good things of this life were packed up in a corner, looking as if there had been a tremendous fight with tables and chairs.

At the lower end there were two or three dispensaries of such luxuries as hot potatoes, stewed prunes, mussels, and beef patties.

They were surrounded by a number of boys and men, whose chief aim seemed to be how long they could keep their hands in their pockets without wearing them out.

The hot potato dealer was in altercation with a man holding a large " tater " in his hand and pointing to an ominous dark speck in the centre.

" Come, you change this," said the purchaser, " or give me back my money."

" My friend," replied the hero of the can, " if I had the heyes of a tater I might be able to see inside of 'em ; but as I haven't, I can't. What I sells, I sells with all faults."

" You won't change it ?"

" I should be doin' my feller tradesmen an injustice if I did."

" Then take it !'

A cry of anguish burst from the lips of the vendor. The potato, hurled with unerring aim, left traces like a snow-ball upon his features, and, staggering against the oven, gingerly poised upon a truck with weak wheels, he over-turned it, fire, salt, butter, pepper, and all.

The luxuries baking in the tin slides flew about in all directions ; and a shout rent the air as the hungry crowd pounced upon them.

" Upon my word," cried Wobstock, " it is too bad to treat a man like that. Here, Ben, Tim, follow me, and we will make mincemeat of this rabble."

But before they could dash into the midst of the scrambling throng, a man holding his eye dashed madly from it.

" My father !" Tim shrieked, and sat down flat.

Alas ! It was Toppem.

After many vicissitudes in the metropolis, and with but two sovereigns, a few odd shillings, and a poor future before him, it struck him that he could not do better than return to his native soil—Cloisterville.

There a man in his position, with forty shillings in his pocket would be received with open arms.

The railway fare being expensive, he walked ; a few miles more or less were nothing to him, and luck favoured him on the journey.

Here and there he picked up an odd job—once to drive some pigs which ran away in different directions at four cross roads, a *contretemps* that caused Mr. Toppem to quicken his pace for fully ten miles, and to leave the owner of the porkers to recover his property. At last he reached Cloisterville, and began to think seriously of doing something for himself, and finally hit upon the potato line.

The weather being warm trade was not brisk, but he had contrived to live fairly well, until the specked tater had brought disaster upon him and ruined his prospects.

" Yes, it's me," he groaned, staggering against a lamp-post. " Oh ! Tim, this is a bitter blow."

" It looks like it," Wobstock observed, grimly. " But I should call it a hot 'un."

" It were a hot 'un," Toppem senior groaned. " The hottest in the oven, and I picked it out specially."

Here, while Tim rose slowly to his feet, he wept silently and bewailed his hard fate.

" I must begin life over again," he said. " I'm always beginnin' life over again, and no sooner do I start afresh than fate comes down on me like a cartload of bricks. Tim, you are clad in silk attire, and siller have to spare ; but your poor father's gone to the bad, and it's enough to lift his hair."

" Look here, father," said Tim, " poetry is not in your line, and I'd wish you'd drop it. Take some money from my purse and go home."

" 'Ome," echoed his despairing parent. " I've forgotten the meanin' of the word. There was a time when the mere mention of it filled my 'eart with joy. Tim, you remember them Saturday night tripe suppers ?"

" Yes," Tim replied, " and I remember something else—no dinner on Sundays, and a hunt for Monday morning's breakfast ; but let it all go. I wish you would stick to your own trade, and become a bricklayer again."

" The man," retorted Tim senior, as he removed the

last piece of smashed potato from his face, "as has fell off three ladders, hout o' two winders, and head fust down one chimbly shaft may be said to have had enough o' the layin' business. Mister Wobstock, we did not part friends; if I offended you I beg your parding. That ten pound note brought a cuss on me."

"Money badly come by never does good," Wobstock observed. "I suppose you have not—ahem!—seen anything of your bosom friend, Ebeneezer Chipps, of late?"

"I've seen him, and I ain't seen him," Toppem replied. "I was down at the old place the other night, and I tumbled over a hold man with a long white beard and a humped back. The beard belonged to another man, but it was Chipps' hump."

"Did you speak to him?"

"No, I only stared 'ard. And suddenly the hump—I mean the hold man, wheeled round and marched orf in the direction o' the cathedral."

"I suppose it never struck you to follow him?" Wobstock said.

"Well," Toppem replied, "the fact is, I was struck myself. While I was starin' with all my heyes, two men rushed out from the archway, and one accidentally for the purpose run a buster ag'in me. It took me quite five minutes to get my wind, and when I came round the street was clear."

"When—at what time did this happen?" Ben Brierton demanded.

"It were last night, and just on the stroke of twelve."

"Oh! father," Tim exclaimed, "where did you come from at such a time?"

His doting parent put his head on one side, and seemed to be mentally searching about for an appropriate reply, which while not wholly departing from the truth would not convict him.

———

CHAPTER XXXVII.

HOW REGINALD BRIERLY WAS STOPPED ON THE WAY.

"My boy," Mr. Toppem said, "a man of my age has a right to be out whatever time he likes."

"You had come from that reeking den of beer and tobacco, the Briton's Arms?"

Mr. Toppem did not deny it, but he indulged in a deep drawn sigh.

"I'm a goin'!" he said, "to find the bits o' my can, and to pick up any stray taters as I see lyin' about. I see I ain't wanted, not even by my own son; him as I had strong 'opes of, him as I thought would be a joy and comfort to me in my hold hage. Ben, you're a bit of a swell now, but well you remember the days when—"

"Really, Mr. Toppem," our hero interposed, "I would rather plead a bad memory to the past."

"And not so much of your Bens," Wobstock put in, wrathfully, "and just listen to me. It seems that you have come a cropper again, and I don't wish to see you standing about the streets like a homeless—er—hyena while your son is in my charge, so if you like I can put you in the way of earning a little money."

"Just you name the job and I'm on," cried Toppem senior.

"Go back to where you were you were last night, and if you see the old man with the white beard let me know at once. We are staying at the Royal Hotel, and when you come there ask for Mister Benjamin Brierly. Be very particular about the Brierly, and still more particular about the Mister. Do you understand?"

"I think I do," Toppem replied, rubbing his chin as he looked at Ben. "What if I should see the hold man in the small hours of the mornin?"

"Ring the night bell and tell the porter to wake us up. Keep away from the Briton's Arms, do your duty like a man, and it will be worth a fiver to you."

"I'll take it in gold," Toppem replied. "The last note was a tenner and that ruined me; all that's left of it is a wreck of hashes and half-baked taters."

. . . .

The sunlight was struggling with the smoke of London, hovering sullenly above the housetops and reluctant to depart, when a hansom cab dashed through Euston-square on its way to the London and North-Western station.

The horse was tired, as was also the driver ; but the latter, waking up thoroughly under the promise of half-a-sovereign if he caught the first train bound for Liverpool, shook up his steed in a manner that astounded the quadruped.

The occupant of the cab was Reginald Brierly.

Haggard, and with frightened eyes, he glanced from the right to left, as if expecting to be challenged every moment.

A waggoner, at the head of a team drawing a heavy load to Covent Garden-market, shouting cheerily to another, caused his heart to beat, brought a rush of blood to his face, and left it livid.

He even suspected the cabman ; for news travels quickly on the wires; and thinking that Wobstock had been foully murdered, the police might have discovered the crime, and flashed the tidings to the remotest village in the United Kingdom.

And again, when any desperate, dastardly deed is perpetrated, men unconsciously become detectives and peer into each others' faces.

Euston station at last !

Reginald Brierly breathed more freely as he stepped from the cab, and forced a smile to his lips as he discharged the driver.

"Take your nag home and give him a good feed," he said ; "he has done the journey in capital style. I find that I have more than a quarter of an hour to wait."

"This ere 'orse and I once took a cove to this werry station," the cabby replied. "He never told me to wait, but I did, and I took him back—not 'xactly where he come from, to be sure, but to quite as safe a place."

"Indeed !" said Reginald Brierley. "Where was that ?"

"To the perlice station," cabby responded. "He was nabbed by the detectives ; and I shall never forget his face when"—pointing with his whip—"they brought him out o' that door. He were whiter than a turnip, and trembled like a cheap willa close to a railway embankment !"

Reginald Brierly felt that his own face was growing

white again, and turned hastily into that spacious but singularly gloomy hall bordered on the right and left by the departure platforms.

"Confound the fellow !" he muttered. "What on earth put it into his head to say such a thing to me ?"

The bookstall was not yet opened, but the newspapers had just arrived, and two or three smart lads were sorting them ready for sale.

"Paper, sir ?" said one. "Horrible tragedy, sir."

"Where ?" Reginald Brierly asked, with an effort.

"I am not quite sure of the name of the place, sir," the boy replied. "We haven't untied the posters yet, but you'll find all about it in the paper."

Reginald Brierly's hand shook as he unfolded the printed sheet, still wet from the press.

In a moment his mind was relieved.

The tragedy had taken place in some remote part of the Black Country, and he felt like a man reprieved from the scaffold.

A heavy-eyed girl, who looked as if she had known no rest for a year, was opening one of the refreshment bars, and Brierly, calling for some brandy, swallowed it at a draught, and walked to the departure platform.

The train was ready for passengers, and a huge engine was shunting slowly towards it.

Reginald Brierly suddenly remembered that in the disordered state of his brain he had not taken a ticket, and he turned back again.

As he did so he ran against a man who appeared to be in a violent hurry.

They exchanged apologies and went their respective ways, and Reginald Brierly soon returned to the train.

There were not half-a-dozen people on the platform, and they were too much engaged in seeing their luggage put into the brake to pay any heed to him.

For the first time since leaving Cloisterville he felt himself safe.

He opened the door of the carriage, and was about to enter it, when somebody touched him lightly on the shoulder.

Swinging sharply round on his heels he found himself

"Gents," said Wobstock, "I beg your pardon for coming so hastily into company, but you'll own that I had good grounds for so doing."

face to face with the man who but a few moments before had run against him.

"Mr. Reginald Brierly?" said the stranger.

"No, sir, you have made a mistake."

"Pardon me, I have done nothing of the kind."

"Well," said Brierly, turning crimson to the roots of his hair, "what do you want with me?"

"A few words."

"I must refuse you," the earth seemed to roll beneath his feet as he spoke. "I am in a hurry—er—you see I am going by this train."

"I would not think of it, if I were you."

"And pray, sir, why not?" said Brierly, plucking up courage. "Are you gifted with double sight, and have you come to warn me of an impending accident?"

"Mr. Brierly," the stranger said, "my name is Herry. Mr. Wobstock employed me on a previous occasion to keep watch over your movements, and last night I received a wire to find you if I could. Luck has fallen in my way, and yet I thought that you would make for America, like many others afflicted with certain kinds of troubles."

"How do you know that I am going to America?' Reginald Brierly asked.

"I am sure of it as I am not going there myself."

"Who are you?"

"A private detective."

"Bah! Let me pass. You have no right to detain, or even to speak to me. Stand out of my way or you will compel me to chastise you."

"Mr. Reginald Brierly," said Herry, slowly, and emphasising each word with a movement of his forefinger, "I wish to behave towards you in a proper spirit, and in exact accordance with my instructions. You will either return with me to Cloisterville, or I am commissioned to call a constable and give you into custody."

"On what charge."

"As an accessory in an attempted murder. You were flying because you thought that Wobstock was dead, but you may put your mind to rest in that respect. A miracle saved him, and let people say what they like, there are miracles in these days as there were in the days of old."

The time for starting the train was up, and the guard, whistle in hand and his eyes on the engine-driver, was shouting, "Take your seats, please. Train going on!"

Uttering a coarse word, Reginald Brierly leaped into the carriage as the wheels began to revolve slowly, and Herry sprang in after him.

"The train stops at Willesden-junction," he said; "and, as I am a man, I will drag you out and give you in charge. If you wish to run your head into a hornets'-nest, you are going the proper way to do it."

Reginald Brierly sat perfectly still and silent for quite a minute.

"You have conquered me," he said. "I will go back with you."

CHAPTER XXXVIII.

MR. TOPPEM FULFILS HIS MISSION—THE MISER'S HOUSE AGAIN.

ALL was peace and slumber at the Royal Hotel.

Everybody had gone to bed, save the hall-porter, and he winked and blinked, and nodded and dosed in his chair, constructed like a sentry-box.

There is a supposition that a hall-porter is an unhappy person, who is denied the luxury of a bed for his sins. But be it as it may, his rest must be of short duration, for after his long vigil he may be seen hard at work when the sun is but young in the sky.

This particular hall-porter was nodding and threatening to go to sleep in right down earnest when the bell rang violently.

He was dreaming that a sporting gentleman with more champagne in his head than brains, had just given him a sovereign in mistake for a shilling. It was a pleasant vision, but melted away as the iron-tongued tormentor spoke.

"Who's this, I wonder?" he growled. "Some fellow without luggage, who wants a bed, I suppose; if so, off he goes."

He opened the door, and Mr. Toppem, red of face,

panting, and with all the signs of excitement upon him, tumbled in.

"What do you want?" growled the porter.

"To see either Mister Bobstock or Wirely."

"No such people here. Be off with you."

"I won't be off!" Toppem gasped. "I'm a little confused—I mean I must see either Mr. Wobstock or Brierly. They're stayin' here, I know, and you'd better knock 'em up or," he added, brilliantly, "they'll knock you down."

The porter counted the sticks and coats as he closed the door, and then vanished into the dim regions of the upper part of the hotel.

In less than a minute he was down again.

"Walk into the room you see on the first landing," he said. "The gents are up and dressing themselves like one o'clock."

Mr. Toppem did not stop to enquire into the nature of this extraordinary description of toilet, but raced upstairs, three at a time, and sank into a chair.

"I've done it at last!" he cried. "I've retrieved my character!"

He had scarcely time to regain his breath when Wobstock, Ben, and Tim appeared.

"I've seen Chipps!" Toppem said, starting up and striking a tragic attitude. "I know it's him, because he was with the rascal that Ben—Mister Brierly—tackled at the fair."

"I have a painful recollection of your share of the business," Wobstock returned. "If it had not been for my hat you would have brained me with the butt-end of the rifle. Well, go on. Where did the rascals go?"

"There was three of 'em," Toppem continued. "They came sneakin' along the street, looking to the right and left, but I was in a shutter-box, and so they missed me. After dodgin' about and makin' sure, as they thought, that nobody was about, they suddenly dived under the archway, and went down to the old house."

"Then they are trapped," Wobstock said, thrusting his hands into his pockets.

The amount of money that he produced and pushed

across the table to Toppem made that lucky individua,
open his mouth to its widest dimensions.

"Now, boys," said Wobstock, "we will beard the
lions—wolves is the proper word—in their dens. Toppem,
run down and ask the hall-porter to lend us some good
thick sticks—as big as the one that killed Captain Cook
—whoppers ; and the more knobs they have on them the
better."

Toppem rushed out of the room, aud returned to it
with quite a selection of weapons under his arm.

"Pick 'em where you like," he said, joyfully.

"We'll try 'em before we buy 'em," Wobstock added.
"Now, then, are you all ready? Quick march, then !"

"Let me go with you," Toppem pleaded.

"You may, if you promise not to get in the way.
Tim, there may be a scrimmage. If you see your father
flourishing about too near my hat, forget that he is your
parent, and floor him."

Tim said nothing, but looked volumes.

They went out into the dark night, their footsteps
awakening the echoes of the silent streets in a strange
and ghostly style.

"We ought to have come hout in slippers," Toppem,
senior, ventured to remark.

"Just so, and run the risk of being locked up for a
band of burglars," Wobstock said. "Really, Toppem,
I wish we had left you behind. That money in your
pocket is jingling like a set of sledge-bells. Leave it
alone, or—or I'll stand you on your head and shake it all
over the street."

Mr. Toppem began to think that perhaps he had better
have remained at the hotel, where, it occurred to him,
that the hall-porter might have been induced to produce
refreshment in a liquid form.

But he abandoned the wicked notion as soon as it was
made, for had he not promised to be a total abstainer?

Leaving the main thoroughfares for the narrow and
badly-lighted ones, they became cautious, and trod
lightly ; and no echoes resounded when they reached the
scene of Ben's early woes.

On reaching the locality of Ben's troubles they became more cautious, and their footsteps fell lighter on the ground.

They stopped under the archway of the court, and never to our hero's eyes did it look more dismal.

It seemed to him as if all the grim shadows of past ages had crept from their lurking-places and added their gloom to the almost awful darkness of the night.

"I think we had better go in Indian file," Wobstock said, in a whisper.

Softly as he spoke, the sound of his voice produced a hollow echo, which might have proceeded from a hideously carved head forming the keystone of the arch ; and Wobstock, in spite of all his nerve and self-control, started.

"What a place for a lonely man to find himself in !" he continued. "Only fancy a scissors-to-grind man wandering down here unawares ! What a mortal crash there would be ! Now, Toppem, you had better go first, as it's ten to one that you will tumble over somebody."

Mr. Toppem did not appear to relish the idea of leading the way.

A little lower down there was a pump, an ungainly, ancient wooden structure, that hid itself away amid a mass of brickwork and beams, and it occurred to him that somebody might be behind it, and ready to pounce out upon the first intruder.

"My eyesight ain't as good as it used to be," he murmured.

"Eyesight has nothing to with it," Wobstock said, testily. "There's not one of us who can see an inch from his nose."

"Well, then, here goes," Toppem returned, desperately ; "but if so be as I should—"

"Mind the three stone steps," Tim said.

Even as the dutiful son spoke the air was rent by a grunting sound, followed by a terrific crash.

"Stand back, there !" Wobstock roared.

Under the impression that a wall or a stack of chimneys had fallen, he seized the two lads by the arm and dragged them forcibly back to the street.

"What was it—something struck with a thunderbolt ?" he gasped.

"I am afraid that my father is the cause of it all," Tim said, nervously.

"Your father? Where is he?"

"I think it most likely that you will find him on his back at the bottom of three stone steps."

Will-i-am Wobstock removed his hat and laid hold of a good handful of hair.

"The monster in hobnailed boots!" he groaned. "If I were a man given to bad language I should say something that would turn some of these old houses upside down. Toppem, you idiot! come here."

"I can't!" moaned the fallen hero. "My right leg has got mixed up with some wooden palings, and I can't get it out."

"What on earth are we to do?" gurgled Wobstock, who had begun to dance about in a frenzied sort of way.

"I think we had better show a light," Ben hinted. "Here is a box of vestas fitted with a small candle. I bought it in London as a curiosity, and it will come in handy now."

"Make haste!" Mr. Toppem shrieked. "Somebody's a-comin', and he's got a big stick with him. I can hear it a-thumpin' on the ground."

Wobstock rushed into the dark entry, and discovering the whereabouts of Toppem by accidentally kicking him violently in the ribs, rescued him at the cost of a short row of wooden palings, guarding a house, before which some unhappy-looking scarlet runners were trying to keep up the reputation of the bean tribe, and bloom under the most trying circumstances.

"Why didn't you fall straight, if you wanted to fall at all?" Wobstock hissed in his ear.

"Fust I went hup, and then I shot hout sideways," Toppem replied, in mournful accents. "Don't shake me like that; I'm a mass of bumps and bruises as it is."

CHAPTER XXXIX.

IN A SHUTTER-BOX—THE END OF THE GAME.

"IF I had my wind, I'd shake your confounded head off your confounded shoulders," Will-i-am rejoined. "I've met with a good many asses in my time, long-eared and short, four-legged and two-legged, but you'd beat all comers in a show, Toppem."

"Hist!" Ben whispered. "The footsteps draw nearer."

They separated, darting away in different directions; but, after all, it was not a person likely to interfere with, or even take notice of them.

The shoemaker, who lived next door to Ebeneezer Chipps, had been paying free homage to things that are strong, ardent, and bewildering, and had gone home to find the door closed against him.

Sundry loud knockings, accompanied by threats, had resulted in an antidote at once cooling and efficacious.

The partner of his joys and sorrows waited until he was thoroughly tired out, and then emerging suddenly, did short but terrific execution with a broom-handle, and then retired within the stronghold flushed with victory and wrath.

As the shoemaker went his way he meditated on the cost of legal proceedings before the magistrates, but remembering that they invariably took the weaker side, he decided upon walking about all night, and settling the breach of domestic peace in his own peculiar manner in the morning.

Meanwhile, Wobstock had worked his way round to the place where Mr. Toppem crouched, guided to the spot by a series of audible pantings and grunts.

"Look here," he said, "you stop that noise, or I'll leave you with no wind to make it. You've spoilt our undertaking—I knew you would. Oh! what a fool I was to allow you to blunder about with us."

Toppem senior remained silent, and clutched the money in his pocket with a trembling hand.

He thought that if he attempted to argue the question Will-i-am Wobstock might carry out the dire threat he had uttered, and plant him upon the apex of his cranium—and Toppem's head bore a slight resemblance to a soda-water bottle upside down.

Soon silence reigned again, broken only by the mournful sighing of the night wind, a dismal cadence that received its chorus from rusty bars, creaking signs, and rattling shutters.

"What say you, Ben," Wobstock said, as our hero came up, "do you think we may venture again ?"

"I think so," our hero replied ; "everything seems quiet enough."

"Then off we go. I say, Toppem !"

"Yes."

"Where's that shutter-box you hid in ?"

"Not fifty yards from where you are standin'."

"Then hide in it again," said Wobstock ; "and if you show your nose out of it until I tell you to, I'll—I'll pull it off."

There was a martyr-like expression on the face of Mr. Toppem as he retired to the shutter-box, but no sooner was he in than he was out again.

"There's somethin' alive in there," he gasped. "I see its heyes a-glarin' like signal-lamps."

"A cat," said Wobstock. "Oh ! here's a pretty fellow to bring out on an adventure. Get in, you fool !"

Toppem drove the cat out, and, planting his back against the wall, reflected mournfully on his many woes.

"Ah ! me," he said, "what's the use o' luck without appiness. Instead of Tim up and protectin' his poor father he gazes sternly upon him with eyes like an 'ungry heagle. Little did I ever think I should live to be stowed away in a box, like a bundle of old clothes. But sich is my fate, and I must abide by it. Now for a pipe o' baccy to soothe my nerves."

Meanwhile our hero, Wobstock, and Tim were on their way down the court.

Will-i-am ran his head against something hard, and concluded that it was the projecting angle of a wall.

"Saved again by my hat !" he muttered ; "the rim's gone this time. Go it ! Couldn't somebody shoot a ton ot bricks on me, iust for fun, or perhaps a cartload of

pickle-jars and old glass bottles might be more effective ?
I'm ready for anything."

"Hush !" Ben whispered ; "here is the house."

As he spoke a light flashed up at one of the windows
and died out, as if somebody had taken alarm and extinguished it suddenly.

"So you are in there, are you, my beauties ?" Wobstock
said. "Good ! Now then to give you a fright."

Walking up to the door, he pounded it with his fists.

"The game is up !" he roared. "Ebeneezer Chipps,
Sable Wallack, and you Sam Rushmore may as well walk
out and surrender quietly. I've come to settle accounts
with you, you murderous dogs !"

Huddled together in one of the darkened rooms, the
three rascals heard the words and trembled.

To them it sounded like a voice from the grave.

"It's Wobstock !" Chipps gasped. "The river gave
him up after all !"

"Keep your teeth from chattering !" Sam Rushmore
hissed in his ear, "and pull yourself together. Is there
no other way out of this den ?"

"Only by the roof. There is a trap in the ceiling of
the tap-room."

"Then," said Rushmore, "we will go, one at a time,
and crawl over the other houses. We must risk everything now, and bolt."

"And most likely drop into the arms of a policeman !"
Chipps groaned. "Keep still—we are safer where we
are. Ah ! pound away, my friend ; the door, as I have
barricaded it, would stand a siege."

Wobstock had nearly exhausted his stock of strength
and patience.

"You cowardly hounds !" he yelled through the keyhole, "are you afraid to face the man you tried to murder ?"

"If I had another chance," Sam Rushmore growled,
"I'd make no mistake, even if the rope was dangling
before my eyes. Well, stay here if you like ; I'm off."

"And so am I," said Sable Wallack.

"What's that ?" Chipps shrieked.

An awful rumbling sound came from the region of the
cellars.

It was like the overturning of several empty barrels, and was followed by a crack as loud as the report of a pistol.

The walls shuddered, and then all was still.

"Wallack! Rushmore!" Chipps said, hoarsely, "speak to me."

He put out his hands, and felt feebly about in the darkness.

He was alone; the ruffians had left him, and now he heard them creeping stealthily up the rickety stairs.

But he did not follow them.

In the very room in which he had starved and ill-treated Ben he stood trying to fashion some definite course.

"I'm too old a man to drag out my few remaining years in a prison," he muttered; "but what else can I expect? What mercy can I hope to find in the breast of the man whom Heaven has saved to punish me? And Ben, too, he is here. I heard his voice just now."

Suddenly he fell upon his knees and clasped his hands upon the crown of his head, and as the first man whose hands were stained with blood cried, so cried he—

"My punishment is more than I can bear."

Then an awful thought stole into his mind.

He would escape, but not in the way of a man thirsting for life and liberty.

It would be but a pang after all. Why not do it?"

There was an old rope in the corner, and a beam over his head.

He laughed as he thought how he would cheat those who had hounded him down at last, but it was the laugh of a man possessed of an evil spirit.

"I will speak to them first," he said.

He went to the window and threw it open.

"You, below there!" he cried. "In two minutes you shall have your revenge."

Without waiting for an answer he banged the window, and then groped his way to a corner and clutched a coil of rope.

"It is old," he said, as he tested its strength; "but it will serve its purpose. Adieu!"

.   .   .   .

BOLD BEN BRIERTON.

When Ebeneezer Chipps opened the window, Wobstock walked backwards a few paces, in the hope of catching sight of him, and as the miser disappeared, he stood with his mouth open and in the very act of speaking, but the words died away on his lips, and he turned to Ben.

"What does he mean by saying that we shall have our revenge in two minutes," he queries, " is he coming down to open the door?"

"I cannot make it out," Ben returned. "Great Heaven! Stand back there."

"Stand back where? Why? What? Are you mad, Ben? Help!"

Ben seized him violently by the arms and dragged him fifty paces from the old house, when a thundering crash shook the earth.

It was like the explosion of a powder mine.

Tim Toppem, who had rushed after Ben, saw something darker than the night reeling in the air, and fell prone upon the earth, scarcely knowing whether the act was voluntary, or whether he was struck with something, or hurled to the earth

The old building had fallen, collapsed like a house of cards, crumbled to atoms like a castle built on sand, under the crash of a thunder-bolt.

Chimney-stacks, dismantled, split and twisted, huge masses of flint and brick, beams, flooring, staircases torn to matchwood, rubbish, dust—and death.

In the very heart of the chaos lay Sable Wallack and Sam Rushmore, battered, mangled, and beyond recognition.

They had reached the roof just as the old house fell, and the shriek that went up from their lips rose high above the mighty din and uproar.

And near them lay the body of a man beneath a beam.

The hand quivering in the last throes of death clutched a rope.

The noose was already made, but Ebeneezer Chipps had been saved from self-destruction.

Then came the lights, the springing of rattles, the hurrying of police, and a crowd of white-faced, half-dressed people startled from their beds.

What followed Ben never really knew.

He saw Wobstock carried away looking something like an alderman who had dined well and not too wisely. He saw Tim rubbing his head and being helped along by a kindly policeman, and when in the street he saw something like a huge letter V near the shutter-box before alluded to

The strange looking object was formed by the manly and ever graceful legs of Mr. Toppem, who, on hearing the crash, had swallowed the best part of his short clay pipe, and had fainted.

Somebody brought him round with a pail of water, a debt of gratitude which he repaid by smiting the Samaritan full on the nose when he was looking the other way. Mr. Toppem then ran ran fully two miles out of Cloister-ville, and would have gone further had he not cannoned against a donkey straying on the road.

    .   .   .   .

On the evening of the same day, while Wobstock was building up his shattered nerves with oysters and champagne at the hotel, Reginald Brierly walked into the room, with Herry close upon his heels.

"I tried to flee like a coward," Brierly said, " but Heaven decreed that it should be otherwise. Here I am; do with me as you please. I am tired of the world, tired of my life."

Ben walked up to him, and looked him full in the eyes.

"Whatever wrong you may have attempted to have done me," he said, "I cannot forget that you are my father's brother. Go to some new country and begin life over again."

"And this is your revenge ?"

"It is the best revenge in all the world—forgiveness."

At this moment an extraordinary sound proceeded from a corner of the room.

Tim was weeping and sobbing at an alarming rate.

Wobstock gazed solemnly at the lining of his hat, and presently, taking Reginald Brierly's hand, put it into Ben's.

"It is best that we should forget and forgive," he said ; "forget our wrongs and forgive our enemies. Mr.

Brierly, I have something to tell you. Only this morning your nephew, the best and bravest boy that ever lived, has put you down for a thousand pounds. That will give you a splendid start."

"It's more than I deserve."

"If we all got our deserts many of us would come poorly off," Wobstock said. "For instance, there's—"

"Mr. Toppem!" a waiter announced.

"I thought so," Wobstock cried. "Tell him to wait. I wonder," he added, "what we are to do with him."

This was a poser which was not satisfactorily settled until some time afterwards when the "white elephant" was started in the greengrocery trade, and, became a steady and persevering man. Reginald Brierly went to Australia and did well, and Ben, restored to his rights of a splendid estate and a princely income, built a number of pretty little houses for the accommodation of his old friends.

They not only lived near him, but near his heart, even when in good time he gave it to a certain young lady, and settled down to the peaceful life of a true English gentleman.

THE END.

www.ingramcontent.com/pod-product-compliance
Lightning Source LLC
Chambersburg PA
CBHW080733250626
47170CB00010B/2815